# DATE DUE

# Findings

## Books by Mary Anna Evans

*Artifacts*
*Relics*
*Effigies*
*Findings*

# Findings

Mary Anna Evans

Poisoned Pen Press

Copyright © 2008 by Mary Anna Evans

First Edition 2008

10 9 8 7 6 5 4 3 2 1

Library of Congress Catalog Card Number: 2007935731

ISBN: 978-1-59058-483-5  Hardcover

Poisoned Pen Press
6962 E. First Ave., Ste. 103
Scottsdale, AZ 85251
www.poisonedpenpress.com
info@poisonedpenpress.com

Printed in the United States of America

Findings *is dedicated to Faye, Joe, and all their friends…*
*and their enemies, too, I guess.*
*I know these people are all imaginary but,*
*in an important way, they're very real to me.*

# Acknowledgments

I'd like to thank everybody who reviewed *Findings* in manuscript form: Michael Garmon, Rachel Garmon, Amanda Evans, Lillian Sellers, Erin Hinnant, Lillian Sellers, Robert Connolly, Faith Wallace, David Reiser, Keith Berg, and Elizabeth Slater. I'd also like to thank Elizabeth Slater and a number of other librarians on the DorothyL mystery listerv for their help in creating a realistic rare book room where the fictional Elizabeth Slater presides.

I am always grateful to my cat Pharoah for his efforts to support my career. Usually, those efforts consist of sitting on my lap between me and my computer screen, while purring at a quite remarkable decibel level. When he's feeling especially supportive, he stands up on my lap to ensure that I'm not distracted from my work by anything so mundane as a computer display. And when he senses that I need extra encouragement, these activities are punctuated by cheek-to-cheek nuzzling and a long striped tail wiping across my face. I find these things quite inspirational. It's astonishing that no cat has appeared in any of my fiction. I guess Pharoah's alter ego is waiting for a story worthy of him.

And finally, as always, my agent, Anne Hawkins, and the hardworking crew at Poisoned Pen Press: Barbara Peters, Rob Rosenwald, Jessica Tribble, Marilyn Pizzo, Nan Beams, and Geetha Perera have done everything in their power to make this *Findings* the best book it can be.

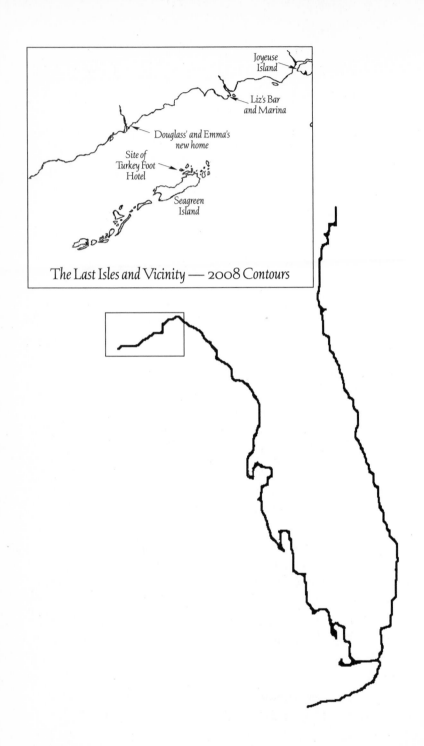

Joyeuse
Island

Liz's Bar
and Marina

Douglass' and Emma's
new home

Site of
Turkey Foot
Hotel

Seagreen
Island

The Last Isles and Vicinity — 2008 Contours

# Prologue

*My dearest Viola,*

*You were right. As ever, my dear, I was wrong and you were right. How many men do you believe are willing to admit as much to anyone, even to their cherished and well-loved wives? Or, should I say, especially to those wives?*

*But you were also wrong, I hasten to add in defense of my manly pride. You once said that my interest in politics—nay, my fascination with politics—was unhealthy and would be my undoing. It is that unwholesome fascination that brings me to admit my wrongheadedness and say a thing you have waited for our entire married life to hear: "We are wrong to bind people to us against their will. We must give our slaves their freedom."*

*How, you may be wondering, has politics brought me to a decision that is, in its way, most personal and intimate? How have scholarly debates over constitutional issues led me to bid good-bye to Bertha, who rocked me to sleep when I was in knee pants? No, long before that. Bertha spooned mashed peaches into my toothless infant mouth. Wave good-bye to Bertha? I might as well bid farewell to Isaiah, who set me on the back of a horse for the first time. But I must, because you—and my infernal politics—have convinced me that it is the just thing to do.*

*I spent all last night in communion with our confederacy's newborn constitution. Do you recall my daily letters to you from Montgomery, detailing every scrap of news that leaked out of the constitutional convention? Do you recall my despair when the delegates elected to begin with the United States Constitution, out of sheer expediency, building our new legal system by editing an old one that could not prevent its society from flying apart? And surely you recall my elation at every reform written into the fabric of our new society?*

*I know your impatience with dry legal issues, but hear me out. The Confederate States of America's new Constitution prevents our congressmen from handing out public money like pork from a barrel. Our president will serve his six years, then a new man will take his place. He will not be allowed to fire public servants, merely because he wishes to replace them with men of his own choosing. Unlike the Congress of the Federals, our Congress will not be able to tax Georgians to pay for projects that benefit only Texans. We can be proud of the things our delegates accomplished in a mere ten days.*

*But the foremost goal accomplished in that ten days was the guarantee of sovereignty to our States. In the end, the threat to that sovereignty led us to secede rather than submit to the tyranny of the majority. I gloried in our Constitution's affirmation of that sovereignty…*

*…until last night. A cold-eyed reading of the document revealed its fatal flaw—its Achilles' heel, if you will.*

*Viola, our Constitution guarantees every State its sovereignty in all things save one: It prohibits any State from outlawing slavery.*

*I am so offended by this hypocrisy that I see only one avenue open to me. If Alabama has been denied her sovereignty in this one area, then I declare my own sovereignty at this moment. My slaves are to be freed.*

*I have resisted this action because of the financial destitution it will likely cause us. I have resisted it because it would mean the dismantling of the agricultural empire my dear father built. I have resisted it because I do not know how the world will treat Bertha and Isaiah and others living among us whom I do truly love. I have resisted it because no one wants to see the whole known world change. And I have resisted it because no man wants to tell his woman that she is right and he is wrong.*

*So do it, my love. Send me the papers that must be signed. Help me work out the knotty problem of how our new freedmen are to be paid, for we minor public servants are not compensated well here in Richmond. I have converted as many of our assets as possible to hard currency, but I dare not send it to you through the mail. More to the point, we will need it to rebuild after this war, which I fear will last long and end poorly.*

*I suggest that you wait until the signed papers arrive, then gather everyone together to tell them of their freedom. Offer them food, lodging, clothing, and a token sum in return for their labor, and a promise of better payment when the war is done. Some may choose to leave, but that is what freedom is.*

*I do not know what this will mean for our future, but we must do the things that God and reason tell us are right. You may find yourself soon penniless, but you will always have me.*

> *Your loving husband,*
> *Jedediah*

# Chapter One

A good day at work typically left Faye Longchamp covered in sweat, rain, dust, dirt, or mud, depending on weather conditions. A more tedious day at work found her sitting in climate-controlled space, clean and comfortable, surrounded by very dirty things. This, unfortunately, had been one of those tedious days.

Faye knew that real archaeology was only just beginning when she hauled an artifact out of the ground. If that artifact wasn't cleaned and measured and expertly described, then digging it up had been a waste of time. When Faye was in the right frame of mind, she enjoyed this painstaking work. Today, however, the early evening air outside was light and balmy, as April air in Florida tended to be.

Faye was having trouble staying indoors.

Not that she could see or feel that April air, because she was sitting in a basement, a rare activity in a part of the world where the groundwater is often so shallow that a toddler can strike water with a plastic shovel. Careful planning and a great deal of money had gone into the design of this house, sunk into a low bluff overlooking the cerulean Gulf of Mexico. There aren't so many bluffs—low or otherwise—in Florida, so a great deal of money had gone into acquiring the land, too. Fortunately, her boss had cash to burn.

The tiny windows in Faye's basement laboratory were well above eye-level, but the room's atmosphere stopped short of being depressing. Its walls were a bright cheery yellow and the stainless steel sink gleamed, because Faye's boss cut no corners on her work space. Thinking of Douglass as her boss always made Faye smile. The word "boss" didn't begin to cover what Douglass Everett was to her. Friend, role model, father figure—those words came closer, but language fails in matters of the heart.

Douglass was mightily proud of Faye's accomplishments. He had sat up so many nights reading the papers she wrote for her graduate archaeology classes that she was seriously thinking about seeking independent study credit for him. Though he had risen from the humblest beginnings to his present status as the richest man in Micco County, Douglass never stopped thinking of himself as the son of a poor black sharecropper. Earning an honors diploma from a white high school in 1964 had been proof enough of his intellect and determination but, oh, how proud he would be to earn a college degree.

Faye decided, without consulting him, that a university education would be the perfect retirement project for her friend Douglass.

She hit the intercom button. "You busy?"

"Just correcting the grammar on your lithics paper."

"Leave my grammar alone. It's fine just the way it is. But I'm really lonely down here in this yellow cave."

The intercom didn't answer her, but she could hear leather-soled shoes thumping down the basement stairs. Those footsteps were heavier than they'd been just a year ago. It hurt Faye to think her friend was getting old. Instead of dwelling on that, she launched her persuasive speech as soon as she saw his face.

"It's time for you to go back to school."

The man's salt-and-pepper eyebrows headed for his hairline. "The museum needs my attention."

She noticed that he didn't say that he didn't *want* to go to school.

"You're the kind of man who needs a whole slew of projects to keep himself occupied. If you try to do just one thing, you'll dry up and get old. You need to keep busy."

"I'm retired. In case you haven't noticed."

"The museum will survive. You've got good employees. I'll make sure they get the tickets taken. Everything will be fine." Douglass' Museum of American Slavery was hardly more than a rich man's hobby, funded by the considerable fortune he had earned with his construction company. Still, he spared no expense in making sure the exhibits accurately told the story of enslaved people in North America, starting shortly after European contact and ending with the Emancipation Proclamation. Faye just wished more visitors walked through the museum's doors. She'd been working on getting the place some publicity, though, so the museum was no reason for Douglass to pass up the chance to go to school.

Faye knew her friend would cut a wide swathe through campus in the same way he'd conquered every other obstacle that life had thrown him. "I can't wait to see you in class. You'll be busting bell curves and making undergrads cry. Really, you're paying me more than enough to take care of things while you do something for yourself."

He didn't say no.

It was so good to spend time with Douglass again. It was even better just to be at home. Faye was overjoyed to be back in her beloved gulf islands for a semester. She had procured funding to work on a tiny islet deep in the Last Isles, excavating the remains of the Turkey Foot Hotel, which had been owned by her family prior to the hotel's destruction in an 1856 hurricane. The hotel site was a short boat ride from her home on Joyeuse Island, so this home-based project gave her the chance to personally manage the ongoing restoration of her cherished two-hundred-year-old house, also known as Joyeuse. And in her spare time, she pointed her skiff toward shore and tied it to Douglass' beautiful new dock, so that she could sit in this lab and catalog treasures. Since Faye thrived on work, she had never been happier.

Faye's squawk distracted Douglass from the paper in his hand.

"You hurt?" he asked.

"Nope. But would you take a look at this?"

While pulling a particularly filthy find from its cleaning solution, she had noticed specks of a color that was not dirt-brown. It was green, her favorite color. It was the color of the live oaks that overhung her home. It was the color of the Gulf of Mexico in early morning.

She swished the object around, anxious to remove the encrusted soil without scratching its surface. Flabbergasted, she watched as an emerald's crystalline facets emerged. She held it in her fingers and its grassy color contrasted with the warm brown of her skin.

The stone was huge, as emeralds go. For some reason, the pure green light reflecting off its surface made her think of the fruit that grew, uncultivated, all over Joyeuse Island. It was the size and shape of a scuppernong grape or a wild plum. Faye, who had never before craved jewelry, felt an unreasoning need to possess this luminous thing.

Because the urge to keep it to herself was so strong, she handed it to Douglass, while she still could. The light in his brown eyes said that he, too, was drawn to its beauty.

He held it up. Light shattered on its surface, flinging green sparks around the room.

"I'll give you credit for this much, Faye. When you go treasure hunting, you don't mess around."

Faye's work day had effectively ended when she cleaned the dirt off a priceless emerald. Since then, she and Douglass had accomplished exactly nothing. Not unless you counted fruitless speculation about what a treasure like that was doing underground on Joyeuse Island, in Faye's own back yard.

"It's not too hard to guess who wore it," Faye pointed out. "My family only had money for one generation before the Civil War wiped them out. I'm talking about the European branch of the family tree. The African branch never had any money at all. The shape and ornate gold setting—what's left of the set-ting—suggest that it would have been the pendant in a grand necklace."

Douglass squinted at the stone's setting, as if he wondered how it was made. "It certainly doesn't look like something a man would have worn."

"In my family's one wealthy generation, there were only two free women on the island: my great-great-great-grandmother Mariah Whitehall and her daughter-in-law, Carole LaFourche. Since I think we can presume that none of the slave women ever wore this thing, it had to be one of them."

"Then I guess it's yours."

"I feel like it belongs in a museum. Fortunately, you've got one handy."

Douglass rolled the bauble around on his palm. "Before you give your treasure away, why don't you sleep on the idea?"

"I couldn't sleep with something that valuable in my house. And I hate to leave it here for you to worry about."

Douglass inclined his head toward a walk-in safe. "I got that thing so I wouldn't *have* to worry about my stuff. Leave it here until you decide what to do."

As Faye gathered her things to go home, she reflected that the reporter had come a week too soon. Six months of nagging phone calls from Faye had finally persuaded the features editor of the Tallahassee newspaper to do an article on Douglass' museum. She was afraid the man had been disappointed by its lack of flashy displays.

The sexiest artifact Faye had been able to show him was an engraved silver hip flask. The reporter had photographed Douglass holding the flask, knowing that it would be interesting to his readers because it was marked with a real person's name—an old-fashioned name, Jedediah Bachelder—because it was made from a precious metal, and because it had once held liquor.

Faye had tried to call his attention to other more significant artifacts—a broken hoe left behind by a long-ago field hand or a shattered pot of African design—but he'd had a magpie's eye for shiny stuff. Only the silver hip flask held his interest. After snapping its photograph, he'd gone on his merry way. This emerald would have impressed him a heckuva lot more.

"How old do you think this thing is?" Douglass was still fondling the emerald.

"Judging from the old-fashioned cut, I'd say it's at least a couple hundred years old. The setting's broken, but it looks about the same age. Mariah and Carole weren't around that long ago, but that doesn't mean they never wore this emerald. It just means that it wasn't new when they bought it. Or maybe Carole inherited it. I don't know anything about Carole's family, but it's for certain sure that Mariah's father never bought her a priceless emerald."

Faye bent down to rifle through a box full of her field notebooks, then another. Victorious, she pulled out the one documenting the find, saying, "I need to refresh my memory on where I found this baby. Maybe it has brothers."

"Maybe they're already here," Douglass says, gesturing at all the artifacts yet to be cleaned.

"That may be," Faye says, "but you keep your hands off. If you want your museum to be taken seriously, we have to do things right."

◇◇◇

Douglass rolled the emerald around on his palm. He was still laughing, an hour after she left, at the bossy angle of Faye's head as she told him to keep his hands off her precious artifacts. He knew better than to try his luck at amateur archaeology. He had learned long ago that it was worth the money to hire smart, competent people. That was why he kept Faye around.

Well, he also kept her around because she fussed over him like the daughter he and Emma had never had. And every now and then, she let him fuss over her, although she remained remarkably resistant to letting him give her things. She continued to let him pay her a nice little salary, but only because she knew she earned it.

Sometimes, he fancied that she looked like the daughter he and his wife should have had. She wore her hair cropped short like Emma, but her glossy and straight black locks looked nothing like his wife's soft, tight curls. Faye's determined jawline reminded him of his own, but he suspected that it was due less to genetics than to sheer, stubborn cussedness. And he and Faye both had cussedness to spare.

He felt in his pocket for the cigar that he was saving for this moment, when neither Faye nor Emma was around to fuss at him for tainting his lungs. Retirement gave a man so few opportunities to do things that met with his womenfolk's disapproval.

A noise at the top of the stairs told him that Emma had finally come home from her regular Saturday-night bridge party. There would be no cigar tonight.

"I'm down here!" he called out, holding the emerald up to the light and knowing how much his wife would appreciate this rarity that Faye had dug up. Maybe Emma would like some emeralds. He'd never bought her any, not that he could remember.

The footsteps on the stairs were loud and hurried, which wasn't like Emma. Maybe if she'd been the kind of woman who drank while she was playing bridge, her step might not be as light and ladylike as it always was. He rose from his chair. "Emma? Are you okay?"

Another set of footsteps and a deep voice told him that he and Emma had an uninvited guest. "Shit. There's somebody down there. I thought you saw two cars leave. Shit." Clattering footfalls echoed down the staircase.

This was a most inopportune time to be balancing a fortune on his palm.

At least two sets of footsteps rushed down the basement steps toward him. The building inspector had approved the room's small, high windows as "emergency escapes," but Douglass knew he could never haul himself out before the intruders arrived. Nor could he leave Emma to a stranger's mercy. For the first time, he wondered if she were even home. He prayed she was still trumping her partner's aces. He'd presumed the first footsteps were hers, but he'd never heard her speak. All he knew was that here were at least two intruders closing in on him. There could be more.

His fist closed over the emerald. He needed to hide it, but the safe mocked him from across the room. It might as well be a million miles away.

With an odd pang of relief, he watched two men, and only two men, clad in dark clothing barrel into the room. Emma wasn't here. Knowing she was safe gave him the strength to face this danger alone.

# Chapter Two

Faye piloted her skiff over the dark waters of the Gulf of Mexico, enjoying this late-night ride home. The silhouette of her beloved island blotted out a sweep of stars near the horizon, and its dark looming shape left her perfectly happy.

Her entire self was bound up in that island. Her African-American ancestors had been slaves there. They had built the glorious mansion for their masters...who were also her ancestors. And before that the island had been held by a succession of Native American tribes. Her romantic imagination insisted that the Creek were among the indigenous peoples who had lived on Joyeuse Island. Since her great-great-great-great-grandmother was half-Creek, imagining them on her island just enhanced her sense of ownership. And since her best friend Joe was mostly Creek, it gave them both a blood connection to their island home, and to each other.

When her cell phone rang, she was almost nostalgic for the days when she couldn't afford one.

"Faye."

Emma's voice was quiet and terrible. Faye cut the motor so she could hear her better.

"Douglass is in the hospital. He's in critical condition. He—"

Knowing full well that she shouldn't interrupt a woman with a voice so full of devastation, Faye couldn't help herself. "What happened? I just left him. He had a heart attack, didn't he? Or a stroke."

Faye remembered his heavy tread on the staircase. She should have stayed with him until Emma got home.

"Faye?" Emma's voice interrupted her dark thoughts. "Did you hear me, Faye? This was no heart attack. Somebody beat him, somebody that wanted him dead. From the look of him, I think they thought he *was* dead when they left him lying there. I surely didn't expect to find him still breathing when I saw what they'd done."

"But who? Who would want to hurt Douglass?"

"I don't know if they came intending to hurt him. Maybe they just wanted his...our...things."

Emma said the word "things" as if she wanted to run through her luxurious new beach house and throw all its beautiful furnishings—antiques, artwork, and all—into the waves.

"I knew right away that something was wrong," Emma raved on, "just as soon as I got home. Somebody had kicked the glass right out of the front door and left it wide open. When I saw that, I started looking for Douglass. The light over the basement stairs was the only one burning in the whole house, so I went down there first. Everything was dumped on the floor, all your artifacts and your file folders and everything, and Douglass was lying bloody in the middle of the mess. Oh, Faye..."

"I'm coming," Faye said, though she didn't move to start the skiff's motor, not yet. She needed to be able to hear everything her tortured friend had to say. "I'm just so glad that whoever did this was gone when you got there."

"I didn't miss them by much. When I walked in the house, I could see out the back windows, all the way down to the water. Two big men were carrying boxes out there. I'm guessing they had a boat tied up to our dock." Emma's voice shook with indignation. "They came here to steal something, but what? It looks like they went straight to the lab in the basement, without touching our stuff upstairs, which is actually worth money. Douglass always told me not to worry when he brought artifacts home. He always said, 'I run a Museum of American *Slavery*, sugar. Slaves were poor folks, by definition. There's nothing in the whole museum worth stealing.'"

But Faye knew that there was. The last time she saw Douglass, he was cradling an emerald in the palm of his hand. No one had seen that emerald since it went in the ground years, maybe centuries, before. How was it possible that anyone other than she and Douglass could have known where it was tonight?

"They don't think he's going to make it," Emma sobbed. "The paramedics wouldn't come out and say so, but I could tell. I rode in the front of the ambulance, and there was a little window where I could look back and watch them work on him. The sight was horrible, but I couldn't look away. It would have been like abandoning him at the very end."

"We don't know that this is the end. Not yet."

"The trauma people put him on a stretcher and wheeled him away from me, then they closed the door behind them. He needs me there. He needs to know that I would never leave him alone."

Tears burned Faye's eyes. "He knows that. He's always known that."

Emma was whispering now. "They called a Code Blue on somebody back there. I heard them. What will I do if they come to tell me...what will I do? I'll be alone, Faye."

"I'm coming." Faye cranked the motor. "This boat makes a mighty lot of racket, but I can still hear you. You just keep talking to me, and you won't be alone."

Hardly ten minutes had passed when Emma's reflexive babbling slowed and she said, "Somebody's coming. His doctor is walking across the waiting room and he's got me in his sights."

"I'm coming. Just hang on to the phone." Faye goosed the motor and wrung a little more speed out of it. "Don't put it down, because I'll be on the other end for as long as you need me."

Joe Wolf Mantooth settled himself behind the wheel. He still gloried in his ability to drive, and it was all thanks to Faye.

She had opened so many doors to the wide world for Joe. First, she'd helped him get his driver's license at the advanced age of twenty-eight. Then, she'd hauled him bodily through the paperwork involved in getting his education back on track, making sure he got every accommodation for his learning disabilities that the law allowed. He wasn't real clear on the details, but he thought it was possible that she'd gotten him some accommodations that the law *didn't* allow. Faye could be scary when she was in hot pursuit of a goal.

Thanks to Faye, Joe had earned his GED, and he was now enrolled in some remedial classes that promised to make him college-ready in time for the fall semester. He was proud of his accomplishments and he wouldn't trade them for anything— except now he was going to school in Tallahassee, and Faye was doing archaeology in the Last Isles. Joe didn't much care for cities, and he didn't much care for being so far away from Faye.

Joe grieved for Douglass as he drove south, but the teachings of his Creek ancestors comforted him, because he knew that Douglass had earned his peace. There was more value, right this minute, in focusing on the needs of those left behind. He would be with Emma and Faye, sharing their burden, just as soon as this car could get him there.

This was no time to think of himself, but even Joe wasn't completely pure of heart. He'd been in Tallahassee for nearly three months, plenty of time for Faye to invite her new friend, Ross Donnelly, to drive his sleek sports car down to Florida from his Atlanta townhouse. And maybe she had. Faye's business was her own.

Still, Joe noticed that, when faced with matters of life and death and love, Faye had chosen to call him. She had asked him to come.

He stomped on the accelerator, but his rusted-out, underpowered excuse for a car was already giving him all it had. Maybe it was time to get a new one.

Faye sat vigil with Emma, in the living room of the elegant home the older woman had shared with her husband. She couldn't believe that Douglass was dead.

Someone tapped on the front door. Faye recognized Joe by the sound of his quiet knock, respectful but not tentative. She went to meet him, but she was stopped short by the sight of him standing calmly outside the shattered door. Splintered glass framed Joe's tall, sturdy body, and she worried that scattered shards of broken glass would slice right through the soles of his moccasins. He stood there patiently, as if it would never occur to him to step through the violated doorway, unless invited.

Joe had brought some necessities with him: bourbon, handkerchiefs, and his two strong arms. He distributed hugs liberally, then settled himself beside the two women. Faye couldn't think of anyone better suited to visit a house of grief. Joe knew how to talk when people wanted to talk, and he knew how to sit still when people didn't want to talk. She thought perhaps the bourbon was a bad idea, since he was visiting the widow of a deacon in the Blessed Assurance African Methodist Episcopal Church. As usual, she thought wrong.

"Let me find some glasses for that stuff," Emma said, rummaging through the kitchen cabinets and coming up with three large tumblers. "The rest of the world drinks it. It can't be all that bad. Besides, the good Lord knows I need something to get me through this night."

Joe sloshed a couple of ounces of bourbon into Emma's glass, ignoring Faye's signals to give her a tiny portion. Emma stifled a little gag and coughed, but she forced down a couple of sips. "Tastes like gasoline," she said. "Or shoe polish. But it *is* distracting."

Faye swirled the brown liquid around in the bottom of her own glass. She wasn't much of a bourbon drinker, being as how she couldn't afford it. She lived in a money pit, so she never had any spare cash. And neither did Joe, on his work-study salary, but he didn't seem to need a lot of money...although she'd bet his grocery bill had gone up, now that he was living in Tallahassee. The hunting and fishing couldn't be good in a town that size.

Faye agreed with Emma about the flavor of bourbon, but she would have compared the flavor to paint stripper. Still, this was a good night for buffering pain, and bourbon was a good enough way to do it.

Crunching glass outside the front door signaled the arrival of another visitor before the doorbell even sounded.

Sheriff Mike McKenzie stood outside, hat off and head slightly bowed. "You know I have to be here on business. First, though, please accept my most sincere personal condolences. God makes very few men as fine as your husband, ma'am."

The four of them sat together for a time. The sound of evidence technicians hustling equipment downstairs and the sheriff's refusal of a glass of bourbon were the only reminders that he was on duty. Soon enough, though, he brought the conversation around to the difficult truth. "Do any of you have any idea who did this thing?"

"If it was somebody looking for something to steal, then they got interrupted." Faye gestured at the walls around them, covered with original artwork.

"Or they were too stupid to know what they were looking at," the sheriff said. Everyone present nodded to acknowledge his point.

"Did your husband have any enemies?"

"Not really. Not any more. When he was just building his construction business, there were people who didn't like him. Competitors who couldn't stand losing a job to a black man. Problem employees who couldn't understand that they were fired for their own bad behavior. Clients who couldn't pay their bills. Business people don't always win a lot of popularity contests. But Douglass was retired. We don't have to deal with those people any more."

"It wouldn't hurt for you to make a list of old enemies, just in case," the sheriff said. "And we can't lose sight of the simple fact that he was widely known to be the richest man in the county. Maybe he just had the awful luck to cross paths with the baddest criminals in the county."

"I wish I'd gotten a better look at them when—" Emma caught a sharp breath. "I just remembered. The two people I saw running away…they were carrying boxes. There's nothing missing upstairs, not that I can tell. Nobody but Faye's going to be able to tell us whether there's anything missing downstairs."

The sheriff turned his attention to Faye. "You were the last person to see him before the attack. Did he seem upset? Worried?"

"Not a bit. I do want you to look at an article about Douglass and his museum that ran in the Tallahassee paper yesterday. I can't think of anything in that article that would have put him in danger, but it's a mighty big coincidence that he was killed so soon after it appeared."

Faye was considering whether this was the time to tell the sheriff about the emerald, when yet another knock sounded. Though broken and useless, that front door was turning out to be the center of the evening.

"Why, Dr. Clark, how nice to see you," Emma said, curiosity faintly coloring her cultured voice. Her unspoken question couldn't have been more obvious. *Do doctors really call on the homes of their deceased patients these days? After midnight?*

"We have procedures to deal with things like this, ordinarily, but—"

Faye could see the man's hands clenching and unclenching in the pockets of his lab coat.

"I'm glad you're here, Sheriff," the doctor began again. "And I'm glad we've got a couple more witnesses, as well. This isn't something I'd trust with just anybody. That's why I came straight to Mrs. Everett. I'm not sure the hospital's security is all that secure, if you know what I mean. I'm not even sure I'd trust everybody at the sheriff's department. No offense."

"None taken. But do you mind spitting out whatever it is you're trying to say?"

The pockets rippled again as the man's fists clenched. "Did any of you know about the secret pocket in the waistband of Mr. Everett's pants?"

Before speaking, the sheriff cast a quizzical glance at Emma, whose expression said exactly nothing. He spoke anyway. "Lots of rich men have places to hide extra cash."

"It wasn't cash that we found." The doctor pulled his right hand out of a lab coat pocket, holding it up, palm outstretched. Resting on it was an emerald the size of a wild plum.

# Chapter Three

Splintered potsherds. Scattered flint chips. And dirt everywhere. Faye longed to sweep it all up, so she could mop the floor. She needed to erase the blood that Douglass had left behind. She needed it badly.

But this was a crime scene, and she wasn't here to clean, but to help the sheriff find enough clues to nail her friend's killers. She stood where the sheriff told her, at the foot of the stairs, and answered the sheriff's questions as best she could.

"Do you know what he stored in the safe?"

"No. He was planning to put the emerald in there, but he must not have had a chance."

The sheriff made a note on his clipboard. "Can you tell if anything else is missing?"

She looked at the wreckage and started to laugh.

He rethought his question. "Okay. Let's take this a piece at a time. What about the walls? They weren't disturbed, not that we can tell. Was there anything hanging on the walls that's not there now?"

Faye shook her head.

"Okay, now look at the big stuff. Has any of the furniture been moved? Besides that overturned desk chair?"

She shook her head again, and he recorded her response.

He asked her another question and she had to ask him to repeat it, because the meticulous preparations of the evidence technicians had distracted her. Lifting fingerprints and collecting loose hairs was painstaking work. Any clues they found would probably be fragile and fragmentary, and it would take expertise and intuition to make any sense of them. Not for the first time, Faye reflected that crime scene investigation wasn't so very different from archaeology.

"Faye," the sheriff said again. "Are you listening? Maybe we should do this tomorrow. I hope I never have a night like the one you just spent."

She shook her head, trying to bring her focus back to the here-and-now. "Are you kidding? There's nothing else left that I can do for Douglass. Or for Emma. If there are any clues here, we need to find them now, before the bastards get any further away. You do have people out there looking for them, don't you?"

Sheriff Mike gave her a look that asked, *Do you truly think I'm an idiot?*, and didn't dignify her question with the answer. No one on his payroll would sleep tonight. The woods, swamp, and gulf were full of his people.

He directed Faye's attention back to the cluttered laboratory. "Okay. Look at the pattern of the stuff on the floor. Can you tell anything about what they were looking for?"

She searched the floor, looking for patterns. That's what science was...a search for patterns that explained something important. And what could be more important than the murder of a friend? She willed herself to see the pattern, but there was none. Only paper and debris and dirt and blood.

If this were an archaeological dig, how would she approach it?

Photographs. Lots of photographs. And sketches. When she dug into history, she was always acutely aware that she wasn't just uncovering evidence of the past. She was destroying evidence, too. No power on earth could put dirt back in the ground and restore a site to its original condition. Everything had to be done right, the first time.

When she dug, she needed to know the exact depth where each artifact had been found. A photograph of a precisely vertical slice through the ground gave her a permanent record of every soil horizon. In a sense, it also gave her a slice through time.

This ransacked room presented a different problem. The debris wasn't distributed vertically through soil; it was spread horizontally across the floor. The most useful photograph would come from directly above. A simple sheet of graph paper laid over that photo would give investigators a plot with the location of every last piece of trash.

But how to get that photo?

The sheriff's voice intruded on her thoughts. "Faye?"

She held up a hand, signaling that she needed just another minute to think. He knew her well, so he held his tongue.

To get the whole floor into one photo would require chopping out the ceiling and the upstairs rooms, then mounting the camera in a helicopter. So that idea could be eliminated. The investigators would have to make do with a composite of several shots.

Should they take the pictures from atop a high ladder? Possibly, but the drawbacks were serious. The legs of the ladder would obscure part of the floor. Also, dragging a ladder around the room would disturb the very crime scene being photographed.

Scaffolding was the only answer. And the key to getting the job done was right in front of her, just above eye level.

"Those windowsills will each support one end of a scaffold," she said, her eyes on the windows, rather than on the sheriff. "For your photographer."

"Do what?" he began, then he caught her meaning. Four high windows were evenly spaced down the opposite wall. If his techs built supports where they sat, snug against the wall pierced by the staircase, then passed scaffolding through those windows, the crime scene would hardly be disturbed. At worst, they'd have to install a single support in the middle of each scaffold. And the benefit of having a perfect record of the location of all this…stuff…would be well worth that drawback.

"You ever thought of going to the police academy? If I had you working for me, every two-bit criminal in the county might as well move on down the road. 'Cause you and me would fill the jail with the sorry asses of every last one that stayed."

◇◇◇

The scaffolding was in place, and the photographer was working diligently. Hours had passed, and Faye thought she saw dawn's pink light seeping through the basement's windows. Sheriff Mike was sitting on the bottom stair with a notebook computer balanced on his lap, and she was perched two steps up, so she could look over his shoulder at the first batch of photos.

He used his pen as a pointer to gesture at the computer screen. "Maybe all this stuff came out of one box." The pen drew a circle in the air over the lower right-hand cover of the screen. "Or maybe the stuff in…say…this area here came out of one box, because they were looking for something in particular…something they thought was stored in that box. Something that's missing now. That's the kind of pattern we're looking for. Nobody would know those things but you."

The sheriff's pen dropped to the clipboard balanced on the stair beside him. He scribbled on it like a man who knew that a computer was more efficient, yet preferred paper because it helped him think. His words echoed in Faye's sleep-addled mind. "Maybe all this stuff came out of one box…"

The sheriff's incessant note-taking bothered her for some reason she couldn't fathom. Didn't her work require her to take whole books full of notes?

This, finally, was the question that shifted her brain out of neutral. Yes, her job did require her to fill up one field notebook after another. Her eyes darted around the room. Where were the boxes that had held her field notebooks?

"They took my field notes." The sheriff kept taking copious notes of his own. "Why would they take my field notes?"

The sheriff's face was troubled. His wife, Dr. Magda Stockard-McKenzie, was an archaeologist and Faye's mentor. He knew exactly what the loss of a boxful of field notes could mean—months of wasted work and the loss of irreplaceable information. "How much work did you lose, Faye?"

Faye cracked a smile, the first one since her last conversation with Douglass. "I didn't lose a second of work, because I always do everything Magda tells me to do. In a file box in my bedroom, I have photocopies of every last page of those notebooks. I used to be sloppy about that kind of thing, until one day when she hid my field notes. I thought I'd lost a whole semester's work. A shock like that leaves a mark on a girl."

It hadn't taken Joe long to pilot Faye's boat out to Joyeuse Island and retrieve her notes. Faye had wanted to go herself, just because she thought the salt spray would clear her head, but the sheriff had made an excellent argument for her to stay right where she was.

First, he'd said, "Stand here and look at the dirt and junk thrown all over that floor." After she'd done that, he'd said, "Now come upstairs for a minute. I want a word with you in private." Once out of earshot of the technicians, he asked, "Could that emerald have been part of a bigger piece of jewelry? A necklace or a bracelet or something?"

"Absolutely. There's really no way to know."

"And you say that it looked like just a clod of dirt before you cleaned it?"

Light had dawned. "You need me to sit on those stairs and help you watch your staff, just in case one of them uncovers a priceless emerald."

"Yep. I've gotta be in and out of the room, talking on the radio to the folks I've got out on the water, looking for the killers and their boat. And I need to be in and out of the house, overseeing the technicians who are looking for evidence inside and outside. I've got Joe busy upstairs, pretending to keep Emma company while he watches out the windows for bad guys. There's nobody else to sit here and watch for emeralds. Besides, you know your lab. It needs to be you keeping an eye on things."

"Do you have doubts about any personnel in particular?"

"Heck, no. But I'd hate to see a bunch of jewels get swept into a dustpan and thrown out the back door. Besides—my techs are real young. They've got bills, and they've got student loans to pay off. A pocket-sized fortune would be a powerful temptation."

"I'd better get back down there."

"Good idea."

So she'd spent hours watching the technicians work, and she was still sitting there when the sheriff told his staff to knock off work before they went to sleep on their feet.

After they were gone, he settled himself heavily on the steps beside her, and Faye remembered that he was almost as old as Douglass had been. Time was wreaking havoc on her friends.

"No emeralds, huh?"

She shook her head. "Anybody find anything upstairs?"

"Emma took me on a tour of their art collection. Nice stuff, too. It's all where it should be. And her jewelry's in the bedroom, right where she left it."

"What can I do to help you find the people who did this to Douglass? And to Emma. Every time they hit Douglass, they were battering Emma, too."

"Well, for starters, you can try not to get your own self killed. Stick close to Joe and don't give any bad guys a chance to get close to you. That means you can't go out looking for bad guys."

Faye rolled her eyes. "I'm not in the habit of doing that."

"But you could keep looking into the information that was published in that newspaper article. Especially that silver hip flask. You know—see if there's anything else that would have attracted thieves or a killer. The emerald's a long shot, since nobody knew about it but you and Douglass, but it wouldn't hurt to keep checking that out. You're gonna do it anyway."

She snorted, but couldn't keep the smile back.

Emma's voice wafted down the stairs. "Faye. The morning's gone and you still haven't slept. I've made up a bed in the room next to mine. It's time for you to take a nap."

Faye wanted to be in her own bed, so she began assembling an excuse, "Oh, Joe and I need to get home to—"

Emma came far enough down the staircase to make eye contact...serious, motherly, no-nonsense eye contact. "I chased Joe into the guest room five minutes ago. He's asleep. Don't make me chase you into your room, too."

Not wanting to upset Emma, Faye did as she was told. As her eyes slid shut, she heard steps in the room next door as Emma walked from one end of the room to the other, paused at the window, then paced back. Sometimes, she paused in the middle of the room for no apparent reason. Or, rather, for a reason known only to her. Perhaps she was studying a carpet stain made when Douglass dropped a coffee cup. Or maybe she was surveying the king-sized bed where she would now be sleeping alone.

After each pause, the deliberate steps began again, at the exact same tempo. *This*, Faye thought, *is what it sounds like to be widowed.*

# Chapter Four

When Faye woke, the glow of late afternoon sun was seeping in her window, and the footsteps in the master bedroom had gone quiet. She would rather eat dirt than wake Emma. Leaving a note on the kitchen table, she slipped out the back door. Joe was on the beach, watching the waves crash. He must have taken his ponytail down when he went to bed, because loose near-black hair played around his face, stirred by the sea wind.

"I want to go home," she said. "I want it bad."

"Got anything to eat out there?"

"Peanut butter and bread. I'm out of honey."

"How long since you ate that ham sandwich the sheriff's folks brought out?"

"Um…"

"You gotta eat, Faye. You should take better care of yourself than that."

Joe reached into the leather bag he wore at his waist and pulled out a handful of jerky. Faye took it, even though she had no notion of what kind of meat Joe had seasoned and desiccated and stored for just such an occasion. It probably wasn't beef jerky, since Joe didn't go around shooting cows with his hand-made arrows. More likely, it was preserved venison or squirrel or rabbit. Regardless of which animal gave its all for this snack, it was unquestionably tasty. Joe was a man of many gifts, and one of those gifts was a pronounced knack for cooking.

He rummaged around some more and fetched out some dried blackberries. Like the jerky, they were chewy but good. Faye wondered if Joe's magic bag held something from every level of the USDA's food pyramid.

"This'll keep you on your feet until we go back inside," Joe said, adding some pecans to the pile of sustenance on Faye's palm. "I did want to let Miss Emma sleep, though."

"Me, too. She needs a few minutes when she can forget everything."

Joe stared at her as if she'd said something idiotic. Faye couldn't remember ever being on the receiving end of such a look from Joe.

"Sleep isn't for forgetting. That's when the dreams come. The healing dreams. Miss Emma needs to sleep so she can know that everything's gonna be okay."

Suddenly, Faye knew how Joe felt, constantly being treated like a remedial student by everyone around him. Lord, she hoped she didn't do that to him often. When it came to spiritual matters, Joe possessed the equivalent of a Ph.D. Why did she keep forgetting that?

Maybe she needed to spend more time dreaming.

Faye didn't know how long she'd sat with her head on Joe's shoulder, watching the sea birds dive for fish. Something made her look over her shoulder—maybe some of Joe's intuitive ways were rubbing off on her—and she saw Emma above them, leaning against the deck railing and staring at the self-same birds. The older woman's face was sleepy and unlined, as if a few hours' healing sleep had washed away whole years.

She and Joe hurried up the wooden steps leading to Emma's vantage point.

Faye reached out a hand and touched Emma's shoulder. "How do you feel?"

"Like I'm living in a brand new world that I don't like much."

"I've been thinking," Faye blurted out. "I want to help you make the arrangements for…"

Emma turned her eyes away from the endless water and focused them on Faye. "I'd like it very much if you'd go with me to the funeral home tomorrow morning. We're having the funeral on Wednesday, and two days isn't much time to plan."

"Planning a funeral is tough on anybody. I definitely think we should do it together," Faye said.

"Oh, it'll be hard, but not the way you're thinking. The funeral director's going to try to sell me a package worthy of the richest man in Micco County. And I'll be trying to follow the wishes of a man who told me to bury him in a pine box."

Faye saw an immediate problem. "I'm not sure they sell those any more. And I'm not sure how the health department feels about them."

"There's plenty of room on Joyeuse Island—" Joe began.

Faye interrupted him before he finished offering to bury Douglass himself, under a big live oak, without bothering with embalming or fancy hymns or a florist's services. She knew that he was well-qualified to give the deceased a Creek-style sendoff, but the fact was that Douglass the Deacon would have wanted a Christian burial. And the health department was likely to be somewhat finicky about pesky details like embalming.

"Joe," Faye said, "I think you're going to have to let us plan a traditional funeral." Then she realized that her statement needed clarifying. "I'm talking about Douglass' traditions, not Creek ones."

Joe nodded that he understood.

"I think we two women can stand against a hard-sell funeral director," Emma said. "We know what Douglass liked. He appreciated beautiful things and he was willing to spend his money on them, but he wouldn't have parted with a nickel just to impress somebody. If we keep our wits about us, nobody will be able to sell us anything we don't want."

Thinking of hermetically sealed metal caskets lined in quilted satin, Faye found herself hoping that Joe would take care of her burial when the time came.

◇◇◇

Joe had a characteristic that was most useful in a colleague. He worked in silence.

He'd been remarkably useful to Faye as she attacked a huge and unpleasant task, sorting through the debris that the burglars left behind. It was like excavating a grievously desecrated historical site, treasures mixed with garbage, then thrown willy-nilly everywhere.

On Monday, once the technicians had finished their photography and their inch-by-inch survey of the crime scene, the sheriff had asked Faye to take the lead. Today, on her second day of sorting through the mess, Faye had found that she could close her eyes and still see scattered junk imprinted on her retinas.

She'd grown to hate the sight of her lab, with its cheerful yellow walls and its dark history as a murder scene. Yet she couldn't leave it. She couldn't stand to see the artifacts that she'd so carefully excavated lying broken on the floor. She needed to make the place neat and orderly again, because there was no other way to set her broken world right.

Joe's skills at cataloging broken bits of flint were nothing short of amazing. As an experienced flintknapper, he could sift through a pile of rock chips and pluck out two pieces that had been broken from the same rock. In a sense, he was gathering up remnants of artifacts that the thieves had damaged and making them whole again. He'd done his darndest to find more emeralds, and so had Faye, but they'd had no luck, so far.

She tried to reconstruct the thieves' activities. They'd broken the front door and run straight downstairs. The muddy footprints on Emma's elegant celery-green carpet made that perfectly clear. Why had they come down here, rather than ransack the house's expensively furnished living quarters?

A few possible answers came to mind. Perhaps Douglass was their only target, and they knew he was in the basement alone. But this begged the question of why they wanted him dead, and how they knew where he was, and why they took anything with them. For there was no question that the two boxes that had held her field notes were missing, and Emma had no doubt that she'd seen two men carrying boxes.

Or perhaps they'd known exactly what they wanted and where to find it. Perhaps they had rushed downstairs, intending to steal one specific thing, but Douglass was unlucky enough to be in the way. Then, after putting him out of commission, they had packed the thing or things they came to steal into the two missing boxes and left. This would make her notebooks innocent bystanders, accidentally kidnapped during a crime. Supporting that theory was the fact that the newspaper article published on the day of the robbery had mentioned that Douglass had a basement lab manned by a professional archaeologist. If they had wanted a particular artifact, then they knew that there was a good chance it was stored in the lab.

Nibbling at Faye's mind was the final and, to her mind, least likely possibility. Perhaps her notebooks hadn't been an unfortunate casualty. Perhaps the thieves hadn't just thrown the objects of their invasion into the boxes storing her notebooks, stealing them accidentally. Perhaps her notes had been their goal all along. But why?

The article had mentioned no artifacts more valuable than the silver flask, which was nearly worthless, so there was no value in stealing the notes documenting all her valueless finds. It hadn't, thank goodness, mentioned her by name, but every page of those notebooks bore her initials. Micco County was no burgeoning metropolis. It wouldn't be too hard to find an archaeologist with the initials F.L.

Faye hadn't discussed these suspicions with anyone. Neither Joe nor Ross could be trusted to react rationally to the idea that Douglass' killers might be looking for Faye. She hadn't even mentioned them to the sheriff, but she sensed that he shared her concern. Otherwise, his not-too-subtle efforts to ensure she was constantly monitored by Joe or someone equally large were nonsensical. And a little insulting.

Faye was no dummy, and she didn't mind taking reasonable precautions. Part of those reasonable precautions had been to use her photocopies of those field notebooks as bedtime stories for the past two nights. Reading those notes had only fed her desire to get back out to Joyeuse Island and look for some more emeralds, but the work she was doing in the lab where Douglass was killed was far more important for the time being.

She had scrutinized every notebook page for some detail that might make her a target. She'd found nothing so far, but she was keeping her eyes open.

# Chapter Five

Every pew in the Blessed Assurance African Methodist Episcopal Church was full, and the ushers had filled the vestibule with folding chairs. Being the survivor of a housefire, Faye found herself scanning the room, looking for a clear path to a window or a door. The open casket made her uncomfortable, but it was what Emma had wanted. She had to admit that, as she watched the mourners file by Douglass' body, many of them seemed to get comfort from one last look at the dead man's face.

She surveyed the casket's polished wood with satisfaction. As she had suspected, there was no modern equivalent of the plain pine box, but neither she nor Emma could bear the thought of putting Douglass into the enameled tin cans that passed for caskets these days. The funeral director's eyes had lit up when Emma asked about wooden coffins.

"Oh, yes, ma'am, we have those, and they are well-worth the extra cost. They feature lovely lines and a hand-rubbed sheen. We can provide any finish you desire—cherry, mahogany, maple, oak...pine..."

With the single word "pine," the solicitous man made his sale. Emma never even asked the price. Douglass had certainly left her enough money to give him exactly what he'd wanted. It was her last chance to do so.

The pine glowed golden, even though its finish was now smudged with the fingerprints of an onslaught of mourners intent on laying hands on the deceased and everything associated with him, even his coffin.

Faye had been honored to sit in the daughter's spot in the family room during the viewing of the body. She had leaned in close to Emma and stayed there while hundreds of people filed past to pay their respects. She had rarely spoken, but Emma seemed to derive strength from her presence, and a newborn widow certainly needed her strength. Faye didn't think that the current Queen Elizabeth herself was ever forced to graciously greet this many people in the space of a single evening.

Joe had long ago stood in the interminable line for a chance to pay his respects to Douglass' widow. Since then, he had stood in the front corner of the family room, near the door, where he could see the face of everyone who entered or left. His intense scrutiny was Faye's most insistent reminder of the fact she would like to forget but couldn't. Douglass had not left this life on his body's schedule or on God's. He had been brutally removed from the side of his loving wife. Joe's clear green eyes were searching the funeral guests, looking for signs of a murderer. Sheriff Mike lingered nearby, doing the same thing.

As Faye sat watching Joe, a familiar figure came into sight and paused, standing framed in the doorway. She had told him not to come. She had called him, weeping and looking for comfort in the face of violent death. In the same breath, she had told him not to come, but here he was.

Why hadn't she wanted him to come? Because she had the feeling that it would be unwise to let herself be alone with him now, when her shattered defenses might prompt her to make a commitment she wasn't ready to make. When dealing with a man like Ross Donnelly, a woman had to know what she wanted. Otherwise, she was going to get what Ross wanted.

◇◇◇

Emma did her best to walk proud during her long trip down the aisle to the front pew, which was reserved for bereaved family members. Douglass had never seen her hang her head and weep, and she knew he was looking down on her from heaven now. Nothing would make Emma lose her grip on her dignity.

And apparently, nothing would make Faye lose her grip on her elbow. The child seemed to believe that Emma would collapse if she let go. That was doubtful. Emma reflected that she had lived sixty years without collapsing even once. She'd never fainted yet, nor succumbed to a fit of the vapors. It seemed unlikely that she would start doing such things now. Still, she wouldn't have wanted to live through this thing without Faye's help.

There had been talk among Douglass' kinfolk about her inviting Faye to sit with the family at the funeral. Emma was not surprised. The Everetts were the kind of family that was very good at that kind of backbiting.

The way Emma saw it, her husband's cousins had been blessed with all the children they wanted. She and Douglass had not. She figured that since God had not given her a daughter, then He had implicitly given her the option to choose her own. Although if Faye didn't stop pushing Kleenexes in her direction, she planned to stuff the whole wad of them into the casket with her late husband.

Lord, how she hated that open casket, but she knew her friends and relatives. If the lid had been closed, they would have talked about it all week.

*Reckon how bad those murderers beat him? Must've been plenty bad, if Emma didn't even let the reverend open the coffin lid.*

Emma wished she had eyes in the back of her head, because two of the seats directly behind her were occupied by intriguing people. Joe Wolf Mantooth remained intriguing, though she'd known him for more than three years now. And Ross Donnelly was newly intriguing.

She and Douglass had met him just a month before. Faye was making her third trip to see Ross in Atlanta, and Douglass had said, "She's apparently not going to bring him home to meet us any time soon. Let's fake an urgent business trip to Atlanta." So they'd done just that, calling Faye on her cell phone when they got close to town and offering to take her and Ross out to dinner.

Faye had known precisely what they were up to. So, probably, had Ross, but they had been very gracious to a meddling old couple, and the four of them had enjoyed a fine evening out on the town.

Ross had made a most favorable impression. Douglass had decided that Faye should marry him immediately, because he had all the qualities men want in their daughters' husbands. He was intelligent, respectful to his elders, financially successful, and he treated Faye like a queen. Emma agreed with her husband's assessment in all of these areas and, as a woman, she would have added that Ross looked like an African god. She thought Faye could be happy with Ross.

But then there was the question of Joe. Douglass had hooted at the idea that his pseudo-daughter should marry this man who needed her help just to get his driver's license. Faye didn't even seem to notice that her steadfast friend was a man—and a man who had put her on a pedestal that was too high even for a physical specimen like Joe to climb. This proved that even brilliant women could be oblivious to bare facts.

When it came to husband material, Emma wasn't so sure that Joe should be dismissed out of hand. He couldn't offer financial stability, it was true, but Faye had been taking care of herself for many years and she didn't seem much the worse for wear. Like Ross, he treated her like a queen, so that race was a dead heat. He couldn't give Faye the deep, scholarly conversation that Ross' wife would enjoy, but Emma believed that only a few people were blessed enough to meet their soulmates. And Joe owned the most beautiful soul she'd ever seen in a man, setting aside her late husband.

Emma had planned to ask Joe to sit with her and Faye in the family pew, until Ross had shown up. Not wanting to put a pseudo-mother's stamp of approval on one man or the other, she had taken the no-action alternative. Neither man was honored with an invitation to sit beside Faye. They weren't told where to sit at all.

Emma didn't have eyes in the back of her head, but she'd sneaked a look in that second pew as she took her long widow's walk to the front of the sanctuary. Both men were there, sitting broad shoulder to broad shoulder. Now they sat together behind Faye, giving her their simple physical presence, which was the same support Faye was giving Emma.

If Joe and Ross felt a sense of competition, it was not evident. They didn't glare at each other or pull away when the fact of a crowded pew forced them to touch each other. Emma thought that, in other circumstances, they might have been friends. Unlikely friends, but friends all the same.

Sooner or later, Faye would have to choose between them. Or maybe she wouldn't choose either of them. Emma wished she could tell Faye what choice to make, but she couldn't. This race was too close to call.

Emma had never seen so much food in her life. Which was saying something, since she'd lived all her life in the South and she had attended southern funerals before. She didn't know about the rest of the country, but she sensed that her friends and neighbors monitored the obituary pages, looking for the name of someone they knew, however vaguely. When a familiar name surfaced, these people flipped their oven switches to "Preheat" and started whipping up delicacies.

She recognized Magda's summer squash soufflé, and she knew that the sheriff grew a dense forest of zucchini every summer, so that their deep freeze could be well-stocked with critical supplies in case somebody died. A generous bowl of his smoked mullet spread sat in the place of honor on Emma's coffee table, surrounded by saltine crackers.

Joe had contributed the pot of oyster stew that was simmering on the stove. Even Faye, who usually relied on Joe to keep her fed, had dragged out her grandmother's recipe for pralines, proving that she did indeed know how to cook.

Ross had shown no signs of any kitchen survival skills whatsoever, but he'd wanted to help, so Emma had suggested that Faye allow him to monitor the candy thermometer. He'd succeeded perfectly, which was what Emma had expected when she nominated him for the task. "Precision" should have been Ross' middle name. The creamy pralines were mouthwateringly good.

The entire congregation of the Blessed Assurance African Methodist Episcopal Church had prepared the rest of the bounty that threatened to collapse Emma's kitchen counter. Each and every congregation member had stopped by after the funeral to pay their respects to the widow, and they'd all done their best to eat their share of the baked offerings, but it was to no avail.

Emma stood in her kitchen, arms outstretched as if to gather up all the excess food, and moaned, "Would you look at this stuff? Have these people missed the point completely? I'm a widow now. One person can't eat all this."

"Food equals love," Magda said, sitting at the kitchen table and spooning applesauce into little Rachel's mouth. Achieving motherhood at an advanced age agreed with her. Her arms and legs were still short, sturdy, and muscular, and no amount of time sitting in a darkened nursery would wash away the tanned and weathered skin of a career archaeologist, but the lines around her mouth and eyes were softer.

Her husband Sheriff Mike, already a grandfather three times over, was well-practiced at doting. He exercised this skill at every opportunity. With parents like hers, Rachel would either grow up to be a princess or the president.

Joe and Ross stood on either side of Emma, each wielding a spoon with aplomb. A stack of filled freezer boxes rose in front of each man. Faye was washing casserole dishes as fast as they got them emptied.

"You'll eat well for a year, Miss Emma," said Ross.

"It's not like I can't buy food. And some of the generous folks who cooked this stuff aren't as comfortable as I am. Fortunately, I've figured out how I'm going to get rid of all this food, without wasting it or hurting the feelings of the people who brought it."

"How you planning to manage that?" asked the sheriff as he tested the temperature of Rachel's rice cereal with a clean fingertip.

"Every time I go to church—Sunday mornings, Sunday evenings, Wednesday nights, every single time—I'm bringing somebody home with me for a meal. Somebody whose months last longer than their money does."

"Well, okay then. I like that plan," Ross said, scooping creamed corn with renewed vigor.

"Just as long as it's somebody you know well," the sheriff said, glancing up from Rachel's bottle with a lawman's gleam in his eye. "None of us needs to forget that there are two murderers out there."

"That worries me, too," Ross replied. "I've been talking to Faye about beefing up security out there on her island. Those killers came a little bit too close to her for my liking." He quickly added, "And to you, too, Miss Emma."

The room's festive atmosphere dampened measurably.

Faye plunged her hands deeper into the hot, soapy water with an annoyed snort. Emma knew Ross had been pressuring her to accept his personal protection since the minister had closed Douglass' funeral service with a heartfelt "Amen."

Emma didn't see that Faye was necessarily in a great deal of jeopardy. The fact that she'd just left Douglass when he was attacked was simply a case of coincidence. What could the burglars have possibly wanted with her?

They would have been quite satisfied to get their hands on her emerald, but they'd had no way to even know that it existed. If they'd given her field notes a quick glance, they'd know that *she* existed, but Faye had explained that those notes described potsherds and flint chips, not emeralds or diamonds. They didn't even have her notes from the day she found the dirt clod that had harbored the emerald. That notebook had been with Faye in the skiff.

"Emma and I can take care of ourselves," Faye piped up.

No, Emma saw no reason to force Faye to accept a bodyguard she didn't need, not even one that looked like Ross. Emma also saw Faye's unspoken objection: being on an island with both Ross and Joe could get a little...crowded.

Fortunately, Emma was significantly older and wiser than Faye, and she saw an elegant, Solomon-like solution to this problem. "Even if Faye needs male protection, which I doubt, she has Joe. I don't mind saying that I'm a trifle nervous to be staying here all alone. Just because those burglars didn't load my art treasures in their boat on their first trip doesn't mean they won't be back. And this time, they've gotten a look inside my house. They'll know what they want, and they'll know there's nobody but a little old lady to stop them from getting it."

There. She'd played the widow card. It had been a little hard to make her lips form the words "little old lady" when she'd put so much effort into remaining attractive for Douglass. Yoga. Facials. Fashionable clothes. She hoped she had the fortitude to continue to put her best face to the world, just for herself.

Poor Ross.

She could see he knew what he had to do. She could see that he was going to do it. But he was finding it hard to make his lips form the words that would hand a victory to his rival, Joe. Did Faye notice? Probably not, since she was so deeply committed to being oblivious. She was certainly blind to the fact that Joe showed every sign of being silently, wordlessly, in love with his best friend Faye.

"Would you mind if I stayed with you for a few days, Miss Emma?" Ross asked. "I mean, Joe will be on Joyeuse Island with Faye, but we're all worried about you, too. I don't need to be back to work for a week or so. Maybe, in the meantime, I could keep the bad guys away."

Emma thought, *Good boy. I knew all along that you were well-brought-up*, but all she said was, "Thank you."

# Chapter Six

The library smelled like Douglass. Faye could smell his after-shave, his favorite brand of deodorant soap, and the cigars that he sneaked when Emma wasn't around. His library's scent seared her heart, but she needed to be alone so badly. It had taken her all afternoon to find a chance at that solitude.

When the sheriff and Magda left the kitchen to put Rachel down for a nap, she saw her chance. Emma was on the phone, returning an interminable list of sympathy calls, Joe was doing something in the kitchen that required intense concentration, and Ross was attacking a sagging drawer with a screwdriver. No one was paying her the slightest bit of attention, so she'd slipped into the library, hoping for a half-hour of quiet time to simply think.

Three minutes later, a creaking door dashed that hope.

"I need to put some WD-40 on that hinge."

Faye reflected that Ross was incredibly sexy when he talked shop. She instantly forgave him for intruding on her quiet time.

"How are you really doing?" he asked, enfolding her in a long pair of arms. At five feet nothing and a hundred pounds, Faye was on the dainty side, but she could usually ignore that fact. Faye knew she was tough. She was fierce. She was large inside.

Usually, Faye felt that her physical size was beside the point, but not when she was in Ross' arms. He made her feel tiny but precious, like a gemstone. Like a rare emerald.

His lips were warm against her jaw, her neck, her ear. "I've missed you every minute. I know it makes sense for me to be here for Miss Emma, but I want to be the one watching over you. I'll have to go back to Atlanta soon, but I want you to come."

"I can't leave—"

"I understand that you can't leave Miss Emma, not for a good long while. I know you, Faye. You'll take care of her for as long as it takes, until she's on her feet and ready to face her new life. But after that, I want you to come to Atlanta. Let me take care of you the way you take care of everybody else."

Faye was an extraordinarily independent person, but she'd also nursed her mother and grandmother through terminal illnesses that had taken years to do their work. Since then, she'd let Joe cook for her and save her life occasionally but, other than that, she'd looked after herself in nearly every way for twenty years. A loud and insistent voice in her head told her that she was ready to hand the reins to someone else. Just for a little while.

If only she were sure that she could fit into Ross' elegant social circle. If only Atlanta weren't so far away. If only.

Ross' kisses slowed and stopped. He rested his cheek on top of her head and just held her. She was glad. Grief left her too wounded for romance. But she was more than ready for love.

Faye and Joe were making a slow exit from Emma's post-funeral party. The sheriff and Magda were packing Rachel's diaper bag, and it was time to go. Faye just wished it were easier to say good-bye.

"Call me on my cell if you need me," she told Emma again, hugging her as she talked. "I don't live that far out in the Gulf. I can be here quick."

"I wish you could stay longer, but I don't like you on the water after dark. Go." Emma made shooing motions with both hands.

Faye met Ross' eyes with a long look, then she took the helping hand Joe offered and stepped down into her skiff. The comforting gulf waters cradled the boat and rocked Faye like a mother.

As the others walked back toward Emma's house, Joe pushed the boat away from the dock, saying, "I saw you pushing food around on your plate. There was enough on the table to feed…well…me. And that's a lot. But you didn't eat a thing." He flipped the choke off and pushed the throttle forward. "I bet you could eat if you weren't in that house where Douglass looks back at you out of every wall. I think we should go see what Liz is cooking this evening."

Faye wasn't sure when Joe got so bossy. He took charge of the skiff—her own personal boat—and pointed it toward Liz's Marina without even waiting for her opinion on the matter.

Fortunately, Joe turned out to be right. As soon as he mentioned the homey cooking dished up in Liz's Bar and Grill, she knew there could be no better cure for a heavy heart. Liz's earthy good humor would help just as much. Maybe nothing but time could fix the empty ache in her chest, but a plate of eggs-and-grits would fill her stomach very nicely. She and Joe tied up the skiff and followed their noses. Liz's food was nothing if not fragrant.

As usual, the grill was full of fishermen, lushes, and ne'er-do-wells, all of them devoted fans of Liz's cooking. Her son Chip was Liz's busboy and sole full-time employee. The menial job was completely unsuitable for a man of his education and ability.

Chip had parlayed a high school football career into a scholarship to play community college ball. Knowing he wasn't cut out for a senior college team—not in the football-obsessed South—he'd earned the grades necessary to transfer to a four-year school as a non-athlete. Liz had been so proud of his scholarly and impractical choice of a major: history.

It had nearly killed Liz when Chip dropped out a semester short of graduation. He'd floated aimlessly until she hired him to help her with the cooking, but even that simple job hadn't worked out. Liz's customers simply refused to eat biscuits formed by anyone else's hands. Chip had been reduced to patting out hamburgers and busing tables.

Faye watched the smart, handsome young man as he dumped other people's half-eaten food in a slop pail, wiping his hands on the bib of his apron now and then. He seemed like an amiable soul, making small talk with the restaurant's patrons as he moved among them. His outgoing nature seemed genuine, too, not the forced friendliness of someone looking for a tip. Faye had a feeling that his sharp eyes missed nothing.

This situation couldn't possibly last. Chip would find something else, because young men with his gifts tended to land on their feet. Maybe that would have happened sooner if he'd been a more take-charge kind of guy but, without a coach to chew his butt out for slacking, it looked to Faye like Chip was content to just drift through life. For Liz's sake, Faye hoped Chip drifted back into college soon.

He picked up a dirty plate sitting on the bar, right next to Faye's steaming hot food.

"Sorry about that. You shouldn't have to sit next to somebody's half-chewed food."

"That's okay. Your mother and her customers keep you pretty busy." She shifted on the stool to get a good look at the young man. Intelligent hazel eyes were set into an affable face that featured full lips and broad cheekbones. Liz had good reasons for her poorly concealed pride. Actually, Faye didn't think it ever occurred to Liz that she *should* conceal it.

"Business is good. There's no sense in complaining about that." He glanced around the room, and Faye could almost see the calculations spinning in his brain. She'd worked food service before, so she knew he, as the son of the proprietor, was figuring the evening's likely gross income, based on his quick headcount of patrons. He could almost surely estimate his own income based on that number and on his personal knowledge of the regular customers tipping habits. The young man had grown up in this bar and grill, and Liz hadn't raised a dummy. Faye knew this, because Liz had told her so on countless occasions.

Chip set down a tray loaded with salt, pepper, ketchup, and hot sauce—everything a girl eating a plateload of eggs could ever want. He gave her a smile that might not have been intended to trigger a healthy tip, but that most assuredly would cause Faye to dig deep into her wallet, and said "Enjoy your meal. Let me know if you need anything else." Then he took his smile elsewhere and left Faye with her eggs and her memories of Douglass.

She rubbed the back of a hand across her teary eyes. Joe noticed—she knew he noticed—but he let her be, which was the right thing to do. On another occasion, she might wipe the same eyes with the same hand, and he would turn his head in her direction and get her to talk about what was bothering her, all without saying a word. And, on that occasion, this would also be the right thing to do. Faye didn't know how Joe knew what she needed, but he always did.

Liz bent her ever-brilliant red head in Faye's direction. "How're you holding up?"

Faye heard herself whisper, "I can't believe he's gone." She'd said the same sentence to herself, over and over, since she received Emma's terrible call.

Liz, whose nurturing tactics tended to involve calories, put a heaping platter of buttered biscuits on the counter in front of Faye and Joe. Faye was astonished to find that plugging an emotional wound with food actually worked.

"Sheriff Mike will find out who did it, and he'll make sure they pay." Liz plunked a pitcher of cane syrup next to the biscuits, in case Faye and Joe found themselves short on carbohydrates.

Looking for something else, anything else, to talk about, Faye settled on a subject that wasn't as painful to Liz as Douglass' death was to Faye, but it was close.

"How's Chip doing?"

"Look at him. Still strong. Still handsome. Still smart as a whip. Still busing tables."

"You don't have any idea why he came home?"

"Not a clue. His grades were fine. I was paying his tuition and dormitory fees, and he had a job that should've covered everything else, so I don't think it was a money problem."

Faye pondered. "Unless his money was going somewhere he doesn't want to talk about."

Liz pursed her lips and did some pondering of her own. "Yeah. Don't you think for a minute that something like that hasn't crossed my mind. I've tried to imagine all the worst things. Drugs. Alcohol, maybe. But he doesn't act drunk or high, not ever. I hug him all the time, sniffing for liquor or cigarettes or pot. He drinks a little, but in this business, you learn to spot real drinking trouble fast. I know kids fool their parents all the time, but I try to be realistic. I just don't see it."

"Gambling."

"Maybe. You can't smell gambling debts. But if he's in deep with a bookie, he sure ain't come to me for money. If it got bad enough that he had to drop out of school, wouldn't he act desperate? Wouldn't he hit me up for a loan, or nag me to pay him more for his work? Or maybe even steal from me? I don't get it."

"No legal troubles?"

Sorrow pinched Liz's brow and lips. Faye was so accustomed to her friend's ever-affable zest for life that she wasn't sure she'd know Liz if she saw her somewhere else, wearing that doleful face.

"He got himself arrested once, but it was a long time ago. He and his football buddies got themselves some fake IDs and they were a-strutting like roosters around some two-bit bar in Sopchoppy, crowing over their big victory. They looked a lot older than seventeen, so they would've got away with it if the quarterback hadn't picked a fight with some of the regular customers. Chip wouldn't ever have done something that stupid on his own, but he'll follow somebody he looks up to. Why is that, I want to know? Men."

"Sometimes I think that Y-chromosome is a birth defect. It sure makes men do some stupid things," Faye said. "That's why they named it 'Why?'"

Joe, who had been studiously ignoring this conversation, cut a pair of eyes in her direction and grunted. Sometime in his GED preparation, he must have learned the purpose of a

Y-chromosome and recognized her insult of the entire male gender for what it was.

Liz turned around to shove a tray of biscuits into the oven. She opened her mouth to resume talking about her favorite subject—her son—when that son turned and walked her way. Faye hid a smile, triggered by Liz's obvious effort to stifle another outburst of maternal pride and concern.

Chip brushed by her, carrying a tray of dirty dishes. He used an elbow to give his mother a playful poke in the ribs as he passed, then he leaned over and kissed her on the top of the head. Liz beamed like an adolescent girl who has caught the attention of a handsome male English teacher.

Chip disappeared through the swinging door that led from the grill to the utility kitchen. Faye could hear the clank of glass on glass as he set the tray down next to the dishwasher. Liz hadn't been smooth enough to manage a change of subject. Over the awkward silence, Faye could hear the sound of a refrigerator door opening and closing. Chip reappeared quickly, this time carrying a tray loaded with raw hamburger patties.

"You're going to need these in a few minutes, Mom. Herbie and his friends are just now getting drunk enough to be hungry. I'll be back in a minute to chop you some onions."

Setting the tray down and squinting critically at the patties, Chip looked like an artist who was dissatisfied with his work. He picked up a lopsided burger and patted it back into shape, nodding as if to say that the patties now met his high standards. Wiping raw meat juice on his apron, he reached for an empty tray and carried it to yet another table that needed busing.

"He's a good boy," Liz said to no one in particular.

"Anyway." She hunkered down and started whispering to Faye as if she'd just realized that she didn't want Chip to overhear her. "He should've known that jumping into a bar fight was a dumb move. After all, he was brought up here in this bar." She gestured at her own establishment and its seedy-looking customers. "He knows that drunken brawls don't ever end well."

"So they got him for underage drinking?"

"And assault. Punched the local tough guy's lights out. He was a juvenile and it was a first offense, so they slapped him on the wrist. Hell. I smacked him harder than that when I heard what he did. Men shouldn't be allowed to drink 'til they're forty."

Faye observed that instituting this law wouldn't put much of a dent in Liz's mature clientele.

"But that happened years ago, before he even started college." Liz sighed. "He and the law have gotten along just fine ever since."

"Then it's gotta be a woman," Faye said. "I bet he got his heart broken."

She squinted in Chip's direction. He didn't look lovelorn. Shaggy chestnut hair and a confident stance made him look more like a heartbreaker himself.

He was chatting with a group of Civil War re-enactors, still half-decked out in their military finery. One of them landed a punch on Chip's upper arm, the kind of punch men give when they like you. Everybody was laughing as he took their dirty dishes. "Well, he's never been such a big ladies' man, but he usually has a serious girlfriend. Not now, but usually. When a relationship goes south, he just crashes and burns. I always have to pick him up and dust him off. Give him a lot of hugs. Tell him some stupid jokes. Make a few cookies…"

Faye stifled the urge to giggle at the image of Liz as a cookie-baking mom.

"Don't you laugh. I make 'em. I eat more of 'em than I strictly should, but I make 'em."

Liz waved her spatula in Faye's general direction, so Faye tried not to keep giggling. She hadn't giggled in a while. At times like this, women friends were good things to have.

"Since he always hits rock-bottom when some girl dumps him," Liz went on. "I've kind of settled on woman trouble as the explanation for why he dropped out. Maybe he needs to take up with a smart, pretty archaeologist."

Joe bristled. He was getting very good at that.

"Don't look at me," Faye said quickly. "What is Chip? Twenty-two? I'm old enough to be his...hip young aunt."

Yeah, right. At thirty-eight, Faye was plenty old enough to have had a youthful indiscretion that resulted in a strapping young man like Chip. That thought called for another cup of coffee. Heavily laced with some of Joe's bourbon.

Liz turned back to the griddle, wielding her spatula over an array of eggs being cooked every-which-way. Four of them, scrambled, were quickly dumped in front of Joe, before Liz bustled off to find someone else who needed feeding. Joe had done his share to help Emma get rid of all that surplus funeral food. Faye glanced sideways to peek at his flat, muscled abdomen. Where did he put all those calories?

Faye had cleared half her plate before she noticed the prickly feeling on the back of her neck. She turned and scanned the room. It was full of people who appeared...perfectly ordinary. They looked pretty much like Liz's usual crowd—loud, jovial, and decked out in extremely casual clothing. In other words, they looked like pleasure boaters, fishermen, and hunters.

Given recent events, two of them might also be killers.

Faye slid her eyes to the left. Two...interesting-looking... young people sat at a table in the corner, and they'd sat there before. She knew their names—Wayland and Nita—and she knew that they were shrimpers and that Wayland, the last in a long family line of shrimpers, had inherited his boat from his father. The plain bands on their left hands told her that they were married. But that was about all she knew. They'd always seemed harmless enough, but now Faye found herself wondering. Were the lightning bolts and eagles tattooed on their arms Nazi symbols? Did their close-cropped hair make them skinheads?

Nita, in particular, was eye-catching. Few women with her striking good looks would choose to be nearly bald. The young couple cultivated a look that said they didn't like the rest of the world much, although they wouldn't mind if everybody looked at them. Were they the kind of losers who would be enraged by the sight of a wealthy black man?

Still furtive, Faye kept eyeballing the couple. Though Nita was of average height, with long and willowy limbs, Wayland was a short, stubby, wiry man, with prominent muscles on arms that showed not the first gram of fat. He had the wizened, sunburned face of a man who made his living on the water. He sure looked like a shrimper. But did he and Nita spend their evenings beating peaceful men to death?

And what about Chip's good buddies, the big table of Civil War re-enactors in the corner? She recognized the biggest, loudest, happiest pseudo-captain as Herbie Canton, who had learned that he could endure his weekdays as an insurance salesman, just as long he could look forward to leading bloodless battles on Saturdays.

Faye had always had a soft spot for re-enactors, being a bit over-fascinated with history herself. She saw nothing wrong with a little harmless obsession in anyone's life, and most re-enactors that she'd met didn't seem like throwbacks who wished the good old days would come back, slavery and all. Heck, a lot of them had two uniforms, one blue and one gray, so that they could be as useful as possible in service of their make-pretend wars. But that didn't mean there weren't two devils lurking in this happy, collegial group.

Faye couldn't sit still. She felt like everybody in the place was looking at her, which was stupid. Even if they'd heard about Douglass' death on the news, they didn't all know he was her friend. She doubted any of them had ever even laid eyes on him, though his house wasn't far up the coastline. Douglass had been a little too upper-crust to hang around a joint like this.

She used her biscuit to mop up the last drops of egg yolk. Leaving enough money on the counter to cover the eggs and a big tip for Chip, she said, "I'm going out to check on my boat."

Liz's worry lines deepened and she came out from behind the counter, following Faye toward the door. "It's nearly dark. Now, why'd you want to go out there by yourself, after what just happened to poor Mr. Everett?"

Joe, who hadn't left his stool yet, laid some money on the counter next to Faye's. He reached out a long arm and tapped Liz on the shoulder. "I'm with her."

Liz gazed up at Joe, who was tall even when he was sitting down, then looked fondly at the way his black ponytail draped over his broad shoulder. "You know what, Faye? If Joe goes with you, you'll be just as safe as a woman can be."

Her dreamy smile followed Joe out the door.

Liz kept a locked cabinet full of boat maintenance supplies out on the dock, and Faye had a key. She reached in and hauled out a jug of bleach. Her world was dirty, but at least her boat could be mildew-free. She and Joe worked while the sun dropped lower.

The lapping of waves against the hull masked any noise made by the happy drunks in Liz's bar. The early evening air was utterly quiet. So when a dark figure lurched off the dock and over the gunwale into Faye's arms, she let out a scream that brought those happy drunks boiling outdoors to see what was going on.

"Wally?" Faye said, when she realized who she was holding. It was her old, two-faced friend Wally, who had owned the marina when Liz was just a short-order cook. Wally, the pothunting scoundrel who would do anything for a buck. Wally, the long-time friend who had kept her secrets back when she lived one step ahead of the law and the tax collector. Wally, the fink who had sold her out to the scavengers who would have killed her for the artifacts buried under her own property.

Wally had disappeared when his crimes came to light, and Faye had missed him in spite of herself. He looked bad, pale and sweaty, like he'd been on one of his legendary benders, which would explain why he'd just staggered and fell into her arms. Where had Wally been all this time?

She reached to wipe the beads of sweat off his forehead and realized that her hand was bloody. A crowd of onlookers was gathering. Joe was already out of the boat, shouting for somebody to call a doctor.

"I'm sorry, Faye. About Douglass." Wally wheezed hard, and Faye could tell it hurt him to talk.

"Don't say anything, Wally. Just lie still. Joe's getting you some help."

Wally's small watery eyes scanned the faces gathering on the dock. He wheezed again. Ignoring Faye's efforts to calm him, he tried and failed to rise up out of her supporting arms. "Need to tell you...sorry...sorry for everything. Tried to stop...never meant to..."

His mouth worked to form the words. "Remember before. You have to remember before," he said, looking hard into her eyes. The light was already fading from his. "Remember. Before," he said one more time, his voice urgent.

"I do remember. We were friends, Wally. We *are* friends." She called out for someone to get a doctor, but it was too late. Wally was gone.

# Chapter Seven

Faye had seen death before, but she'd never seen this much blood. Everything in her world was red. The blood. The fiery sunset that reflected in the eyes of a sea of confused bar patrons. Liz's hair, hanging over her face as she wept for Wally, who had been her friend and her boss and maybe her lover.

Even the warm highlights in Chip's chestnut hair were red, as he cradled his weeping mother against his chest. And that chest was covered with a cherry red polo shirt, wet with her tears. The sheriff's mechanical pencil was the color of blood as it scratched notes on a white sheet of paper. There was a red ambulance and its red lights circled pointlessly, because the patient was dead.

Blood coated Faye's hands and arms and chest—the parts of her that had touched Wally as she cradled him in her lap. It still lay in red puddles around her feet, even though the emergency personnel had gently lifted his body onto a stretcher quite some time ago.

She couldn't focus her mind enough to get up and get out of the boat. Where would she go? Joe, God bless him, didn't try to tell her what to do. He just sat beside her and held her hand.

The sheriff and his forensics team seemed happy to let them sit in the gory mess, probably because it meant they weren't messing up the crime scene. They weren't tracking through the blood, dropping hairs, or strewing fibers hither and yon. All they were doing was sitting there in a pool of congealing gore while they answered questions.

No, she hadn't seen anybody lurking in the shadows when she walked out to her boat. And neither, Joe said, had he.

No, she hadn't even seen Wally until he dropped into her lap. Neither had Joe. And neither of them had seen the knife that had gouged a hole in his back. It seemed to have disappeared into that mysterious place where Wally had been hiding for years now.

No, Wally didn't say any more about Douglass, beyond being sorry. Sorry for killing him? Sorry somebody else killed him? Sorry for Faye's pain? Sorry he cheated him at poker? Neither Faye nor Joe could say.

No, neither of them knew of anyone in particular who would have wanted Wally dead. Wally had been the kind of person who generated murderous feelings in everyone around him at one time or another. He lied at the drop of a hat. He manipulated people for the sheer hell of it. He cheated at cards, even when he wasn't playing for money. If Faye had been asked to guess which of her friends was most likely to wind up dead of a stab wound, it would have been Wally. But, no, she didn't know who did it.

She noticed that Joe had climbed onto the dock, and he was talking to the sheriff. When had he done that? Even Joe was wearing Wally's blood. The red smear on Joe's cheek contrasted with the near-black of his sleek hair and the clear green of his eyes. His moccasins were soaked. Faye suspected he'd have to make himself a new pair.

Lanky Joe had to stoop over to get his mouth close to the stocky lawman's ear. Clearly he didn't want someone to hear what he was saying. Maybe that someone was her.

Faye knew she was sitting in a puddle of blood, but she felt like her brain could use a little boost in its blood flow. The hum in her ears was drowning out all ambient noise, and black dots swam in her field of vision.

The sheriff squinted in her direction. "Why hasn't someone gotten that woman out of there? Look at her. Merciful God."

He gave Joe a short nod, then jerked his head in the direction of one of his deputies. As Faye watched, Joe boarded a little aluminum johnboat belonging to the sheriff's department and piloted it expertly, pulling alongside her and holding out a hand. Faye gathered her wits well enough to scramble out of Wally's blood and into the boat. By moving carefully, she was able to accomplish this without disturbing the crime scene much at all.

"The sheriff said I could take you home. He said he'd make sure your skiff was cleaned up. We can swap it for this one tomorrow."

Home. Faye could already feel the sand of Joyeuse Island under her feet. She could see her elegant home, rising high on its sturdy foundation, an above-ground basement, and two floors of cavernous living space, crowned with a magnificent cupola and surrounded by a forest of Grecian columns. Trying to restore this grand old ruin would be a lifelong project, but that was okay with Faye. She could hear the footsteps of six generations of her ancestors echoing through its halls. She wanted to go home.

Joe opened the throttle, and they left all that blood behind.

Faye's finances had improved in recent years, so she'd been able to add a number of modern conveniences to Joyeuse. A few solar panels enabled her to run some electric lights and a small appliance or two, though not necessarily at the same time. Gas-powered appliances—refrigerator, range, and oven—gave her a near-normal kitchen. A diesel generator filled in the gaps in her newly modern lifestyle.

Still, beyond patching a few leaks, she'd never had to update the old house's original plumbing. A rooftop cistern installed before the Civil War brought running water to her modern bathroom, sun-warmed and with ample pressure, any time she wanted it. And, tonight, she wanted it. Faye needed, more than anything else, to be clean.

Peeling off her clothes, stiff with drying blood, she shrank from the notion of tossing them on the bathroom floor or into the hamper. She vastly preferred the notion of burning them.

Pushing open a casement window, she threw the ruined shirt and pants out of the house.

Naked and barefoot, she padded back to the shower, stopping only when something small and damp stuck to her foot. She stooped to pick up the folded paper and noticed, with a sigh, that it was bloody, too.

What on earth had she tucked in her pocket? In her headlong rush to purge her life of Wally's blood, she was tempted to simply pitch it, until she recognized the stationery. The scrap of paper was torn from a piece of university letterhead. Graduate students like Faye could hardly afford to overlook correspondence from the entity that held their futures in its figurative hands. She uncrumpled the paper, wondering what the university wanted from her now.

How odd that she couldn't remember opening any mail from the university in weeks. It had been longer than that since she visited the campus. She looked at the paper again, and she thought she saw the outlines of four bloody fingers. Could Wally have slipped this into her pocket?

Spreading the sticky paper out in the sink, she saw that it wasn't a letter, just a hand-scrawled note. No, not even a note. Just eight characters: RARE F301.

Faye recognized the cryptic letters and numbers instantly. Any student in a graduate program that still required extensive research on hard copy documents would recognize it. This was a Library of Congress call number.

Actually, it was only part of a call number. RARE signified a book shelved with rare documents. The F said that the book's topic was American history. She'd need to look it up, but she was pretty sure that 301 was one of the numbers assigned to the states ringing the Gulf of Mexico. There should have been a period after the 301, and some additional characters identifying the exact document, but they were missing.

Without those characters, this call number would leave her standing helplessly in front of a whole row of shelves full of books on southeastern history. Without some clue about what

Wally had wanted her to know, she could paw through all those books for months without finding anything.

Baffled, Faye left Wally's note in the sink to dry and got in the shower. Sometime in her shampoo cycle, between lather, rinse, and repeat, Wally's contorted face crept into her mind and wouldn't leave. He may have been a scoundrel, but he'd been her friend, too. Faye was just so sad to get him back, only to lose him forever.

His last words came back to her. *Remember before, Faye.* She and Wally went back a long way. There was plenty of "before" for her to remember.

Faye considered a night of dreamless sleep in her own bed to be the very definition of heaven. When she woke, Joe had already gone fishing and cleaned the morning's catch, which was a fair measure of how badly she'd needed the sleep. A breakfast of grilled fish that couldn't have been fresher quelled her nervous stomach.

If she purposefully kept her thoughts on the here-and-now, ignoring her insistent memories of Douglass in his coffin and Wally lying dead in her lap, then she felt almost ordinary...until she flashed back on the sound of Emma's voice as she told her that Douglass was gone. Or until Wally's weak, thready voice intruded on her ears, insisting that she "remember before."

"The sheriff told me to bring you back to see him this morning. He said he'd want to talk to you some more. About Wally and all that stuff."

Faye nodded. The fish in her mouth tasted like smoke and sea. It seemed a lot more real than the bizarre happenings that had taken the lives of two of her friends. The sand, the fish, the warm air, the sea smells, the fresh breeze—these things were real. The dead bodies of her friends were not.

What had left their bodies at the moment of their death? She had watched Wally pass from this world to the next, yet she couldn't say what had happened. One minute, he was himself, alive, carrying around with him the memories of their past together. The next minute, her friend was inarguably dead, but she couldn't say how she knew it. She certainly couldn't say how it happened. Well, there was the bleeding hole in his back, but that wasn't what she meant. What had changed when Wally went away and left her sitting alone, with a man's empty shell in his lap?

Thinking of these things gave Faye vertigo. She regained her balance by reminding herself that she had no control over the things life hit her with, but she could control how she reacted to these blows. Her natural response to pain was to fight it. She could fight her friends' murderers by helping Sheriff Mike bring them to justice.

Faye was a little fuzzy on how she might do that. The sheriff had said he wanted her to pursue the stories behind Bachelder's flask and the emerald. It wasn't clear to her how learning that history would help but, like the sheriff, she had a tenuous feeling that the events of the past week were connected. She would follow the story as best she could, for Douglass and Wally, and to satisfy her own ferocious curiosity. One topic that she was uniquely qualified to pursue was the emerald. At the first opportunity, she would be retracing her professional steps, trying to find the precise spot where she dug it up, so she could dig there again.

Her pulse quickened when she thought of what she might find. Anything. That was the part of archaeology that had ensnared her like a narcotic. She might find more emeralds. She might find golden links of the chain that had held them together. She might find a clue to identify the person who lost them, or who put them in the ground. Or she could find nothing but dirt.

But first, she would do something that was more immediately and obviously useful. She would meet with the sheriff and dredge up every last memory of her final moments with Douglass and Wally. It would be painful, but it was the least she could do for her dead friends.

◇◇◇

Emma had bought a new door. Of course, she'd bought a new door. She couldn't exactly leave the front of her house open to the wind and rain. Faye realized that she must have had the door replaced before the funeral, because Emma was a woman who showed the public her best face. She would not have let half of Micco County walk through a mangled entryway. This meant that Faye had walked blindly through the new door, many times, oblivious to the change.

Coming upon the new door caught her up short. It was beautiful, with ornate patterns of leaded glass, but it wasn't the door she'd shuffled through over the years, carrying loads of books or boxes of dirty artifacts. It wasn't the door where Douglass had met her so many times with a smile and a hug. He would never see this door. She hurried into the house so that she wouldn't have to look at it.

Emma led Faye and Joe to the kitchen table, where she and the sheriff and Ross were already nursing huge mugs of coffee. Magda was frowning at the glass of milk in front of her. Coffee had kept her afloat through graduate school and all her years of chasing tenure and then the late-night hours that even tenured professors kept. But coffee taints breast milk, so Magda was stuck drinking cow's milk for a while longer. Caffeine hunger did not improve her disposition. Cuddling a baby did, but she'd left Rachel with a babysitter so that she could concentrate on the task at hand.

"I liked Wally," she said, "but he could be a son-of-a-bitch. Several people at this table have felt like killing him from time to time. Does anybody have a clue who actually did it?"

The sheriff riffled through the papers in front of him. "It *looks* like everybody in the restaurant…bar…whatever Liz calls it…was accounted for. I'd say some of those alibis were stronger than others. For example, we've got that big table of re-enactors in the back corner. They were all drinking. They all say that nobody left the table for at least half an hour before Wally was killed. I'm not so sure anybody would've noticed if one of 'em got up and went to the bathroom, though. As much as they were drinking, I'd be jiggered if there wasn't a steady stream of guys going to take a piss."

"I remember Wayland and Nita were sitting off to themselves," Joe said. "Doesn't seem like anybody would've been keeping a real close eye on them."

Emma, whose head had been bowed over her coffee cup in deep thought, jerked her head up. The sheriff was trying to say "Liz says they never left the bar," but Emma wasn't letting him hold the floor.

"Did you say Wayland? Wayland Curry?"

"Yes," the sheriff said, shoving his reading glasses down his nose so that he could focus on Emma. "You know him?"

"He was the biggest problem employee Douglass ever had. You name it, he did it. Sleeping on the job. Fighting on the job. Faking an injury. Douglass kept giving him chances, until he stole a wad of bills out of the petty cash. Then, after he got fired, the guy had the gall to sue for wrongful termination. He had no case, but Douglass fought hard, anyway, because he felt like the accusation was such a blot on his reputation."

"Do you remember what Wayland Curry looked like?"

"I could never forget his wormy little face."

Faye thought those were pretty harsh words, coming from ladylike Emma.

"Could he have been one of the two men you saw on the night Douglass died?" Ross asked.

Emma shook her head. "I wish I could tell you he was, but like I said, Wayland is wormy-looking. He's way too small to be one of those men."

The sheriff regained control of the conversation. "What about Wally? Was he the right size?"

"I didn't actually know the man, so I can't…oh. I guess you need me to look at him, don't you?" Emma swallowed hard. "If it will help, I'll look at the body and see if Wally could be one of our killers."

"I'll go with you, Miss Emma," Joe offered.

"No, I'll go. I want to go," said Faye, though her stomach churned at the thought of spending more time in the company of a corpse. If Emma could do it, then she could.

"All right. I'll take you two ladies over there. Now. Back to Wayland and Nita…let me see…." The sheriff plucked a paper out of the stack and studied it. "Here's my notes on the tattooed pair. They alibied each other. Big surprise. And nobody noticed either of them leaving the room. Liz says she'd taken their order and served it, both within ten minutes of Wally's death, and the two of them were sitting there both times she went to the table."

"Speaking of Liz…" Emma started. After a moment's hesitation, she went on. "I don't know her, but I understand she's friends with everybody here. So I hate to ask. But you say she used to work for Wally and that he wasn't always a nice person. So…"

"Liz was definitely behind the counter the whole time Joe and I were eating," Faye offered. "We were talking to her. After that, who knows?"

The sheriff held up another piece of paper. "She gave me records of her cash register receipts for the whole evening, so we've got the time of each transaction. And we've got the names of the customers, except for them that paid cash."

Ross looked over his shoulder. "Looks like Liz was pretty busy."

"Let me see that." Faye reached for the paper and ran her finger down the column of numbers. "There. See those two cash transactions? That has to be me and Joe. She'd checked out a half-dozen others in the twenty minutes before we left. And four more customers paid her after that, just in the time it took us to go out to my boat and start cleaning it up. She didn't have much time to go outside and stab Wally."

"Liz isn't the only one that ever works the register." Everybody looked at Joe. This was the advantage of keeping quiet most of the time. On the rare occasion that Joe spoke up in front of a crowd, people listened. "Chip works the register sometimes."

"You got a point," the sheriff said. "Liz almost runs the whole show—cooking, waiting tables, taking the money—but Chip does the food prep…which takes him into the back room and out to the meat locker and the utility shed. That keeps him out of people's sight on a regular basis. And he helps her out at the register when she's busy." He held up the list of receipts. "She sure was busy the night that Wally died. Which I guess means they were both pretty busy. Everybody in the place mentioned seeing Liz and Chip during the last few minutes before the killing. Their alibis aren't air-tight, but they're better than most."

Emma was talking again. "Do you…do you think that Wally killed my husband? What did Faye say he said while he was dying? 'I'm sorry about Douglass….' And didn't he say something like 'Tried to stop…' What was he trying to stop? Maybe he wished he'd stopped beating a defenseless old man."

"We don't know, Emma, but his last words make him a prime suspect. That's one reason it's so important for you to go look at his body. Today. This morning would be good. It will help if we know whether he was one of the men who broke into your house that night."

Faye sensed that the sheriff was closing the conversation down and she had another question. "One more thing—I saw all the people we're talking about, right at the time of Wally's death. They came boiling out of the restaurant, just as soon as they heard me scream. Now I remember being very, very bloody. I didn't see anybody wearing any blood but me and Joe. And Wally. Was there enough time for the killer to wash up? Or are we dealing with someone who was never in the bar at all?"

"I doubt there was much time to wash up," the sheriff said. "Though there might not have been all that much blood, not at first. Wally was bleeding from a major artery. From the trail of blood we found, it looks like it might have burst after Wally got up and tried to get some help. The significant bleeding you saw may not have started until the killer was gone."

"Can you tell us what you know about Wally's stabbing?"

"Well, we know where it happened. We found some of Wally's blood out in the parking lot, in the corner next to the utility shed, so you're right. For all we know, the murderer could have been somebody who never set foot in the bar, somebody who drove up, did his killing—"

"You sure it wasn't a her?" Faye asked.

"Can't be sure. I just usually say 'him,' because not so many women go around killing people. Humor me on this one."

There were exceptions to that rule, and Faye knew it well, but she let the subject drop.

"Where was I? The killer could have been someone in the bar, or it could've been someone we don't know anything about, somebody who drove up, killed Wally, and left. It looks like the first blow dropped Wally to the ground, then the killer stabbed him again and left in a hurry. Probably because he was afraid of being seen. Or maybe he thought he was finished, because Wally was doing such a good job of looking dead."

"Then Wally got up off the ground and came looking for me, because he wanted to give me that note I told you about. I sure wish he'd lived long enough to tell me why."

"Assuming that's true—that he was looking for you so that he could give you a message—then we have to also assume that he saw you when you walked from the restaurant to the boat dock. Being as how nobody's seen him since the hurricane, we have to wonder if he came back just to get some kind of information to you. We just don't know what that information was. Whether he'd already been stabbed by the time he saw you walk past, we can't say. We do know that when that artery blew, Wally didn't have much time, and he knew it. He went looking for help, and you were it."

Ross leaned forward, trying to enter the conversation. "What about the knife? You still haven't found it?"

"I've got divers in the water. We've looked in the woods, in sheds, in toolboxes—at least the coroner was able to tell me it was definitely a knife, not a screwdriver. That made the toolboxes a lot easier to search. The bar...well, that's a hell of a thing. There's knives everywhere in there. Steak knives on the tables. Butcher knives in the meat locker. Paring knives in the kitchen. Chip and Liz looked like they wanted to laugh when I asked 'em if any knives were missing, but it's too damn awful a question to laugh at. They want to help, but they just can't."

"Could the killer have washed off the knife, then left it in on a dining table or in the kitchen?" Faye swallowed hard, thinking that she might never want to eat at Liz's again.

The sheriff shrugged, and Faye felt her appetite leave, perhaps permanently. The silence around the table suggested that everyone was digesting the same information.

Magda spoke up, briskly changing the subject. "Any footprints? Or anything else that could identify the killer?"

"Nope. That gravel parking lot doesn't do much to preserve prints."

Emma's mind hadn't left her husband, nor the possibility that Wally might have been his killer. "After Wally mentioned Douglass," Emma said, taking Faye's hand and looking her in the eye, "did he say anything else?"

"He said he was sorry. And, like you said, he wanted badly to tell me about trying to stop…something…but he wasn't able to get the words out. Then he told me to remember. He said that several times. It was clearly important to him that I remember the friendship we had before he sold me out and ran."

"*Do* you remember anything else, dear? Anything that would help the sheriff?" Emma's eyes were pleading.

"I remember that the whole time Wally was double-crossing me…the whole time he was choosing money over me…he was pretending to be my friend. It's hard to put much stock in anything Wally says. I mean, anything he said. The man was a lie walking around on two legs."

◇◇◇

The morgue was cold, and it smelled exactly like Faye expected it to smell. Wally looked almost like he'd looked as he lay dead in her lap, only worse. He was nothing more than a waxy lump of flesh. The only warm things in the room were Emma's hand and the tears on Faye's face.

The sheriff said, "Take a good look at him, Emma. Look at his size—he was five-eleven and weighed about two-ten. Could he have been one of the men we're looking for?"

Emma walked around the body, checking it from all angles. Then she closed her eyes and consulted her memory. "Could have been. Yes. He could have been. But it was dark and they were far away. You know I can't be sure."

"I know. But we had to try."

◇◇◇

Ross drove Emma's big, expensive American car just as expertly as he drove his little, expensive, German sports car. Faye had her window down, trying to blow the morgue smell out of her hair.

"I wish I could have done that for you. Visit the morgue, I mean. You two have been through enough lately."

"We appreciate the ride and the moral support." Emma noticed Faye's window and rolled down her own. "This is not the first time in my life that I've found myself utterly surprised at the things that have happened to me. And at the things I have to do to make them right."

The April countryside flashed past Faye's window, cheerful and green, as if death and betrayal and decay didn't happen. As if they didn't matter.

"This sure is a nice car, Miss Emma." Ross was ordinarily smooth and debonair, but this obvious attempt to divert the subject to something innocuous jangled Faye's nerves. "The turning radius is amazing for a car this size."

Faye's mind was too fried by now to follow the thread of any conversation, however banal. She found herself ignoring what Ross was saying and merely listening to the unfamiliar cadences of his over-educated speech. Had he once had a Brooklyn accent that he'd worked to overcome? Or had his parents spoken with these measured, cultured tones? Maybe he'd absorbed his perfect diction at his mother's knee.

"I've never driven a Cadillac before. I had no idea they had this much power."

An echo of his words banged around in her brain. *I've never driven a Cadillac before.* Did her thick southern accent set his teeth on edge? When she spoke, did he hear something like *Ah've nevah drivuhn uh Caddylack buh-fore*?

Faye wasn't sure she knew anybody else besides Ross who actually pronounced the first "e" in "before." Ross almost said "bee-fore," in a caricature of correct speech.

That settled it. His diction was too self-conscious. He'd learned it from a speech coach. Who ever heard of saying "bee-fore?"

Suddenly, she was sorry she'd allowed her brain to chase this rabbit trail, because she heard an echo of Wally's last words.

*Remember before. You have to remember before.*

What had Wally meant?

*Remember. Before.*

Before. Bee-fore.

Or did Wally really say, "before?" The question knocked her out of her shell-shocked haze.

Maybe she'd had it all wrong. Maybe Wally had said, "Remember B4"?

Somehow, he'd slipped a note that said only RARE F301 into her pocket.

And RARE F301.B4 was a complete call number.

Faye didn't know the entire Library of Congress system of cataloging books by heart, but she knew parts of it well enough. She knew that the B signified that the author's last name began with a B. The 4 was the identifier that distinguished the book Wally wanted her to see from all the other books on the same shelf. And the university letterhead told her which library's rare book collection held Wally's secret.

Ross drove along, unaware that she was sitting in the back seat, piecing together a message from a dead man. Emma dozed in the passenger seat beside him. Faye would just as soon Emma didn't know what she was thinking. The woman had been through enough. Let her rest until Faye helped the sheriff bring the heads of her husband's murderers to her on a silver platter.

Why had Wally given her the information in this way? Maybe he'd wanted to make sure nobody got the message but Faye.

Even if someone else had found the note, few people thought automatically in terms of Library of Congress call numbers in the way Faye did, and Wally knew it. And of those few scholarly folks, Faye was the only one that heard Wally's final clue: B4. This code was designed just for her. But why didn't he just tell her what he wanted her to know?

Perhaps because the person who killed him was standing nearby.

Somewhere in the university library was a rare book written by someone whose last name started with a B. There was a message in it for Faye, left for her by a dead friend. Tomorrow, after she filled the sheriff in on her discovery, she would be driving to Tallahassee.

# Chapter Eight

Faye was wearing white cotton gloves, and so was Joe. They were also trying to look trustworthy for the benefit of the rare books librarian, who looked like she wished her assistant hadn't let them put their grubby hands on the merchandise. Nevertheless, Faye was a graduate student with full library privileges, and Joe was a harmless undergrad, obeying all the pertinent rules. The librarian had no choice but to let them read the book.

It was a collection of letters from an official in the Confederacy, Jedediah Bachelder, to his wife, Viola. The aged volume in her hand was interesting in itself. Sometime in the late 19th century, someone had bound Bachelder's actual letters into a leather-bound book, making this volume one-of-a-kind. Because Bachelder hadn't been particularly interesting to historians, the letters had never been published in a printed volume. This book was all there was. No wonder the librarian had been loathe to have them touch it.

Faye found Bachelder's letters intriguing, simply because she'd held one of his personal items in her hands a century after his death. The silver hip flask that had so fascinated the newspaper reporter had been engraved with Bachelder's name. When she found it, Faye had done some research showing that Jedediah Bachelder was a prominent slaveholder who had owned several plantations in Florida and Alabama, one of them on a river south of Tallahassee. Based on the man's history as a slave owner, Douglass had agreed to put the flask into his museum of slavery.

Library research wasn't often so immediately rewarding as it had been this morning. Before she even opened the book, Bachelder's very name had told Faye that he was a link between Wally's library reference number and Douglass' museum pieces. But the simple existence of Bachelder's flask and these letters didn't explain why Douglass' house was targeted for burglary, or by whom. And it certainly didn't explain Wally's death. The old hip flask was interesting, but it wasn't worth doing murder.

It might, however, explain the timing of the burglary. The reporter had run a photo of the flask in the newspaper on the very morning of Douglass' murder. Once that article appeared, anybody in Tallahassee and the surrounding area could have feasibly been aware that he owned a 19th-century hip flask engraved with the name J.L. Bachelder. Less than 24 hours after the paper hit Tallahassee's doorsteps, Douglass lay dead. The sheriff would want to let officials in Tallahassee know about the flask's possible connection to the murder, so that they could put a guard on the museum.

She handed the collection of letters to Joe, so he could leaf through it. His arsenal of educational aids was arrayed around him. A voice recorder freed him from having to take laborious notes. A straight-edge helped his eyes focus on the line of text that he was reading. A transparent sheet of blue plastic filtered out visual noise in a way Faye didn't understand, dramatically improving his reading accuracy.

Joe's tutors certainly knew what they were doing when they prescribed these strategies for circumventing his reading difficulties. For a man who preferred to use tools that he'd chipped himself out of stone, Joe was very high-tech when it came to learning.

While Joe used his modern tricks to decipher 19th-century letters, Faye searched the library's collection for more information on Bachelder. A reference book of biographical sketches identified him as a functionary of the Confederate States of

America government. President Jefferson Davis himself was said to have frequently sought his counsel.

More surprising was the fact that Bachelder's wife, Viola, merited her own biographical sketch. In her day and age, a lady's name only appeared in print when she was born and when she died, if then. Viola Bachelder, though to all appearances a lady of unblemished character, had not lived a quiet, retiring life—at least, not in her last years.

She had spent the last part of the war in a townhouse located in a small Alabama town near one of Bachelder's larger plantations. Turning the townhouse into a hospital, she had ministered to soldiers wearing either uniform. Civilians were also welcome in her hospital....all civilians. Much ink was spilled over the fact that Mrs. Bachelder turned away no one, not even slaves and freedmen. The redoubtable woman had succumbed to typhoid fever at age 44, only a month before Appomattox, and Faye was very sad to read of her early death.

Faye returned the biographical sketches to the librarian, whose desk plate gave her name as Elizabeth Slater, and settled herself beside Joe again. He removed the blue plastic sheet from the page he was reading and handed over the book of Bachelder's letters, clicking off his voice recorder as he did so.

She silently blessed him for taking the initiative to record the text of the first few letters. Ms. Slater had informed them that special permission would be required to get copies of these fragile and irreplaceable documents, and that would take time. Meanwhile, Joe's recordings would have to do. She'd gotten him some voice recognition software for Christmas, so they could have transcriptions of these letters with a touch of the button. Heaven only knew what the software would make of Bachelder's Victorian turn-of-phrase or Joe's Oklahoma accent, but maybe the result would be readable enough.

Faye scanned the letters, promising herself more time with them later. They seemed to be of little historical value on a national scale—Bachelder revealed little about the workings of the Confederate government—but they were a touching tribute to a marriage of long standing. Jedediah spent the war years away from home, and his concern for how his wife fared in his absence grew as the Confederacy's fortunes waned. Faye sat bolt upright in her chair when she read about his solution to the problem of rampant inflation and its effect on their fortunes.

*Whilst here in Europe, I have converted my paper currency, soon valueless, I fear, into something more concrete. Having been offered the purchase of a fabulous emerald necklace purported—without proof—to have belonged to the luckless Marie Antoinette, I acquired it. If we are left with nothing else at the end of this interminable war, its sale will provide us with the means to begin again. And if we retain our fortunes, I can think of nothing so lovely as the gleam of these green jewels around your slender white throat.*

Had Wally wanted her to know about this necklace? She was sorely tempted to believe it was the source of the emerald that she had found. A necklace of emeralds fit for a queen would be valuable enough to provoke murder. The possible linkage to Marie Antoinette could only serve to enhance its market value. Was Douglass killed by someone who wanted it? Did the killer know that it lay buried here in the islands off the Florida Panhandle?

Still, no one could have known that Faye had found the necklace. Well, part of it. Was its fate buried in the text of this crumbling book in her hands? It might well be, but closing time had come, and dragon-faced Ms. Slater was standing in front of Faye with hands outstretched, reminding her that rare books didn't circulate.

It wasn't so far from Tallahassee to Liz's Marina, where Faye kept her car or a boat, depending on whether she was on land or sea. And it wasn't so far from the marina to Joyeuse Island. If it weren't for the problem of changing from land transportation to water transportation, she and Joe could have been home even quicker. Joyeuse Island was snugged close up against the mainland, but there was no place in the surrounding swamp to park a car or leave a boat. Liz's place was the best option Faye had.

Liz could have charged any amount for parking or docking, and Faye would have had to pay it. Fortunately, Liz was a friend, so she let Faye take advantage of her facilities for free—just as Wally had, back when his empire had included the bar and the grill and the tiny grocery store and the marina. Faye would have squinched her eyes shut to block out the memory of Wally lying dead in the morgue, but she was piloting a boat and needed to see.

She'd made a cell phone call to the sheriff to tell him what she'd learned at the library, but he wasn't home. It was just as well. Magda was the one who would want to hear every word of what she'd learned about Jedediah Bachelder.

Magda had responded precisely as expected. She'd crowed over Faye's victory in finding Bachelder's letters, then she'd shifted into research mode.

"Let me just do a web search for 'Jedediah Bachelder' right quick and see what turns up…damn. One measly hit. A web page on a man called Duncan Kenner mentions him in passing. I have no idea why, but I'll check it out. That's all I've got." The silence on the other end of the line had been thick with Magda's frustration. "Well. I guess I'll have to do some more scholarly research. Check some professional databases. Comb through my personal library. Call some reference librarians. Stuff like that. I'll let you know what I find out."

Faye had told her not to waste her time with the university's rare book collection, since Ms. Slater had been quite clear that she had no other information on Bachelder.

Magda's response had been characteristic. "There's more than one way to skin a cat. And there are plenty of librarians in this world."

It was full dark when she and Joe got home. By the time they rustled up something to eat, it was well-past time for bed. He'd disappeared quickly into his bedroom, and neither light nor sound leaked under the door.

Joe seemed to waste neither motion nor thought. He could crouch, relaxed, for hours, waiting for a clear shot at a deer. He could stand utterly motionless when motion wasn't needed, yet launch himself instantaneously into a full run when it was. She imagined that he had the same relationship with sleep. When he needed to be alert, he was. When he needed to sleep, he did, without having to quiet a humming, singing, nagging brain.

Faye, on the other hand, had the kind of brain that keeps its owner awake at night. It worried over money. It agonized constantly over the evidence surrounding Douglass' and Wally's deaths, utterly convinced that those mysteries could be solved by sheer intellect and doggedness. It flitted around the subject of Ross and his invitation for her to come to Atlanta. Why did he want her to come? For fun? For love? Forever?

Her brain wondered if she'd ever finish school. It worried that she would never have children. These days, it dwelled on Douglass and Wally, and on Emma's pain, and on her own pain. If she didn't stop her brain in its tracks, she might never sleep again. Perhaps a little work was what she needed.

Wide awake, she opened her laptop and searched for the file she'd uploaded from Joe's digital recorder. Bachelder's written letters weren't accessible to her outside the rare books library, but this recording gave her a few of those letters to study until she returned to the rare book room.

Faye was a visual learner, so she had an almost perfect retention of anything she read, but she didn't do so well at remembering things she'd heard. It couldn't be helped. She hadn't thought to put the voice recognition software on this computer, and she wasn't about to wake up Joe.

Faye curled up in bed and listened to the words of a man a hundred years dead. At first, she thought that Joe's Oklahoma accent clashed with the formal language of a wealthy southern gentleman, but then she rethought that impression. Who knew what wealthy southern gentlemen had sounded like at that time? Joe's twang might be perfectly appropriate.

Joe's reading was occasionally marred by a stumble over a tricky word, but these mistakes only served to remind her of how far he'd come. Joe had worked hard for every bit of schooling he'd ever gotten. She was glad he was getting the accommodations that could boost him past his learning disabilities. However far he wanted to go in school, even if those plans included a Ph.D., Joe could count on Faye's help.

*January 7, 1863*

*My dearest Viola,*

*This will be a very brief message, when I consider how much I have to tell you and how much it means to our future. In the shortest and bluntest of terms—I am being sent abroad. I am to be part of a delegation charged with enlisting England to join our side in this war. No doubt, you are as surprised to hear this news as I was. I am no ambassador, and I don't possess a politician's gift for crafting words that sway opinions. I am merely a lawyer whose career has been spent in service of the citizens of a small and unimportant town.*

*Since I came into my father's properties and amassed properties of my own, even the law has slipped from my daily life. One may graft fancy words onto plain occupations, but words do not change truth. I am a farmer. My farms are large and rich, but a farmer is what I am.*

*I will speak plainly now, for I will not be able to do so again until I return home to you. Our domestic mail seems still to be secure enough, but the danger of my letters being intercepted on the high seas is too great, so I must tell you now of the way that political realities have impinged on our personal lives.*

*I feel certain that I was carefully chosen for this duty because of our joint decision to free our slaves.*

*The English are said to hope that our cause prevails, because the Federals' tariffs on our cotton is a great burden on their mills. Alas, they are hesitant to help us, because they do not wish to be seen as in support of slavery. My inclusion in the delegation is a not subtle reminder that everyone in our fair newborn country does not own slaves. I feel sure that I will be told to remain silent during negotiations, so as not to offend by my lack of diplomacy.*

*At the first opportunity, someone will point out that I employ only free people. After that, my presence will speak for itself.*

*At the second opportunity, I predict that someone will make mention of the fact that General Lee himself has freed his slaves. After that, no more will be said, because no one else in the delegation can claim the same status. Nor do they want to.*

*I must bare my personal feelings on this page, as the urgency of our mission does not allow time for a visit home. I miss you, Viola. And beyond that, I grieve for what this war may cost us. We married late, though not so late that we could not hope for children. Yet no children have come. Such a long separation at this point in our lives may take away our last hope for a family. I regret that loss deeply. But it is time with you that I miss most.*

*I love you, Viola, and I will come home to you.*

     *Your adoring husband,*
     *Jedediah*

In his basement bedroom, Joe lay staring at the ceiling. He worried about Faye most of the time, but the worries spoke louder in his ear these days.

Was she safe? Was she happy? If she wasn't safe or if she wasn't happy, was there anything he could do about it?

He knew she wasn't sleeping, though an entire floor of the vast old mansion separated them. He knew this because he knew Faye, and he had recognized the signs that she had an obsessive fit coming on. Her eyes were bright. Her voice was tense. She had a knotty problem in her sights—solving the murders of Douglass and Wally—and nothing so unnecessary as sleep would interfere with her efforts to unravel it.

He didn't know how to help her in that quest, but he did know how to lie still and think calming thoughts. He'd always believed that an undisturbed mind sees straight to the heart of a problem. For the time being, the best thing he could do for Faye was to help her comb the tangles out of her mind. He meditated on the problem and, when he thought Faye was finally asleep, he slept, too.

# Chapter Nine

"So you went to Tallahassee yesterday? You took Joe with you?"

Faye took exception to the implication that she was dim-witted or a liar. "I told you I would, and I did. I need to go back and finish yesterday's research and I'm going the first chance I get. I'll take Joe then, too. I'm not planning to take a bodyguard everywhere I go for the rest of my life, but I'll keep him around for the time being, if you think it's important. Do you really think I'm in so much danger?"

Sheriff Mike glanced around his office as if he'd rather do just about anything than argue with Faye. Such an argument would be a losing proposition, and Faye knew he lost pretty much all of the arguments at his house. He shifted in his desk chair and sighed. "I haven't the slightest idea. You could've been hurt if you'd still been with Douglass when the burglars arrived, but I don't think you were their target. Since I don't know who stabbed Wally or why, I can't say whether the killer would have gone after you if big, strong Joe hadn't been standing there."

"Why would they?"

"Well, I don't know. But it sure doesn't hurt to have a six-and-a-half-foot-tall man standing next to you when there's bad guys afoot. Joe's not complaining. I think he kinda likes looking after you. And having Joe be your bodyguard gives me something to tell your friend Ross when he calls me up, worrying about your safety. Which he does on a daily basis." He reached in his desk drawer for his cigarettes, which weren't there and hadn't been there since Magda made him quit. "You have an interesting effect on men, sugar. I never met a woman who needed a male protector less—other than my wife—yet you've got guys fighting for the privilege. I say let them look after you, until we figure out what's going on. After that…if they get on your nerves, I say you should kick 'em both in the butt. That's what my charming bride would do."

Faye pulled a file folder out of her briefcase and tapped its corner on the sheriff's desk. "Let's forget about my bodyguard problem. Do you want to hear what I learned in Tallahassee?"

"You bet."

"Remember I told you that Wally gave me a note on the night he died? Well, it took me straight to an old book—a collection of letters from a Confederate official named Jedediah Bachelder."

Sheriff Mike leaned forward to hear, reaching for the desk drawer at the same time. He drew his hand back with a sigh and pulled a stick of gum out of his shirt pocket. "What did the letters say? Did they give you any clue about why Wally got killed?"

"Nope. But there *was* a connection to Douglass' murder. Remember that newspaper feature? The one that ran the morning before he was killed? Well, the picture that ran with the article was of Douglass holding a silver hip flask…that was engraved with the name J.L. Bachelder. And when I got my hands on the book of his letters…surprise! One of those letters mentioned an emerald necklace."

"And that triggered the attack on Douglass? How? Nobody knew about the necklace, not unless Douglass called somebody and told them as soon as you left. And I still don't think they'd have had time to get to his house and kill him, even if he was so foolheaded as to do that."

"Haven't got a clue. The flask wasn't worth enough to be a motive for murder, and nobody knew about the emerald. Yet they're both linked through Jedediah Bachelder to two people who wound up dead. Now do you understand why I'm going back to Tallahassee, first chance I get, for another look at that book?"

"You can't just check it out?"

"Not a rare book. And the librarian says it's too fragile for me to get permission to photocopy it, not until I jump through a few more bureaucratic hoops. One day, somebody'll transcribe the text and post it on the Internet, and I'll be able to peruse Mr. Bachelder's deepest thoughts from the privacy of my own home. But not now. So I'm going back to Tallahassee, but not today or tomorrow. The rare book collection keeps short hours."

"If I know you, you've got some other plans that involve dirt. Library work is so…clean."

Faye checked her fingernails. She scrubbed them every time she brushed her teeth and every time she went to the bathroom and every time she showered, yet dirt still collected there, even when she couldn't recall doing any digging. Today, they looked presentable. "It only makes sense for me to go back to the spot where I found the emerald and see what else I can find. And I'd like to lay eyes on Bachelder's homesite. I've got the property records and an aerial photograph, so I'm pretty sure I can find it. Best I can tell, the house is long-gone, and I don't really know what I hope to accomplish, but it's something my gut tells me I need to do."

She left her real reason for visiting Bachelder's home unsaid. Archaeologists do what they do because they crave a physical connection to the past. If they'd been happy learning out of books, then they would have majored in history and spent the rest of their lives in libraries, museums, and classrooms, all of which are blessed with air conditioning and functional heaters.

Faye felt a bond with Bachelder when she held his hip flask and when she read his personal letters. She knew he'd been a plantation owner, which was just a glorified farmer. He himself had said as much. There could be no closer connection to him than walking over the land that he'd worked. And that his slaves had worked. She could never forget them. Bachelder had owned slaves, and then he had set them free. She needed to understand a man capable of doing both those things in a single lifetime.

"Wherever you wind up going, Bachelder's land, Joyeuse, the library—I don't care. Just promise me you'll take Joe."

Faye blew an exasperated breath through pursed lips. "I'm not dim-witted and I'm not a liar. I told you I'd take Joe."

"Speaking of dim-witted, here's a little something you might want to know. When Ross calls me up—every day—he lets me know exactly why he thinks he should be your bodyguard, and not Joe."

"And his reason would be…"

"He doesn't think Joe's smart enough."

Faye leaned back in the chair and crossed her arms. "I'd like to see Mr. High-falutin' Lawyer shoot a rabbit with an arrow he made himself. Shot from a bow that he'd also made himself. I'd like to see him track that rabbit all the way across Joyeuse Island. I'd like to see him tell time by the sun and predict the weather by the sounds the birds make. I'd—"

"I hear you, Faye. I know what Joe can do, and I know what he can't do. I just thought you might want to know what's going on."

"I thank you. And when the time is right, I'm planning to explain to Ross Donnelly exactly what's going on, too."

# Chapter Ten

Faye woke up with three goals driving her. She liked it when she had goals. She could control her approach to reaching those milestones. Focusing on concrete goals distracted her from those messy elements of her life where she had no control.

She couldn't bring her friends back from the dead, but she could by God do all she could to help the sheriff track down their killers.

Her conversation with the sheriff had solidified in her mind the three things she needed to do. She needed to continue sifting through Bachelder's letters, trying to find the information Wally had wanted her to have. She couldn't say why, but she also felt like she needed to go to Bachelder's homestead, just to get a feel for the man. And, though the search might prove fruitless, she burned to go back to the spot where she found the emerald.

Maybe there were more priceless jewels waiting for her there. Or maybe Jedediah Bachelder had left a letter buried with the emerald, conveniently explaining why his name kept cropping up in connection to murders committed a hundred years after his death. Of course, he'd have had to write it in waterproof ink on paper capable of staying underground for a century without rotting, but hey…stranger things had happened.

So which of these windmills was she tilting at today? Or rather, which of these windmills were she and Joe tilting at today? Because the sheriff had made her promise to keep Joe around as a bodyguard, and Faye kept her promises.

The library kept short hours. The drive to Tallahassee made book research a lot less efficient on Saturday and Sunday. It made more sense to wait until Monday to go to the library. So should she strike out into the unknown and pursue Bachelder's homeplace today, or should she dig for buried treasure in her own back yard? Faye knew from soggy experience that the weather in April could be iffy, but there wasn't a cloud in the sky today.

She stuck her head out the window and squinted at the clear blue dome above her. There was always a chance in this climate that a roiling black thundercloud would blow in and drench her world in rain, but that prospect was as unlikely today as it ever would be. It made sense to attack the goal that would require her to venture farthest from home on this cloudless morning. If she had to, she could dig for an emerald in her back yard on any old blustery day.

Faye had a long history of working frenetically while a thunderhead loomed on the horizon, only dashing indoors when the deluge hit, and she hadn't been struck by lightning yet. When she thought about being caught in a deluge in the swamp in a metal johnboat under a forest of trees shaped like lightning rods—and she had been in just that precarious situation on many occasions—Faye considered working at home, even in bad weather, a comparative piece of cake.

Having come to her decision rationally, Faye started gathering her maps of the area around Jedediah Bachelder's old home place. She also started packing food. Joe could go all day out in the woods without eating, but she most certainly couldn't.

Their destination had been so clear-cut on the maps. Who would have expected Faye and Joe to still be poking fruitlessly around in the swamp, after spending most of the morning in the boat?

The springtime air was warm, promising that the gators and mosquitoes and snakes would be out soon, if they weren't already. Property records had shown her where Jedediah Bachelder's plantation had been, acres and acres of it. Existing documents gave her his property boundaries, but they didn't tell her where the house had been located. This was not a trivial problem when you considered the hundreds of acres Bachelder had owned.

Without overt information on his home site, Faye had gone looking for indirect evidence, and she'd found some. Topographic maps showed a small area of high ground on the margin of a broad, flat area that would have been perfect for large-scale agriculture.

Faye would have bet money that Bachelder chose the high ground for his homesite. It would have been a typical choice for his historical period. Besides, a good-sized river snaked past the presumed house site. In an era before UPS and highways and big rigs, Bachelder would have needed a way to get his crops to a port or a railroad, so that they could be shipped to market.

Conversely, without access to a river, he would have had a devilish time getting supplies. Bachelder's slaves could have grown food for everyone on the plantation, but they couldn't have conjured up the mechanical equipment that was, even then, growing more critical to a successful farm every day. And they certainly couldn't have provided the luxuries that wealthy planters expected: oysters on ice, rosewood furniture, velvet window hangings, pianofortes...

In Faye's search for Bachelder's home, the river had been a dead giveaway. Too bad it looked a lot different from a boat than it did on the map. She and Joe had been puttering around in the swamp for quite some time now. Fortunately, Faye rather liked cypress trees and tea-colored water and heavy draperies of Spanish moss.

The shallow draft of Joe's johnboat meant that they weren't constrained by the river channel. They could explore the creeks and bayous and wetlands that fed the river and kept it healthy, and they could do it legally. A landowner can throw a tres-passer off private property, but the waters of the state belong to everybody. At the moment, Faye and Joe were perfectly legal, although she hadn't promised herself that they would remain that way. Being this deep in the swamp more or less guaranteed that trespassing could be accomplished without consequence.

The sight of a crumbling brick foundation, topped with the leaning remnant of a single column, pulled her right out of the boat. Sometimes trespassing just had to be done.

Joe was handy with a machete, but Faye had known that for years. He had already cleared much of the undergrowth away from the old foundations of Bachelder's house, enough for Faye to see its layout. There were no surprises. It had been a big square house with porches, front and back. Sturdy piers as tall as Joe had lifted its bulk off the ground so that cool breezes and periodic floods could pass beneath the floors. A broad hallway had split the house in two, and each half had been split into just two tremendous chambers. People liked their rooms spacious in those days.

The length of a toppled brick column told her that the house had been at least two stories tall. This had been a lot of house for a childless couple who owned several other homes. Standing within its walls made Faye feel a connection to Jedediah and Viola Bachelder. It made them real.

The ground within the foundations was pocked with holes. Faye could see dozens more pits scattered around the house site in all directions. One or two of them looked new, with fresh dirt piled at their edge. The rest of them had been eroded into a shallow dish shape. Were pothunters really this active out here, so far from everything?

She sighed and said, "Let's look out back."

Joe brandished the machete, ready to clear her a path before she even told him why.

Faye started wading through the weeds, heading for the rear of the old house. "I want to find the family cemetery."

More bricks. They were handmade and they were everywhere. They lay where they had fallen when the house collapsed, one wall at a time. They protruded from the earth, scattered relics of a garden path. And a low ridge of them enclosed a rectangular spot of earth dotted with leaning tombstones that were as chipped and stained as an old man's teeth.

The graves had not been desecrated. Faye thanked heaven for small miracles. Some of the markers were so old that their faces had been smoothed by wind and rain. One of the less ancient ones, a tall marble obelisk, still bore most of the name that had been carved on it, long ago. Many of the letters were lost to time, but the capital letters had been carved large and bold. There was no mistaking the J and the L and the B. The letters following the B were blurred, but Faye could make out an "a" and an "l" and two "e"s, all of them in the right positions. She felt sure that this was Jedediah L. Bachelder's final resting place.

She looked around for Viola, but realized that Mrs. Bachelder would have been buried where she died, in Alabama. Their brief biographies had told Faye that Viola's husband survived her by thirty years. He might even have remarried. When the government Bachelder had served lost its war, he had become less worthy of a biography, so the information in the book of biographical notes was sketchy in the post-war period.

There might or might not be any useful reason for Faye to know the rest of Jedediah's story, but she knew she'd keep looking for the Bachelders and their history. The man's letters had spoken to her. If she neglected his story, it would have been like abandoning a friend.

"Faye."

She realized that Joe had been repeating her name quietly, trying to get her attention.

"Faye," he murmured in a voice just loud enough to be heard over the wind through the swamp grasses. "There's somebody out there. We're not alone."

Joe belonged in the swamp, with its palpable air and mucky soil. Many are frightened by the hard-edged black shadows of thick-chested oaks, or by the blurry Spanish moss that drifts down from their branches like a soft collection of wraiths, but not Joe. The ruined house held no ghosts for him; it was nothing but a pile of bricks that time had brought to its knees.

He might have been chilled by the cemetery, being Creek and thus aware of the need to respect the dead. But this graveyard had been undisturbed so long that the air around it felt untroubled. The dead here truly slept.

No, the intruder did not disturb these dead ones, only Joe and Faye. Joe could almost feel the vibrations of the man's footfalls through the soles of his moccasins. The man's labored breathing stirred the air, and Joe could sense that disruption. Like a wild beast, Joe's hearing was keen, and his senses went beyond mere sight, sound, smell, taste, touch. When he heard a change in a blue jay's cry, he knew there had been a sound to upset the bird, even if he couldn't hear that sound himself.

During his recent studies, he'd learned that sound waves could be thought of as a disruption in air. This made sense to Joe. Sometimes it seemed to him that he detected faint sounds as a breath of wind on the skin of his face. He inclined his head toward the subtle sound that had caught his attention, pointing with his chin, so that Faye would know where the trouble lay.

A buzzing noise that even Faye could hear struck their ears, and they both smiled. It was the sound of a zipper, followed by the rustling of a man adjusting his fly so that the cloth would be out of the line of fire, so to speak. Somebody had stepped out of the open field that lay just inside Joe's field of vision and into the woods to relieve himself. A second's thought made this situation more troubling. If the man had been alone, he wouldn't have bothered to step into the woods for privacy.

Who was out there in this empty wilderness? And why?

If Joe intended to live up to his job as Faye's protector—and he did—then he needed the answers to those questions.

Faye and Joe didn't have to lurk long in the dark, quiet swamp, wondering how much to worry over being detected by their new companion. Before long, he had walked out of the trees and back into the sunny clearing beyond.

Within a few minutes, any noise they might have made would have been drowned out by the racket of large trucks using four-wheel-drive to navigate rough and rutted woodland trails. Periodically, the ringing impact of hammer on nail echoed through the air.

"We're mighty far out in the woods for a camp-out," Joe observed. "And they're not here to hunt, or they wouldn't be making so much noise."

"Even if they were hunters—isn't deer season over? What's left? Squirrels?"

Joe grunted, which said pretty much all he had to say about the need to honor governmental hunting restrictions out here on the edge of civilization. "Doesn't matter about the season. Like I said, these noisy folks aren't hunters."

Joe counted twenty-two trucks and jeeps in the grassy clearing, and at least that many ATVs, all fully loaded with passengers. Ten minutes ago, he and Faye had been alone. Now the population of a small town had burst into the pristine wilderness. Well, not so pristine, he guessed, since somebody'd had a big farm out here a hundred-and-fifty years ago. But it was fixing to get a whole lot worse, now that these guys were out here scaring the wildlife and just generally making nuisances of themselves. The birds had made a big ruckus when the invasion had first begun, but they'd quickly gone silent.

Metal detectors began emerging from pickup beds, and Faye swore. Joe was a little surprised. She didn't swear much. For a woman who shopped for clothes at the Army surplus store, Faye's habits were remarkably ladylike.

"They're having a pothunting party," she whispered.

Joe raised an eyebrow. No sense talking when it wasn't necessary. Not until he figured out how important it was to stay hidden from these people.

"Landowners who own property where artifacts are common can make a good little profit by charging people to dig there." Faye was whispering, but she sure was talking a lot. "Pay a flat fee, pitch a tent, and go home with a piece of history. These are people who would be willing to strip mine a battlefield to find a new prize for their collections."

Joe had crept a few feet forward to get a better look at the jovial newcomers as they fanned out with their shovels and their metal detectors. "We know some of these people."

◇◇◇

The crowd was so far away that Faye could barely make them out as individuals but, after a few minutes of squinting, she realized that Joe was right. They did know some of the people gathered in the clearing. She saw the small wiry form of Wayland. His wife Nita stood beside him with the posture of a dancer. Her graceful carriage should have been incongruous with her near-bald head and violent tattoos, but the look somehow worked for her.

They stood close to each other, almost shoulder to shoulder. Faye realized that she'd never seen them more than an arms'-length apart, as if their marriage bond was extraordinarily strong. Or as if they didn't trust each other.

She saw Chip's tall, athletic shape and the portly profile of Herbie, the re-enactors' natural leader. The faces of the crowd around him were indistinct, but they moved like people who looked to Herbie for guidance in all things.

Wayland and Nita separated themselves from the crowd, walking so directly toward the shadows where Faye and Joe stood that she was sure they'd been seen. Herbie continued moving through the group, shouting instructions Faye couldn't understand because they were garbled by distance.

Wayland and Nita's lean-hipped swagger was as different from Herbie's brawny stride as a king cobra was from a diamondback rattler. They didn't move like shrimpers. They moved like rock stars. She shrunk back into the inky shadow of a live oak.

"Does it matter if they see us?" Joe's voice was as quiet as the running river water.

Faye tried to think through her kneejerk reaction to hide. The landowner was within his rights to dig on his own property, or to allow these people to dig there. She and Joe were trespassing, but they weren't interrupting criminals in the act. Still, the landowner would obviously want to avoid trouble. Also, some of these people would recognize her, and it was no secret that she was an archaeologist. That might not be a good thing among this gathering of pothunters.

"We don't want to be recognized." She thought for a second, then added, "And that means we don't want to be seen. We do stand out in a crowd, you know."

There weren't all that many women with *café-au-lait* complexions and short black hair wearing size-four Army pants roaming the Florida Panhandle, but Faye might have had a faint hope of anonymity. Joe, on the other hand, was…distinctive.

Joe reached up and untied the leather thong holding his ponytail back. Elbow-length hair spread itself over his shoulders.

Faye shook her head at his idea of a disguise. Joe was still wearing buckskin pants and moccasins, he was still memorably tall and broad, and he still had the face of a romance novel cover model. "Nice try. But it doesn't help."

Wayland and Nita kept coming. They stepped out of the clearing and into the trees, heading for the high and dry homesite as if they'd been there before. When Wayland pointed Nita toward the crumbling garden path, Faye understood that he, at least, knew where he was going.

"The house site is right over there," he said.

"How come Herbie keeps us off this part of his land?" Nita asked.

When Nita and Wayland took a dozen more steps, they would stumble onto Faye and Joe huddling in the underbrush like two rabbits. They were going to be discovered. There was no help for it. Faye figured they might as well control the situation.

She made eye contact with Joe and he nodded. They rose together, interrupting Nita saying, "I always wondered about this place. I heard tell—"

Faye cursed her timing. Whenever a rural person says, "I heard tell—", anyone interested in the past should shut up and listen. Stories live a long time in oral history. She wondered what Nita had heard told about Bachelder.

Sticking out her hand, she mumbled something inane like "Nice to see you two out here."

Nita and Wayland looked back and forth from Joe's face to Faye's. She could tell that they did in fact recognize them. Despite Joe's excellent disguise.

Nita looked at Wayland. "Do archaeologists spy?"

"Apparently."

So these two scary-looking people knew who she was and what she did, and they were savvy enough to realize that she might pose a threat to their treasure-hunting escapade. Joe, with his uncanny intuitive sense, did just the right thing. He straightened up, displaying his full height and the machete in his hand, and glowered silently down at Wayland.

"We came out here to look at the old house," Faye said with an ingratiating smile. "Just like you. Joe cleared the foundation, so we could see. Want a look?"

Nita cut her eyes in the direction of the piles of brick. She did indeed want a look.

Wayland turned out to be the kind of person who felt the need to bluster when faced with a larger man. "Wait. Where'd you two come from? You weren't here on any of the other days. You didn't drive out with us, and there wasn't any cars around when we got here. I'm thinking you didn't pay any two-hundred-and-fifty dollars, either."

Two-hundred-and-fifty dollars? Coming out of the pockets of more than a hundred pothunters? Faye did the math, and the number was big. How often did the landowner—had Nita said it was Herbie?—throw these parties? A person could quit working on that kind of tax-free income…for as long as the artifacts lasted.

Her professional journals were full of articles cataloging the sordid details of these events. As soon as the paying customers went home, treasures would start turning up on EBay. They would start with common and cheap finds, like the stone points that were often offered by the dozen. The artifacts' significance—and their prices—went up from there. In fact, they went up substantially.

The most disturbing thing Faye had ever seen being offered on the Internet was a complete set of buttons from a Civil-War-era Confederate uniform, ostensibly found at a battlefield located on private land in Tennessee. Now a man might conceivably lose a button in battle. He might lose two. But if a person considered how likely it was that a complete set would be unearthed, unless the jacket had been buried intact, the commercial offering of those buttons began to take on a new look. And if that person meditated for long on how likely it was that a jacket would be discarded by a soldier whose army was losing and whose government couldn't provide him with another uniform, then there was only one conclusion to be drawn.

Those buttons came off a jacket that had lain in the ground and moldered with its fallen wearer. The person selling them had robbed a grave.

Faye's own hands weren't completely clean of the stain of illicit trading in artifacts, though it had been a long time since the need for money had backed her into that corner. One thing she didn't do, however, was profit by stealing from the dead.

Nita gestured at Faye and Joe. "I think we need to ask Herbie why these two people are on his property."

"Are we still on Herbie's property?" Wayland asked. "Seems like he'd be taking us over here to dig, if he owned the home site. Bound to be a lot of interesting stuff laying around an old house like this."

"Those guys don't want bricks and old bottles and trash like that. Herbie knows it's the battlefield they want. And he knows who's paid their money, too." Nita grabbed Faye by the elbow and bellowed, "Herbie!"

Joe took a big step forward.

Faye held up a hand to calm Joe. Nobody'd hurt her, not yet. Herbie was hustling in their direction. Behind him, she saw a sight that intrigued her and made her heart sink, all at the same time. Several treasure hunters were donning SCUBA gear. Some of the most intrepid were already in the river.

"What's going on here?" Herbie asked. "My rules are simple, and here they are. I've nailed them to half the trees in these woods."

He held out a sheet of paper with a heading that said **THESE ARE THE RULES. READ THEM!** As Faye reached out a hand and took it, recognition dawned on Herbie's face. He knew who she was, so he knew there was an archaeologist crashing his pothunting party. He tried to snatch his sheet of rules back, but Faye already had it firmly in her grasp.

Faye could read uncertainty in Herbie's eyes. For an instant, he wasn't sure how to proceed. Recovering his equilibrium, he quickly adopted an attitude of arrogant bluster.

"I don't have many rules," he said, though the densely typed sheet in Faye's hand put the lie to that claim. "You four people are already breaking the biggest one. I marked the boundaries as clear as I knew how."

He pointed at two trees marked at breast-height with a ring of orange tape. Flashes of orange peeked through the woods in all directions. Herbie was telling the truth on that point. He'd marked his boundaries clearly, and she was on the wrong side of the line.

Suddenly, confusion erupted in the clearing, rather near the spot where Nita and Wayland had stepped into the woods and found them. People were running from all directions. Faye's first impression was that a fight had broken out. Then some of the louder, clearer voices reached her ears over the general hubbub.

"Chip found a rifle. Look at that!

"Can you tell anything about it?"

"What's that sticking out of the ground under it? Hey, Herbie! Get over here and tell us what this is."

Then Wayland spoke in a voice so loud that it silenced the others. He took a few steps in the direction of the diggers, then pointed to the shadows where Faye and Joe stood. "Ask her. She's an archaeologist. She'll know what you've got there."

The silence deepened. This was not a crowd to welcome an archaeologist who had crashed their party. Except for Chip. He rushed to her side, holding out the muddy remnants of an old rifle. "Faye—can you tell me anything about this? Do you think it's from the Civil War?"

"'Course it's from the Civil War," Herbie rumbled, trying to get between them. "This is a battlefield, ain't it?"

Chip was wiping at the metal barrel with a shirttail. "I don't know. Could be a hunting rifle some hunter dropped last year. Could be from the Indian Wars, for all I know. It's kinda cool to think maybe it belonged to Osceola or somebody like that. What do you think, Faye? Is it old?"

Liz had said that Chip was a history major. He sure acted like one. She reached for the gun barrel, but Herbie succeeded in getting between them.

The crowd was quiet...waiting. If Herbie wanted Faye and Joe gone, she wasn't sure what these people would do.

Herbie clapped a pudgy hand on Chip's shoulder. "I got somebody who'll appraise that thing for you, Chip. You don't need this trespasser to tell you what it's worth."

Chip hadn't asked her what it was worth. He'd asked her how old it was.

Chip looked at Faye over Herbie's head. "What *do* you think it's worth?"

Her heart sank. If Chip, a known history buff, was willing to sell his prize, then the whole lot of them were. Well, there had been a time when she'd have been willing to sell it, too, if it would have helped save Joyeuse.

She opened her mouth to tell him she'd have to spend some time with it to assign an age or a value. Herbie stopped her. "I think it's time for you to go home. We don't want any trouble around here."

Still, the crowd said nothing. More than a hundred faces were turned toward Herbie, waiting to follow his lead. She sure hoped he was sincere when he said he didn't want any trouble. Joe was still bristling and holding his machete in plain view, so that was a point in their favor.

"We'll walk her back to her car," Wayland said. Nita was still holding Faye's elbow. "We know how to keep a lady safe," he added. "Safe enough."

Was this guy anxious to display the chivalry that typified his romantic view of the Civil War era? Or was he dangerous?

Herbie considered the offer as if he himself wasn't sure what Wayland's motivation was. Finally, he said, "I think I'll be the lady's escort. Because I don't want any trouble around here."

Faye eyeballed Joe, wondering why no one had noticed that the lady had a perfectly good escort. Herbie didn't take the hint.

"Where's your car?" he demanded.

"We have a boat." Faye noticed that Joe spoke in an appropriately dangerous tone of voice. The sheriff would approve. Ross might even approve, though Faye doubted it.

Faye could feel a hundred or more pairs of eyes boring into her back as Herbie marched them to the river bank where Joe's boat waited. She amused herself by trying to calculate how many of those watchers were carrying a concealed weapon. A fascination with military history tended to go hand-in-hand with a passion for weapons.

A person shot and killed on this spot might never be found, not unless a witness came forward. Surely nobody in the crowd was so utterly confident in this motley crew of pothunters as to commit murder in front of dozens of them. For the first time, Faye was glad of the large crowd.

As if reading her thoughts, Herbie leaned close and murmured, "You should be careful where you go poking around, ma'am. I have friends here who've parlayed their finds into a nice little income. They live off those sales, some of them. And I do all right myself, charging people for the right to dig. There's more than one here who'd kill you as soon as look at you, if you was to get between them and their money."

Faye refrained from pointing out that he might consider looking for better friends.

Soon enough, they reached the boat. When Herbie saw them safely in it, he used his foot to push the boat away from the bank. Only when they had started the motor and begun to head downstream did he turn and walk away.

Joyeuse Island was a nice little boat ride from the ruins of Bachelder's home, and Joe was at the helm, so Faye had plenty of time to read Herbie's rules. They were:

1. You find it, you keep it.

2. No trespassing outside the boundaries marked in orange. I mean it.

3. No littering. I don't feel like picking up after you. And pack your trash out with you when you go home.

4. Use the latrines provided and use the shovel afterwards. I'm serious.

5. No fighting. I will kick you out. I won't refund your payment, either.

6. People who paid the camping fee should pitch their tents in the camping area only. People who didn't pay the camping fee should go home at night. I know it's a long way. Deal with it or pay the fee.

7. If you rented diving gear or a metal detector from me, take care of it, or I'll keep your deposit.

8. If you find something worth selling, I know people with money who like old things. I can act as your broker. My fee is 25%. Take it or leave it.

9. If you mess with somebody else's finds, you'll get hurt. What are you going to do? Call the law?

At the bottom of the list of rules, Herbie had posted his fees for campsites, equipment rental, and food.

"Herbie's making out like a bandit!" Joe said, looking over her shoulder. Faye wasn't sure he should be trying to read while he steered the boat through these shallow waters. "I'm surprised he's not charging for the latrine."

"He wants people to use it."

"You got a point there. But did you see what he's charging for a ham sandwich? And I'd have to want a beer real bad before I'd pay that much."

"After a long hot day of digging, I imagine Herbie can charge whatever he wants to for a cold beer. If he could keep this racket going, he could retire from the insurance business, except he's gonna run out of artifacts, sooner or later. Looks like he's trying to make his money while he can."

"Should we tell Sheriff Mike?"

Faye sighed. "It's not his county. And I don't know that there's any laws being broken. Except maybe Herbie should be paying sales tax on all that money. It's his land and he can dig it up if he wants to. I guess he can charge people to do it for him. If they don't disturb any burials, they're probably in the clear, legally. But, yeah. We should tell Sheriff Mike. He's working two murder cases, and we just got a look at several dozen people who are willing to skirt the law in a pretty serious fashion."

"Why do you think there's so much treasure for those people to hunt way out here? One of those guys said something about a battlefield. Did the Civil War come through here? Why?"

Joe scanned a landscape that didn't look like a strategic military target. Unless you were an alligator. This swamp would look especially good to a gator.

"You taking American History this fall?"

Joe nodded.

"Then listen and learn, my young apprentice. You can get a paper out of this. An A-plus paper. The Confederacy started life as a nation under some severe disadvantages. Name some."

"Well…they were in a war, right away."

"Yep. They were at war before they'd had time to set up a government, generate some income, acquire some weapons, form a military hierarchy…it's a wonder they managed as well as they did. What else?"

"They didn't have the factories they needed to make guns and ammunition and ships."

"Nor the raw materials. Anything else?"

"They could've used a few thousand more soldiers. A lot of thousands of more soldiers."

"Very good. But that's all military stuff. What does everybody need?"

"Um…food and water?"

Faye slapped him on the shoulder. "Good. I hope I'm the teaching assistant in your class this fall. Most of the South had water, plenty of it. It was a farming culture, so food wasn't an immediate issue, but it became one. First, they had to feed an army that wasn't producing food. Then the war destroyed crops and disrupted transportation. The coastline was blockaded the whole time to keep foreign imports out. All those disadvantages added up. As early as 1863, women were rioting for bread in the streets of Richmond."

Joe looked around him again, surveying this gator haven for the solution to the Confederacy's food supply problem. "Not much to eat here but fish."

"Precisely. There were canneries on the Florida coast. Saltworks, too. Bachelder may well have sold this property to an industrialist—someone who could make more money off salt and fish than he was making by growing cotton that he couldn't sell, anyway. Or maybe he was businessman enough to run those enterprises himself."

"The Yankees sent an army down here because somebody was selling fish and salt?"

"Sure. The Confederacy needed food to keep their army on its feet, and the Federals knew it. There were battles in this area with the sole purpose of keeping that protein out of the hands of the rebel army. I'm thinking that Herbie owns the site of one of those skirmishes. Those divers may be looting a ship sent to the bottom of the river nearly a hundred-and-fifty years ago. It's tragic." She fell silent.

"You're not sneaking back out here to look for a sunk ship or a fish cannery, Faye. You'll get shot."

The sound of Joe's voice caught her up short. It had a harsher edge than usual.

"You telling me what to do?"

"I'm hoping you'll listen to good sense."

"Well, okay. If you put it that way, I'll leave Herbie and his friends to rape history in peace."

# Chapter Eleven

Why was Faye surprised to see Ross sitting in Sheriff Mike's office? She should have been no more surprised to see him there than she was to see Sheriff Mike working today, on a Saturday.

Ross looked very comfortable, leaning back in his chair, feet flat on the floor, legs spread, hands resting palms-down on his thighs. But then, Ross always looked relaxed, strong, and in charge.

The snippet of conversation that she overheard before both men rose to greet her involved squirrels, dogs, and ammunition, so she knew that Ross had gotten the sheriff to talking about his favorite subject: hunting. Did Ross hunt? She had no idea. She doubted he'd spent much time stalking squirrels during his formative years in Brooklyn, but he lived in Atlanta now. He was also a lobbyist. She supposed that people who hoped to influence Georgia politicians would do well to learn how to shoot woodland creatures. If Ross needed any help developing those skills, all he had to do was to ask Joe.

Perhaps Ross' newly acquired hunting expertise had stood him in good stead today. Perhaps he had wanted to see her and had made his daily call in person Sheriff Mike as a way to "accidentally" bump into her.

Now she was being paranoid and silly. She had a cell phone. If Ross wanted to see her, he would call her like a normal human being. He had no need to manipulate events like a...well, like a lobbyist or a politician.

"Where in the world have you two been?" Sheriff Mike asked. Responding to Faye's blank look, he ran his fingers through his graying hair like a comb.

She did the same, and pulled a twig and two leaves out of her hair. Peeking at Joe out of the corner of her eye, she saw that he had a good deal more than that caught in his mane. Because he had a lot more hair that she did. Right now, he seemed to be wearing the equivalent of half a tree. He was also muddy to his knees.

She sneaked a peek at her own feet. Yes. A good portion of Bachelder's swamp had come home with her.

"I told you I was planning to get dirty. Remember? We went to look for Jedediah Bachelder's homesite."

"Found it, too," Joe added proudly. "Also, we found a bunch of people I didn't like much."

Faye wished Joe had kept this bit of information to himself. She'd planned to tell the sheriff privately about stumbling onto the pothunting party. And she'd planned to make their encounter with a host of dangerous characters sound tame and non-threatening. Like a walk in the park. Swamp. Whatever.

"Were they dangerous?" Ross reached a hand toward Faye, then stopped himself.

"One of them was holding a gun..." she began.

Ross' face was the very picture of consternation. So was the sheriff's.

"...but it was a hundred-and-fifty years old. Give or take. And it was real rusty."

"I think the barrel was jammed full of clay, too," Joe offered.

"You two are going to be the death of me." Sheriff Mike looked a little stressed. He had jumped to his feet at Faye's mention of a gun, and Faye regretted teasing him about such a thing. It was in really poor taste, considering the events of the past few days. She almost told him to sit down, then she remembered that he had Magda to nag him into a healthy old age.

"Who were these people and why were they carrying an old, dirty gun?" Ross asked in a tone of infinite patience.

"Pothunters. Collectors. Connoisseurs of historical artifacts. Call them what you like. They were tearing up a Civil War battlefield with gusto. And they were paying through the nose for the privilege."

"Listen to me carefully, Faye." The sheriff still hadn't sat down. His badge glittered under the fluorescent lights, as if to remind Faye that his words carried serious authority. "Stay away from unsavory characters. There are murderers out there."

Ross nodded at the sheriff's words.

"We thought we'd be alone with the snakes. Really. We should have been alone. Who knew these idiots would be there, too? But I thought you'd want to know who we saw out there. Herbie, the Civil War re-enactor. It's his land. And a bunch of his re-enactor friends. Also, two skinhead-types that hang out at Liz's place—Wayland and Nita. I think they're married. To each other, I mean. And speaking of Liz, I saw Chip, too."

"Sit, everybody," the sheriff said, pulling in a chair from another room. "Does it seem weird to you that you recognized so many of those people?"

"Not really. Herbie and Wayland and Nita are regulars at Liz's. They must live around here. And Chip obviously does. The rest of them were new to me this weekend, but according to this, they've been digging that battlefield for days." She pulled Herbie's rules out of her pocket and pointed to the dates posted on the bottom. "Liz's place is the closest restaurant by miles. I imagine everybody got tired of Herbie's overpriced ham sandwiches fairly quickly. Even Herbie."

The sheriff finally sat, taking the paper from her hand and adjusting the glasses on his nose. "Where is this swamp where you and Joe went wading?"

"Out of your jurisdiction. Wakulla County. And I don't think Herbie and his bunch are breaking any laws, beyond selling beer without a liquor license. But you might want to let your counterpart there know what's going on."

"Do you tell everybody their business, Faye?"

"Yes," Joe said. "She does."

A smile was flirting with the corner of Ross' mouth. He took her hand and squeezed it.

She liked him a lot. Because he liked her the way she was.

"Well. That's enough business for today, I think. Faye, you stay out of trouble. You hear me? And Joe. How'd you like to spend some time with your goddaughter?" Sheriff Mike pointed to this week's photo of Rachel, displayed prominently on his desktop next to three others. "She and my wife are bothering Miss Emma this afternoon. And Ross tells me that he wants to take a boat ride."

"Wanna show me Joyeuse?" Ross asked. "You've told me so much about it that I don't really need to see it for myself. But I want to."

So there it was. The political maneuver that had brought Ross here. A few minutes of hunting talk with the sheriff had camouflaged the larger topic—replacing Joe as her bodyguard, for an afternoon or, if Ross had his way, forever.

Faye considered whether she should be offended. She thought about refusing to cooperate with this clumsy effort to take care of her, when she didn't really need it. She decided, instead, to go with the flow. Joe's face was alight with the thought of spending the afternoon on his hands and knees, following Rachel as she crawled all over Emma's satiny wood floors. The sheriff looked satisfied with his efforts to keep Faye safe from harm. And an afternoon in her island paradise with Ross, alone, sounded irresistible…once she'd set him straight on a thing or two.

"You want to see Joyeuse? Then let's do it. I've got a boat at Liz's, so we won't have to take Joe's and leave him stranded. But we'll need to stop at Miss Emma's and get you a bathing suit."

"I stashed one in the car. Just in case I wangled an invitation."

Faye had to give the man credit. He made a plan. He implemented that plan. And he forgot not the first detail.

Liz was giving Ross the same all-over scrutiny that she habitually gave Joe. Joe usually didn't notice, but Ross did. Faye felt for him.

Liz leaned over the bar and said, "I need to talk to you, Faye," in a hoarse whisper. Ross gratefully excused himself and escaped into the men's room.

"Good God, girl," the red-headed restaurateur said in a voice that boomed off the back wall and echoed back. "Where do you find these men? You never come in here without some kinda arm candy."

"I wonder how Sheriff Mike would feel if he knew you called him 'arm candy.'"

"Wasn't talking about the sheriff. And you know it."

"Magda thinks he's cute."

"You're not gonna tell me where you find them, are you? You're gonna pretend they just drop out of the sky." Liz turned around, flipped a half-dozen burgers, then turned back to Faye. "Anyway. I wanted to tell you that Chip was back at school."

"That's great!" Faye started to say more but stopped, confused. "But it's the end of the semester. He can't be back at school until the summer term, at the earliest."

Liz waved the question away with a grease-smeared spatula. "I didn't say he was back *in* school. I said he was back *at* school. One of my customers saw him on campus yesterday, and she called me on the spot. Everybody around this place knows how much I want to see that boy back in college where he belongs."

"Have you talked to Chip about it?"

Liz snorted. "Are you nuts? He's twenty-two, and those three-and-a-half years of college make him a whole world smarter than his old mother. At least, he thinks so. If I told him the sky was blue, he'd say it was green. Also, he'd shake his head because I was 'clinging to outmoded tropes to form my world view.' Or something like that. But I don't care if he thinks I'm ignorant or outmoded or just stupid. I want him to go back to Tallahassee long enough to get that last semester done. You can't know how valuable a flimsy scrap of diploma paper is until you try to get by without one."

"You still don't know why he dropped out in the first place?"

Liz leaned forward with a gossip's smile. "It was woman trouble, for sure. My customer saw him walking around campus, following some girl like a lost puppy. So here's what I think. He had a girlfriend. She dumped him and he came home to lick his wounds. Now she's taking him back. That'll make him happy. He'll go back to school, just to be with her, and that'll make me happy. End of story."

Ross stepped out of the bathroom, so Liz lowered her voice. "My customer says the woman was a little skinny and plain, compared to how good-looking Chip is. But she walked tall, like somebody who knew where she was going. My boy needs somebody to keep him straight, because I can't do it forever. She sounds like marriage material to me."

Faye didn't respond. She just grinned and took Ross' arm, saying "Let's take a boat ride."

But she was thinking, *Marriage material? You don't even know her.* She hoped for Liz's sake that Chip's girlfriend stayed with him long enough to see him through school. After that, they could marry or not, but he'd have that all-important bachelor's degree. Like Liz, Faye had spent a lot of years trying to do without one of those.

Faye couldn't resist forming a mental picture of Chip bringing a woman home to meet his mom. Any ordinary woman would be intimidated by her tough demeanor. Maybe Liz would make some kind of effort to be less scary. It was a good thing Chip had chosen somebody who walked tall.

The thought of Liz dressed like somebody's mother—demure dress, sensible shoes, and all—made Faye laugh out loud.

Faye enjoyed watching Ross sit back and surrender control. He didn't look like he was enjoying it much, but he was doing it.

It seemed only fair that she should be in control of the boat. On land, he was a confident driver who owned a high-powered driving machine. So he should drive, if he wanted to. On water, she had a lifetime of experience. Also, she owned two boats which, though battered and ugly, purred like kittens and moved like barracudas. So she should be the boat pilot, if she wanted to. And she did.

Ross sat beside her, looking like a man who didn't know what to do with his hands. Since he was noticeably off-balance and since he had no way to walk away, this was as good a time as any to pick a fight.

"So. You went behind my back and talked to Sheriff Mike about Joe. What have you got against Joe?"

He had the good grace to look sheepish. "I don't have anything against Joe. He seems like a good guy. I'm just worried about you. Some terrible things have happened and—"

"You don't think Joe can protect me from the bad guys? He's done it before. And I take care of myself pretty well, too. In case you haven't noticed."

"Oh, I noticed."

She could tell he was trying not to smile. Faye was pretty sure he wasn't taking her complaint seriously, so she pressed harder. "I also hear tell that you think Joe's too dumb to be trusted with my safety."

"I never said that."

"Sheriff Mike says you did." That would teach Ross to try to manipulate her friends and presume that they wouldn't tell her.

"I didn't use the word 'dumb.' I wouldn't do that. But, yes, I did ask Sheriff Mike if he didn't want someone looking after you who…um…could think quicker."

Faye cut the motor. They were as far from land as they were going to get. The mainland was a dark band reflecting in the water behind them. They were just close enough to Joyeuse Island to see individual live oak trees reaching their gnarled branches out into the air. If Ross didn't want to hear what she had to say, then he was going to have to jump out of the boat. And it was a powerful long swim to dry land in either direction.

"You don't believe Joe thinks quickly? Go hunting with him sometime. He thinks quicker than a dove can fly. I know, because I've eaten the doves. And you don't think he can protect me? Once, a man was trying to kill me. He almost got the job done, too, but Joe put a stone spear point right through his throat. Another time, a woman was about to shoot me at point-blank range, and Joe took her out with one shot. Could you do those things?"

Rather than answer her question, Ross said, "My point is that maybe Joe shouldn't let you get into those situations. Maybe I could think of a way to avoid them altogether, if I were the one looking after you." A withering glance from Faye prompted him to amend his statement. "Maybe you and I *together* could figure out a way to stay safe."

Faye snorted to acknowledge that this suggestion was a step in the right direction. "I don't think you like Joe, and I can't figure out why. Do you require all your friends to have advanced degrees?"

"Faye. He's young. He's good-looking. He lives with you. I'm human enough to be jealous. So sue me."

"Here's how things are. Joe's lived on my island for three or four years. Most of that time, he didn't even live in the house. He sort of...camped. During that time, he's had girlfriends. I've dated several men, including you. Joe and I are friends. Roommates. Um, I guess 'housemates' is a better word. And when you see my house you'll know that you can be housemates and live about a quarter-mile apart." She couldn't keep the smile off her face when she thought of showing Joyeuse off to Ross. "If Joe and I were going at it like rabbits, I wouldn't be driving all the way to Atlanta to see you. So give it a rest, okay?"

She started the motor. "Besides, you and I don't get much of a chance to be alone lately. Let's quit wasting time."

If Ross had ever wondered why Faye was always short on cash, his question began to be answered as soon as she tied the boat to her nearly new dock. He supposed it had been built since the big hurricane, because Category 5 storms don't tend to spare puny things like boat docks. Hefting a bag packed with his bathing suit and towel, he followed Faye up a dirt path leading through a dense thicket of bushes and undergrowth. Huge trees lay toppled in all directions, their thirsty roots reaching for the clouds.

"The hurricane wrecked the tree canopy on this side of the island," she said, pointing at the trees' carcasses. "These vines and brushy plants had never had much sunlight before, but they're really growing now. It's interesting to watch the plant life change from month to month, just because we had a big storm. Joe cut up some of the downed trees for firewood, but I think we'll leave most of them for wildlife habitat."

Ross had hoped that they'd exhausted the topic of Joe. Apparently not.

The path curved to the left and Faye plunged on, pushing the over-eager vines out of their way. The verdant leaves blocked his view, so that Faye's home revealed itself suddenly. One minute, he was pushing his way through a wild and unkempt piece of nature. The next minute, he was standing at the edge of a neatly mown clearing with a monumental edifice gleaming against the grass like a white jewel.

The house was encircled with slender white columns and delicate balustrades. A broad staircase swept upward to a finely detailed double door. Palladian windows ornamented the dormers that brought light to the top floor, and a proud cupola rose over the whole confection. If ever a woman was house-poor, it was Faye.

The roof was obviously new. The paint job was fresh. Faye had told him about her fruitless struggle to find someone able to reconstruct the exterior staircases using the original methods. In the end, she and Joe had taught themselves how to do it.

He hoped she'd taken advantage of every source of historical preservation funding available—hurricane recovery funds, too. He didn't know anything about 19th-century carpentry tech-niques, though he was willing to learn, but he knew quite a lot about how to navigate governmental mazes. He could help Faye get money for her quixotic project. And he had a good bit of money of his own that he was willing to spend. He was willing to do pretty much anything to make Faye happy.

She'd struggled so hard. Losing her mother and grandmother when she was hardly out of high school. Flipping burgers to pay for college, until the money just wouldn't stretch far enough to make school possible. Digging for bits of her ancestors' past, then selling them to artifact collectors, just to raise the money to pay the taxes on Joyeuse and keep it standing. And now she was back in school, working for Douglass' museum, doing her doctoral research, and continuing the work on Joyeuse.

He knew she would always continue restoring this old house. It was the legacy passed down from her mother and her mother's mother, all the way back to a freed slave named Cally. Faye had told him Cally's story, and she'd made it her story. Any man who hoped to make a life with Faye would be making a life with Joyeuse, as well.

She was slapping a hand on the smooth masonry wall of the bottom floor. "This above-ground basement was built sometime shortly after 1798, according to a family journal. It was probably just a modest building built out of tabby, a kind of cement people made with the ingredients at hand—sand, shells, stuff like that. Sometime before 1829, my great-great-great-grandfather turned that little cement building into a rich man's dream."

She led him into the ground floor basement, where the thick, dense walls had kept the air cool all day long. "There's a bathroom to your left. Do you still want to go for a swim?"

He nodded silently, still occupied by the sight of the wrought iron hinges and the irregular shapes of the tiles under his feet and all the other obvious signs that he was standing in a structure built completely by hand.

"I'll go put on my suit. See you in a few minutes." Faye stepped into a closet-sized room where a cramped staircase was hidden. Her erect carriage emphasized the shapely figure beneath the baggy clothes. He wondered whether bathing suits were strictly necessary, this far from civilization.

◇◇◇

As a true island dweller, Faye owned more bathing suits than dresses. She had a dresser drawer packed full of them.

Unfortunately, as the owner of two aging boats, most of her bathing suits sported grease stains in strategic places. They were all bikinis, so she pawed through the pieces, hoping to find a clean-ish top and a clean-ish bottom in coordinating colors. Maybe she should just take a heavily stained suit and dip it in motor oil, rendering it all one color—a nasty color, to be true, but still one color.

A glint of fuchsia in the bottom of her drawer spoke to her, and she answered it.

"Come to Mama."

She'd bought the fuchsia suit for a long-ago date with a long-ago fiancé, and it had been way too cute to do engine work in. It had flirty white polka-dots, a flirtily low-cut top, and flirty knots on the hips. It was perfect. An old memory stirred, and she dug around in the back of the drawer. With a triumphant yank, she pulled out the matching sarong. A few minutes later, Faye sauntered down the sneak staircase, looking like a woman who had no idea how to keep a boat engine humming.

The sand on Faye's little tiny beach was fine-grained and perfectly white. The water was still a bit cool for her Florida-girl tastes, but she couldn't resist its transparent turquoise. Ross surprised her by shedding his oh-so-cultured lawyer persona. He tossed his towel on the sand and ran headlong into the water with a whoop.

"You look so...dry," he said, shaking water out of his tight curls.

She responded by running almost as fast as he had and whooping just as loud. The water closed over her head and she knew that, in a minute or two, it wouldn't feel quite so cold.

Ross' hands closed on her waist. He pulled her to him and, as her face broke the water, he kissed her. Then he dunked her back beneath the waves. Clearly, he was unaware how dangerous it was for a city boy to declare water war on an island woman.

Yes, he was taller and sometimes he reached out a long arm and grabbed whatever he could reach, tossing her into the air. And, yes, he was stronger, so he could sometimes fend off her submarine attacks. Often enough, though, he was toppled when she dove down and grabbed one of his big feet.

Faye had known for a long time that a small person could splash as well as a large one, so she used her watery ammunition well. Ross might have declared water war on her, but she was proud of fighting him to a draw. They were still laughing when they waded onto the beach.

She was shaking the sand out of her towel when she felt something come between her skin and the chilly spring breeze. Ross had wrapped one end of his towel around her and, because a big man requires an oversized towel, it was long enough for him to wrap the other end around himself. Faye had to admit that this was a most attractive way to warm up after a swim.

He leaned close and said, "I like your beach, and your basement is very nice. Why don't you show me the rest of your house?"

A historian's fantasy. Or, to be more accurate, an archaeologist's fantasy. Ross could think of no better way to describe Faye's cherished home. She'd escorted him through the above-ground basement's open-centered passageway, pointing out the rooms that had once been the plantation office, the dispensary, the wine cellar, and all the other service rooms used to run a large household and a tremendous agricultural business.

Upon opening the doors to those service rooms, he found that Faye had converted them into comfortable living quarters. A modern sofa and easy chair adorned the old office, and groaning bookshelves lined its walls. A quick glance at the books' titles gave him a glimpse of the woman. Her library included tomes like *Make Your Restored House a Home*, the collected works of Shakespeare and Austen, *The Martian Chronicles*, and *The Complete Tightwad Gazette*.

She had already moved on into the old infirmary, where she had installed a sleek and functional kitchen. "I love my gas-powered refrigerator. I can't tell you how long I lived out of ice chests. It seemed like forever."

"Is that an electric light?"

"I have solar panels."

"Were they expensive?"

"The tax credit helped a lot."

Ross thought, *Good girl. Let the government help you with this place.* Then he realized that maybe Faye didn't even need him to help her find funding for this mammoth home improvement project.

She gave a careless gesture toward one door and said, "That's Joe's room," then moved on quickly as if to avoid a difficult subject.

Pointing at the bathroom where Ross had dressed, she said, "Joyeuse is amazingly livable these days. I've always had bathrooms—my grandmother installed them, using the original cisterns and pipes—but I was able to spruce them up a lot last year. I'm especially partial to the humongous claw-foot bathtub."

"It's authentic, I'm sure. You don't seem to be very fond of reproductions."

Faye grinned and nodded. "If it looks old, I want it to be old. If it's not old, then it can look modern, because I'm not into fakes. It took me a long time to find just the right tub for this room. My job gets me dirty and I do love a nice hot bath."

Ross found himself distracted by some enticing mental pictures.

Faye opened the sneak staircase door, thought for a second, then closed it. "Let's go outside and walk up the grand staircase. That's the way you were intended to enter the main floor."

The steps were broad and deep enough to be negotiated by a lady in a hoopskirt, or a man in riding boots and spurs. The wood was new, but the design of the staircase meshed seamlessly with the style of the house. The craftsmanship of the stairs was superb, which wasn't surprising, considering who had built them. Ross suspected that, together, Faye and Joe could build anything they damn well pleased.

The color of the wood under his feet changed as he reached the top of the stairs, turning to a dull, weathered gray. The boards of the broad porch felt strong and sandy under his feet—old, strong, and sandy. A porch swing hung to his right, and the vibrations of their footsteps had set it into motion. It swayed back and forth, inviting him with its slight motion to sit and rest.

"The main floor didn't suffer as much as the rest of the house over the years, not until the hurricane. I've cleaned it up, but restoration is a long way off. And Lord knows how much it'll cost me to furnish it."

The heavy doors swung open and Ross found himself looking into a cavernous space that could have been described as a domestic cathedral. The spacious rooms flowed into one another—Faye explained that she couldn't yet afford to replace the pocket doors that had once divided them—but their absence only made the space seem more vast.

There wasn't a stick of furniture in sight. Ross' last girlfriend had been an interior designer. She'd have had a spasm if she'd gotten a look at this place.

"None of the wallpaper was salvageable after it had a nice little soak in saltwater. I've been researching the paper patterns, hoping to find designs that come as close as possible to the originals, because I'm pretty sure I'm gonna be stuck with reproduction paper. I guess it's too much to hope that some wallpaper company might have rolls of paper from the 1800s just lying around its warehouse."

Reading between the lines, Ross figured Faye was planning a full-out assault on those warehouses, just in case.

"I know how to patch the plaster work," she said, pointing up to a finely detailed medallion on the ceiling. The moldings at the top of the walls were almost as elaborate. "I just need to find some time. I'll need a whole lot of time to touch up the faux marbling on the mantels and the painted graining on the woodwork, too. You can't rush that stuff."

She opened a little door in the dining room to reveal the sneak staircase. "One more floor. Well, two, counting the cupola. I used to have a spiral staircase that took you as far as the bedrooms, but the hurricane got it. I can't get it rebuilt until somebody figures out how it was built in the first place. It looks like Joe and I may have to do that ourselves, too, if we don't die of old age first."

So she was planning to keep Joe around until she died of old age. Perfect. Ross almost groaned out loud.

The sneak staircase ended in the master bedroom. The décor here looked...frothy...to Ross' masculine eyes. Each square inch of wall and ceiling space was covered with murals in every shade of off-white he could imagine. Lilies, roses, magnolias, lace, ribbons—the room was white-on-white, shaded with gold, and it was too fresh for the house.

"You did this?"

"I restored the original murals, yes." She smiled as his astonishment.

"Now I understand why you don't have a TV. When would you watch it?"

She toured him through a music room adorned with tiny harps and a gentleman's bedchamber painted with foxhunting scenes. Her own room was a lavender confection of swans and wisteria so beautiful and so feminine that it was clear why she had chosen it for her own, over a master bedroom that was a lovely but sterile vision in white.

There was little furniture on this floor, either, just beds in her room and in the master bedroom. There was a chest of drawers where Faye kept her clothes, and several display cases where she kept her most treasured archaeological finds, but that was about all. Everything he laid eyes on seemed to be an artifact or an antique or simply something old that still worked. Ross hoped she was able to find some antique wallpaper stashed in a warehouse somewhere. It would be a shame to paste something fake onto something as completely authentic as Joyeuse. It was as authentic as Faye herself.

The sparse furnishings told him that Faye didn't throw away anything that might still be useful. She slept on an antique convent bed. The display cases housing her finds looked like they'd been discarded from a musty old university laboratory. Ross could almost smell the formaldehyde.

In one jam-packed closet, he saw a camp stove, a large cooler, and a radio so old that it looked like something geeky boys had used to talk to faraway geeky boys back in the 1950s. She must be keeping these things as a defense against the day she lost the modern conveniences that she'd so recently acquired. If her range and her refrigerator and her cell phone evaporated, Faye would still survive, just as she had before she'd owned such things.

She fetched a long tool with a hook on the end, then led him onto the reconstructed landing, where an empty hole waited for the spiral staircase to be rebuilt. Using the tool to hook a metal loop in the ceiling, she yanked open a trap door, from which a ladder unfolded.

The ladder mechanism screeched in protest, and Ross couldn't help himself. "I need to put some WD-40 on that."

Faye grinned and scrambled up the ladder. He followed her up into a square room that was practically all windows.

"We're in the cupola," she said. "The mainland is that way." She pointed to a vast expanse of deep green cypress swamp. "The Last Isles, including the site of the Turkey Foot Hotel, are over there." She waved in the general direction of dark blotches in the crystalline water. "And out there is the open Gulf of Mexico." Perfectly turquoise waves rolled under a perfectly blue sky.

"My ancestors built this place. With their own hands." Faye waved a loving hand of her own over the sprawling roof below them.

Ross turned to look at the dark mainland, because he knew that way was north. Atlanta was a long, long way from this spot.

He could live here with Faye and be happy, but there wasn't a hell of a lot of legal work to be had on a private island. Faye could certainly live with him in Atlanta and continue to go to school, but he wasn't clear how happy she could be without this aged pile of wood beneath her feet.

All this time, he'd seen Joe as the one thing between him and the woman he wanted. Now he'd seen the face of his true rival, and her name was Joyeuse.

◇◇◇

Faye took care to tie her boat properly for the night, as she always did. She missed Ross, but she understood his unspoken reason for going back to shore so soon. Emma would notice if he didn't come in until morning. And there was the question of what Joe would do…would he stay the night at Emma's, or come back to sleep at Joyeuse—which was, after all, his home—even though Faye had a guest and might wish for privacy?

Within the hour, she heard Joe as he dragged his johnboat onto the beach and tied it to a tree. She didn't expect him to come upstairs to tell her good-night, and he didn't.

Joe's recording of Jedediah Bachelder's letters was still trapped deep in the memory of her laptop computer. The analytical part of her brain, the part of her that belonged to the world of science, begged her to listen to another letter, but the emotional part of her brain said no.

She needed to grieve for Wally and Douglass. She needed to obsess over the problem of Ross. He radiated the confidence of a man who was always in charge. Could she be happy with that? And could she be happy in Atlanta, far from Joyeuse? It was obvious to anyone with a brain that Ross was not born to live on an island.

She banished Bachelder from her mind and cataloged her grief for Douglass and Wally, knowing that she would revisit it compulsively for years and years. Instead, she drifted off to sleep while thinking of Ross' kindness and strength. Surely those things were enough for real happiness. Could it really matter so much where they lived or what either of them did for a living?

In her dreams that night, she was motherless, alone, and lost. She couldn't find her way home, because she had no home. Her subconscious mind was screaming at her, trying to tell her what she knew already—that home would always matter to Faye. It mattered far more than her career. Maybe it even mattered more than love. When she was awake, she could argue with that part of herself. But not while she was asleep.

# Chapter Twelve

Grief woke Faye early. She'd done this before, waking from a dream she longed to share with her mother, then realizing that her mother wasn't there. And never would be again.

She knew Douglass would have enjoyed an afternoon like Joe had spent yesterday, talking baby talk to Rachel and sipping coffee with Emma. He would have enjoyed hearing about Bachelder's letters and, like Faye, he would have burned to know the history behind the emerald he'd had in his hand on the night he died.

The sheriff agreed with her that she should continue to pursue the link between the emerald and Bachelder and Douglass' death. It wasn't traditional crimefighting, but he had people to do that. Also, she was a civilian and officially had no reason to stick her nose into the murder investigation.

But the emerald was her business. She'd found it on her own land, and she would have been scouring the countryside for the rest of the necklace, even if Douglass were where he belonged, snoring in bed beside Emma. If she could help find his killer by doing archaeological work that she'd be doing anyway, so much the better.

Today was the day that she went out and looked for that emerald's brothers and sisters. Her heartbeat quickened. Faye knew that if the day ever came when her heart wasn't stirred by the possibility of what she might find, that was the day she should hang up her trowel.

◇◇◇

With field notes in hand, Faye stood in a weedy area between her house and the beach, trying to reconstruct her activities on the day she found the emerald. She remembered squinting through a break in the brushy vegetation, trying to get a glimpse of the Last Isles so that she could orient herself. Most of the trees in that area were gone, victims of the hurricane, so she'd pounded a metal stake into the sandy soil to give herself a reference point.

The stake was there, right where she'd left it. Finding any location listed in her field notes would be a simple matter of measuring its distance from the stake in the north-south direction, then doing the same thing in the east-west direction. Any sixth-grader could do it.

As she squatted to leaf through her notes, Joe walked into the underbrush, following a lizard and studying its movement. Some of the deepest silence on earth settled around them.

The beach was far away and the waves were calm. Their movement added a subtle bit of rhythmic background noise. Sometimes the wind stirred the palm fronds overhead or the hair over Faye's ear. Those faint sounds only accentuated the lack of non-natural noise. Come sunset, the waterbirds would be diving for their supper, and their caws and splashes would seem earsplitting compared to the present hush.

Had they been anywhere else, the shushing grind of a shovel slicing through sandy dirt would have been drowned out by regular, everyday noise. Faye and Joe would never have heard it.

There had been treasure hunters on Joyeuse Island before, and there would be again. This did not mean that they would ever stop making Faye blindingly angry. Before any consideration of danger had time to reach her forebrain, she was running. The thought of someone else probing beneath the surface of her own island was as horrific to her as the idea of an amateur surgeon slicing open her mother.

Joe was stumbling out of the bushes and hollering at Faye to stop, but he was wasting precious time fumbling at the leather pouch hanging at his waist. Also, Faye had a head start. She just might manage to stay more than an arm's-length ahead of Joe for as long as it took to track the source of the noise.

At the treeline where Faye's beach met the tangled bushes, Nita the lady shrimper was perched on the edge of a sizeable hole, with her back to Faye. She was digging with a long-handled shovel, turning over great clumps of soil and scattering the back-dirt hither-and-yon, as if it were of no importance. Since it had no monetary value, it *was* of no importance to Nita.

Faye was so angry that her brain was wiped clean of common sense. People had lived and died on this island, hundreds of them. No, their graves weren't right there where Nita was digging, not that she knew of. But the things they'd made and used, the artifacts that still told the stories of their lives—those things might be.

Yes, Faye's archaeological work disturbed the physical record of those lives, but she strove to minimize that disturbance. She thought of her work as a memorial to them. It was a way to reach across time. Learning about long-ago people put a face on them. It brought history to life.

There was a difference between what she did and what Nita was doing.

There *was* a difference.

Nita was doing nothing but destroying the bridges that bound humans to their past.

"Hey! You can't do that on my property!"

Faye didn't know how she'd thought Nita would respond to her challenge. Probably, she'd thought the artifact thief would just run away. Or maybe she'd expected the woman to make excuses for what she was doing. Later, Faye would tell herself she should stop expecting criminals to act like ordinary people.

Nita swung the shovel hard, blade out. Its corner caught Faye in the hip, the only fleshy part of her scrawny body. The blade drew blood and its impact would leave a magnificent bruise, but if such a blow had struck Faye anywhere else, it would have broken a bone.

Common sense returned. Faye's immediate goal changed. She still wanted Nita gone, but first she intended to avoid getting hit with that shovel again.

The momentum of Nita's powerful swing carried her torso around like a golfer with perfect follow-through. Faye took the opportunity to launch herself at Nita's exposed back. The two women were about the same size, but Faye had an advantage: her opponent was off-balance. Her weight carried Nita to the ground on top of the shovel that was doing all that damage. Grasping its handle, one hand on either side of Nita's neck, Faye pulled it back against her assailant's throat to immobilize her.

Faye was ridiculously proud that Joe had not had to take down this particular criminal. She was a little tired of him saving her butt.

But where was Joe, anyway? She'd had a devil of a time staying out of his reach. He should have reached her at about the time Nita swung the shovel.

The sound of someone running in heavy boots stopped her breath in her throat. Joe didn't wear boots.

The beginnings of a grin on Nita's face prompted Faye to yell, "Joe! Watch out!"

Nita's husband Wayland had been standing lookout, though he'd been expecting trouble to come by sea and had been looking in the wrong direction. His inattention had bought Faye and Joe a few seconds, but no more.

Wayland was running toward them with an evil-looking rifle in his hand. Faye knew that she would only be in control of this situation for as long as it took Wayland to stop running and take aim, but she wasn't about to give Nita the satisfaction of letting her loose even a moment sooner than she had to.

There weren't many things that would make Faye let go of Nita's neck, but a bullet would be one of them. She wanted to close her eyes and hunker down, bracing herself for pain far beyond a bruised and bloody hip, but sight was one of the few things left that she had going for her. It would have been stupid to shut it down out of cowardice. She looked directly into Wayland's face and tried to guess whether he'd really pull the trigger.

Then something alien flew through Faye's peripheral vision and wrapped itself around Wayland's legs, taking him down and sending the rifle flying from his hands. Joe had pulled a bolo out of his bag of tricks. While a bolo is a simple weapon made of weights attached to a leather thong, its operation isn't simple at all. In Joe's hands, it could drop a rhino.

It took forever for the sheriff and his crew to get out to Joyeuse Island, but Faye didn't care much. With the judicious use of Joe's bolo and some rope from her boat, and a few episodes of brandishing Wayland's gun in their prisoners' faces, she and Joe had managed to keep things under control until the law arrived.

When the sheriff arrived to take the prisoners' off Faye's and Joe's hands, he didn't say, "Hello." He didn't say, "Nice work." All he said was, "My wife wants to have a word with you." Then he handed Faye his cell phone and walked over to get a good look at Wayland and Nita. He looked amused at how thoroughly Joe and Faye had trussed the criminals up.

"I've been an archaeologist for twenty-five years," Magda began, in a tone of voice that suggested that quite a bit more time would pass before she was through with this tirade. Faye held the phone out a couple of inches from her head. Her eardrum could only take so much of Magda when she was in full harangue. "A quarter-century. In all that time, nobody's pointed any guns at me. Well, maybe once. And I don't believe I've ever had to fist-fight anybody. Why do these things happen to you?"

"There were no fists involved. It was a shovel fight."

"I heard that shovel drew blood. Where did she hurt you?"

"On my cheek."

"Your face? Faye! You're too pretty for that. You tell my husband to get you to a plastic surgeon right now and—"

"Magda. It was a butt cheek."

"Oh. Well—but still—archaeology is not supposed to be a blood sport. I don't like being worried about you all the time. Can you answer my question? Why do these things happen to you?"

Faye fought the urge to say, *I don't know, ma'am. I'm sorry, ma'am. It'll never happen again.* Instead, she opted for, "I think it's because I'm spending my career out here in the islands. There are a lot of out-of-the-way spots where people do bad things, because there's no one to see them. And there's a lot of valuable stuff to dig up—you know, from the hotel and the plantation and all—and the local people know it. It looked to me like Nita and Wayland were pothunting, planning to sell whatever they found. When people get caught breaking the law, they tend to point guns at people. Especially when there's money involved."

"But why were they there, Faye? There are a lot of islands out there. Yours is just one of the biggest. Why'd they pick your island, and why'd they pick that spot? And don't tell me you presume it was random. Assuming that an important event has no explanation is the last refuge of people who don't want to use their heads."

*Why were they there in the first place?* This was a question a scientist would ask. It had crossed Faye's mind, but she'd really been too busy to deal with it. "I don't know. It looked like she'd just picked a random spot and started shoveling."

As it passed her lips, Faye realized that she'd just used Magda's least favorite word: "random." She kept talking fast, hoping Magda hadn't noticed.

"We've had some problems lately with pothunters at the hotel site—nothing too serious yet—but it only makes sense that they'd come there. The newspapers all did stories on the Turkey Foot Hotel and Joyeuse after the hurricane. Treasure-hunters aren't dumb. The plantation and hotel were full of rich people and they didn't have a chance to get their valuables to shore before the 1857 hurricane. They're high-probability places to look for the good stuff. Well, the expensive stuff, anyway. As far as pothunting on Joyeuse Island goes, though, I can't think of a specific reason for Nita to pick the spot where she was digging."

"Well, don't let that question get away from you. It might be important. You sure don't want to have my husband hauling trespassers off your island on a daily basis. I'm actually glad they were pothunting, instead of just prowling around. That means they weren't necessarily looking for you."

"I just happened to be here. That's all."

"You're so sure? There's no chance of a connection to the two killings?"

"Wayland and Nita wouldn't be my first suspects, no. They're way too small to be the people Emma saw after Douglass' attack."

"That doesn't mean they couldn't have killed you."

It was true so there wasn't much for Faye to say but, "Thank you. For worrying about me. For caring. For all that stuff."

Magda said, "Hmmph," and hung up.

The sheriff, seeing Faye thumb the phone's off button, ambled over and said, "Let me count these criminals. One. Two."

"Too bad they're not the two people Emma saw the night Douglass died," Faye said. "In the dark, Nita might pass for a man...a very, very delicate man. However, neither she nor Wayland would ever pass for large."

"My thoughts, exactly. I'll put them in a lineup and show them to Emma, but these aren't our killers."

"Maybe they're not Douglass' killers—" Faye began.

"Yeah, I know they were around when Wally was stabbed. I'll keep them in custody as long as I can, trying to get a lead on his killing. But if I can't get anything on them besides trespassing and assault, I may not be able to keep them all that long."

Faye knew a lot of large men. The sheriff. Joe. The only large men she remembered at Liz's bar when Wally died were among the Civil War re-enactors. Certainly not Wayland. And Nita wasn't big in the least. Emma would never have mistaken her for a man, even on the dark night her husband was killed. Nita's sinuous body practically shouted femininity.

The sheriff knew those things as well as Faye did. He could hardly haul in everybody who was a certain size, just because they'd eaten too many plates of Liz's eggs and grits.

Sheriff Mike leaned closer to Faye and lowered his voice. "We got a lead on Douglass' murder today. It's not much of a lead, but it's something." He motioned for Joe to come listen. "Emma was wrong about one thing. The thieves did go upstairs—probably after they were finished downstairs, and probably after Douglass was out of commission. That's why the muddy footprints only went downstairs. They were down there long enough to wipe most of the dirt off their feet."

"Did they take anything?" Faye figured it couldn't be anything valuable, or Emma would have noticed by now.

"The original copy of your catalog of the museum's entire collection."

"That's all?"

"It's all Emma can come up with. I've got technicians in Douglass' office, looking for evidence. So far, we've got no fingerprints, so I guess they were wearing gloves. There were a few fibers, mostly cotton, white and blue. Not much we can do with that, unless we get a specific pair of jeans of or a t-shirt or a pair of gloves to check them against. We did get a couple of hairs that look to be Caucasian, so they're not Douglass' or Emma's—"

"That's great! Can you get DNA from those?"

"Maybe. But we've got to have some subjects to match it with."

Faye cut her eyes toward Nita and Wayland who were being hustled along by a couple of deputies.

"Yes, we'll look at their DNA first thing. It'll take time and I don't think it'll match. If it doesn't, then we'll be back to Square One."

Faye blew an exasperated breath through pursed lips. "It may be even worse than that. The DNA may turn out to mean nothing. You know the whole countryside came through that house after the funeral."

"Exactly. Half the people in Micco County could've left those hairs. Heck, one of the funeral-goers could've taken the catalog as a souvenir, meaning that even following up on that is a waste of precious time. Here's the bottom line. As far as we can tell, there's nothing missing but paper—your notes and the catalog you prepared."

"I don't like the way all this stuff keeps coming back to Faye," Joe said.

"Neither do I," said the sheriff. "And neither does my wife."

Faye couldn't argue with any of them.

# Chapter Thirteen

The antibiotic ointment did nothing to ease the throb in Faye's wounded hip. She twisted around to get a look at the cut—thank goodness, it hadn't needed stitches—but she couldn't do much more than spin around, chin over her shoulder, like a cat chasing its tail. A mirror helped her get a bandage on it, which was good, because she had no intention of asking Joe to help her with that little chore.

She'd called Ross, intending only a short, happy, reassuring call to tell him how perfectly safe she was. Instead, she got a dozen variations of, "What was in that catalog that the thieves wanted so badly? What was in your notes? Think, Faye!"

Exhausted by a day spent dealing with an unprovoked attack and hours of subsequent law enforcement activity—not to mention the need to keep all her protectors calm—she pulled some pajama bottoms over the fresh bandage and crawled into bed.

Was she safe here in her home? The sheriff had seemed unsure. Nita and Wayland were in jail, and they'd be staying there overnight, at least. Were they working alone? Or would someone else come to take their place? She was glad Joe was downstairs. And she was glad that Liz had lent him a gun, just in case.

Was it possible that Douglass' killers really came looking for nothing more than paper? What did they think was hidden in those notes or in the catalog that was worth the risk of breaking into Douglass' house? When they'd found him standing between themselves and their goal, they'd killed him. What piece of paper, short of a piece of paper money with a heckuva lot of zeros on the front, was worth that? And, just maybe, those same people killed Wally rather than let him tell anybody about the letters from Jedediah Bachelder to his wife. That book didn't hold anything but letters. More paper.

Everything kept pointing to the emerald. Any crook worth his salt would do whatever it took to steal a treasure like that. But only if they knew where it was, and that was so very unlikely. Douglass hadn't been stupid enough to tell a soul what he had stored in his safe, much less tell someone he was holding a queen's ransom in the form of a precious stone. Besides, there had simply been no time for someone to take a call from Douglass, decide to steal the emerald, then boat over to his house to kill him and steal...a lot of nothing.

Presuming for the moment that the thieves had managed to circumvent the time problem, and presuming that they did know about the emerald, Faye asked herself whether that was the only thing they'd come to Douglass' house to find. Perhaps they would have thought that the location of the rest of the necklace, and its many still-missing emeralds, was hidden in all the paperwork that they'd stolen.

What made them presume Douglass had that information? If they'd read Bachelder's letters, they would know that he'd once owned an emerald necklace. If they'd read the newspaper, they'd know that Douglass owned one of Bachelder's many possessions, the silver hip flask. Could this have led them to Douglass' door?

All this speculation was fruitless, because she knew deep down that nobody but Faye and Douglass were aware that the emerald was in the laboratory that night. Was there any other link, however tenuous, between the necklace and Douglass that someone else *could* have known about? What was that link?

The word "link" bounced around in her brain. If the emerald had once been part of the necklace, it had hung from a chain, presumably a gold one, based on the fragments of its setting that were still attached. She didn't have a single link of that chain. The stone's setting would have been attached to its chain with a piece of gold hardware called jeweler's finding…and, long ago, she had unearthed a gold finding.

When she found that finding, all those years ago, had she been digging in the area where she'd found the emerald? She thought it was possible. Yes, she was pretty sure that the two objects were found with a few feet of each other.

The finding had been nothing more than a tiny gleam, easy to spot in the sandy soil of Joyeuse Island. She'd found no chain, no pendant, no jewel, just a bit of gold and twisted golden wire. It had been engraved with an *M*, barely visible after so many years in the abrasive soil. At the time, she'd thought perhaps it had once belonged to her great-great-great-great grandmother Mariah Whitehall LaFourche. With a sense of vertigo, she now realized that it might have adorned the doomed neck of Marie Antoinette.

It was a tiny thing, but an interested person who saw the article about Jedediah Bachelder and his flask would surely visit the museum to see whether anything more interesting had surfaced. Anyone who'd read Bachelder's letters—which had been in a library accessible to the public for many years—would know that the owner of the little silver flask had once owned something far more valuable. Might someone have visited the museum to see what else Douglass had that could be linked to Bachelder?

It wouldn't have taken long to scan the little museum for gold or emeralds, for few things in the building fits that description. It was, after all, a museum dedicated to the lives of slaves, who were not known for owning jewels. Douglass' entire collection of precious metals with some link to slavery—the broken finding, a worn pocket watch, a couple of wedding rings, the silver hip flask—were all displayed together in a small case. They would be quickly found by anyone looking for precious stones or metals.

Would there have been time for someone to read the morning paper, search the museum and find evidence of the necklace in the form of a gold finding, then plan a late-night raid on the laboratory to steal information on where that finding had been found? Yes. But wasn't it risky doing such things so fast?

Among the sheriff's suspects was a double truckload of re-enactors and treasure hunters. They would know plenty of arcane history of the time. Perhaps it was common knowledge among Civil War buffs that Jedediah Bachelder had once owned a treasure. Once Bachelder's flask had been printed in the paper for everybody in Tallahassee to see, the burglars would have been in a hurry to make sure nobody else got there first. If they were sufficiently motivated by greed, they wouldn't have worried about one old man who got in their way.

If all this were true, then there was enough information publicly available to lead treasure hunters to Joyeuse Island. Perhaps Nita and Wayland were only the first scavengers to come looking for Bachelder's jewels. And perhaps they wouldn't be the last.

She reached for her computer. She wished she had enough time to drive to Tallahassee and read every last one of them at a single sitting, even if reading the prolific Bachelder's correspondence took days. The site work related to Bachelder's necklace—the visit to his house and the abortive effort to excavate the site where the emerald had lain—had taken so much of her time and mental energy that she hadn't even finished listening to the ones Joe had recorded for her. Another of Bachelder's letters would make a good bedtime story.

*September 10, 1863*

*My dearest Viola,*
    *I send this letter by private messenger, because I am nearer to you than I was. Not so near that I might come to you, I fear. Hundreds of miles separate us still, and with the disruption of the railroads, there is no easy way to cross those miles. Growing disorder guarantees that unsavory characters litter the territory between us. No matter. My messenger has a fast horse and he is a crack shot. I feel confident that this most important and private missive will reach you.*
    *Our mission to England was not successful. Another group, sent to France with similar orders, met with the same result.*

There is talk that Duncan Kenner, a respected Louisiana planter, may attempt to succeed where we could not. He has the ear of President Davis, and I understand that he wishes to take with him an incentive that we could not offer: an offer to emancipate our country's slaves. In my opinion, full emancipation would obtain us important allies in Europe, and such aid might hand us full victory. Unfortunately, from my association with our president, I do not imagine that he would ever agree to such a thing.

And so, we must struggle on alone, cut off from the world by the damnable blockade. I wish I could know that you are well-fed and free from the want of some critical item, such as medicine. I dare not hope that you are comfortable, for we are at war and few among us has everything needed for comfort.

The blockade—I seem unable to leave that subject—has enabled me to see much of the world. A blockade runner smuggled us out of Wilmington, and we landed on lovely Bermuda for too short a time. Because the English cannot receive a ship from our Confederacy without violating their position of neutrality, we were forced to play a shell game, booking passage on a ship—any ship—registered to a country England is willing to recognize.

The briefness of our sojourn in Bermuda will speak to the fact that these tricks are played on a daily basis. The ship captains who pause in this harbor are well-versed in deception. Our travels home brought us through Nova Scotia, a landscape as alien to my Florida upbringing as it is possible to find on this earth.

The irony of these maneuvers is highlighted by the fact that the Federals themselves have been forced to recognize our sovereignty, though they do not admit it. A country may close its own ports, but it cannot declare a blockade on them. Lincoln knows that this action signifies recognition under international law, but he had no better choice.

We are in a war between sovereign states, not a rebellion, but such semantics hardly matter in the face of so much *death and suffering. It may be treasonous, but I have come to think that not even defeat or victory matter so much, not when one considers the blood spilt on our soil and on that of the Federals.*

*On the subject of death...it has been much on my mind that I might not survive this war. No, I am not in battle, but my ship might have been sunk at any time on either of my interminable voyages. When I am in Richmond, I am part of a military target. I cannot risk leaving you destitute.*

*I have written you of a necklace that I purchased in England. It was unwise of me to trust that information to the erratic mails, but I was thoughtless in my despair at our separation. Sending this letter by messenger is far safer. I pray that my first letter reached you, and that no other eyes saw it while it traveled to Alabama. That necklace is our future. What remains of our fortune is far safer, bound up in gold and emeralds that will not perish, than it would be if it were tied to bonds or currency that might be nothing but paper tomorrow.*

*This necklace has been a much more pleasant traveling companion than paper money. It was easily concealed on my person, whereas the equivalent value of paper money would be far more than I could carry, even if I still possessed the strength of a young man. Our treasure has been as safe as I. I have lately come to understand that I would like it to be safer than I.*

*Last month, I traveled to our Florida plantation, with plans to conceal the necklace there, only to find that you had been forced to sell that property. I commend you for finding a way around the laws that would prohibit a woman from such commerce. Do not worry that I grieve over my childhood home. I know that it cost your heart dearly to sell it. I pray that the proceeds have kept you safe and fed. But its loss meant that I was forced to find another safe haven for the jewels.*

*I know you recall the holiday we spent, just before the war, at the island plantation once owned by a friend of my father's. There was a time when the two families visited often, for they were our close neighbors when one traveled by water. Though the property had passed from the man I knew, Andrew, to his young step-son, Courtney, by the time of our visit, you remember the compatibility of our interests and the even-tempered graciousness of Courtney's character.*

*I wished before our visit that Courtney had been married, for I feared that you would lack feminine companionship during our long time on his island. My worries were for naught. The lady of the house, Courtney's young cousin, managed to entertain you delightfully, without sparing herself the duties of a household. You may remember remarking on the beauty of the house and the delicacy of the foods her cooks served us.*

*Ah, I must not think of delicate foods in this difficult time.*

*With Courtney's assistance, I have secreted our future, in the form of that exquisite and rare necklace, on his island. I will say no more in future letters of the necklace or of its hiding place, for fear of my letters falling into hands other than yours. Either destroy this epistle or give it to Isaiah, for I know that you have taught him to read by now, as surely as I know that I love you. Should the war find our home, it might be ransacked for valuables, but I deeply doubt that the invaders would look to a freed slave for treasure.*

*If I should not return, Isaiah can help you find the island. The necklace is buried in a copse of trees southwest of the great house. Courtney observed that it would be a lovely location for a summerhouse. He expected to have his men begin construction the following day. You and Isaiah will find a crawlspace under the elegant new structure. And buried there you will find a treasure.*

*Though I rather hope you don't. I'd prefer to fetch the treasure myself and fasten it around your willowy neck.*

*Your adoring husband,*
*Jedediah*

# Chapter Fourteen

Faye had stopped being sleepy by the time she'd heard the first paragraph of Bachelder's letter. Her first thought had been *Why didn't Joe tell me about this?* Then she read back over the letter. Bachelder had mentioned visiting an island plantation, yes. But he'd mentioned no last names, and only two first names: Andrew and Courtney. There was no reason to expect Joe to remember every name on her family tree. Also, by the time he'd read half-a-dozen letters into the recorder, his brain would have been on automatic pilot. He might not have noticed his own name as he mumbled it into the machine.

When she'd turned on the voice recorder and started listening to Joe's soothing voice, Faye had been at a dead end in so many ways. She'd had no clue about who killed Douglass and Wally, and neither had the sheriff. And she'd been stymied by the problem of fitting together the emerald and the silver flask and her friends' murders. There was no reason they *should* fit together, other than the circumstantial fact that something significant happened to each piece of the puzzle—the emerald was found, the flask's photo was in the newspaper, Douglass and Wally died, and Nita and Wayland showed up with shovels and a gun—all within the space of a few days.

The letter changed everything. It told anyone perusing the worn volume of Bachelder's collected letters that a fabulous necklace was hidden somewhere in the islands near his childhood home. Anyone who read the local paper would also have known that Douglass possessed one of Bachelder's personal items and that he employed a personal archaeologist. If they were sufficiently interested to visit Douglass' museum—and who wouldn't be sufficiently interested in a handful of emeralds and gold?—then they might even have seen the gold finding

The first names of Joyeuse's Civil-War-era owners, Andrew and Courtney, might have already led them straight to Joyeuse Island, but for the fact that the Micco County Courthouse had burned in the 1890s. So far as the killers knew, the only key to finding their home—and the treasure that had been buried there under a summer house—lay in the field notes that documented where Faye had found the hip flask and the finding.

Nobody but Faye and her closest friends knew that a piece of Bachelder's necklace had already been found. Its location had been documented in her notes, but it hadn't been labeled, "Priceless emerald." Probably her notes said something like "Unidentified object, possibly manmade." And the thieves didn't get that notebook, anyway. They were still working blind.

They did get the notebook that documented the finding. Faye would have bet good money that this information was what had brought Nita and Wayland to her island. Too bad they didn't know how to figure out where the finding had been, based on her notes.

Given the thieves' limited knowledge, it was no surprise that someone had come to Douglass' house, looking for Faye's notes and the catalog. Those innocuous papers could be the modern equivalent of a treasure map, minus an X marking the spot.

She told herself not to jump to conclusions, but there was no way to stifle her first excited thought. She was pretty sure the spot where she and Joe had been attacked by Nita and Wayland—the spot where she'd found the emerald—was southwest of the house, right where Bachelder said he'd buried the necklace. A quick look at her site sketch would give her that answer, but she had more pressing issues.

First and obviously, she needed to call the sheriff. If the killers were after the emerald necklace, which seemed even more possible than it had an hour before, then Sheriff Mike needed to know everything she did.

It was the middle of the night, but the parents of babies didn't tend to keep regular hours. It was time to call the sheriff. Besides, if he found out that she'd kept something so important from him for even a few hours, he'd...what? Sheriff Mike was a very gentle man, but he had ways to keep people in line. If Sheriff Mike were ever really mad at Faye, he'd sic Magda on her.

Faye shivered at the thought.

Her plan for the night followed a logical sequence of events: First, she'd call Sheriff Mike. Then, she'd scour her field notes to remind herself exactly where she'd dug up the emerald and the finding. Next, she'd see if voice recognition software could recognize Joe's rural way with a vowel, because she wanted hard copies of those letters. No. She *needed* hard copies of those letters.

Finally, she'd reward herself with the chore she was looking forward to most. She'd pull out her old family journal and see if Great-great-grandmother Cally had mentioned any of the Bachelders' visits.

◇◇◇

The sheriff had been properly appreciative of Faye's exciting new information, and he hadn't once squawked because she called him in the middle of the night. He was not, however, the one who had gone to his office at midnight to fetch the extra copies of Faye's field notes filed there. Magda went, because she was on fire to read them and she couldn't wait till he got home. Also, somebody had to stay with little Rachel.

Faye knew that Magda was even now pawing through the notes, looking for something that would tell them where Courtney had built his summer house. If God was good, she'd also find something that linked it to the jewel and the tiny gold finding that might once have cradled it.

In the meantime, Sheriff Mike wasted Faye's time asking questions like, "Is Joe out there with you? I know Liz slipped him a gun, and I don't want to know whether it's registered. I just want to know that he has it with him. We can deal with the paperwork crap some other time."

Faye was patient with him.

Yes, the house was locked up tight.

Yes, Joe was with her.

Yes, Joe had the gun.

Joe also had an arsenal of homemade stone weapons. There were always a few of them scattered around any place he frequented—his bedroom, his boat, the spot in the woods where he went to meditate and chip stone. He had accepted Liz's handgun, but he'd held it slightly away from him, as if it smelled. Maybe, to Joe, it did.

Finally, Sheriff Mike hung up, so she'd accomplished the first task on her list. Magda was looking for clues in the field notes, so she was taking care of Task Two. A few keyclicks on the laptop had put the voice recognition software to work transcribing Joe's recordings, which gave her a good start on Task Three. The slowest link in this chain of events was Faye's ancient printer. She left it printing the transcripts and used the time to spend a few moments with her great-great-grandmother.

Cally hadn't actually written in the old family journal, started by *her* great-grandfather, William Whitehall, in 1798. She'd spent her whole life keeping Joyeuse from rotting down and keeping the farm surrounding the house solvent. There had been little time for niceties like journal writing.

Instead, during her last years, Cally had described her long and eventful life to an interviewer for the Federal Writers' Project, a program that had documented the stories of former slaves while creating work for writers left unemployed by the Great Depression. Long ago, someone had tucked a copy of the interview into William Whitehall's journal. It seemed fitting to Faye that she keep it there.

*Excerpt from the oral history of former slave Cally Stanton,*
*recorded 1935*

When the first master was over Joyeuse, you wouldn't ever
have known we lived on an island out in the water. People
came and went all the time and they didn't just come for
dinner and leave, not back then. They'd come to stay, and
the master would throw a ball, because his guests had to have
something to do. Wasn't any radio then, and the master's
friends weren't big on doing anything useful with their time.
So there wasn't an awful lot to do but throw a formal ball.
Besides, how else would the ladies get to wear those ballgowns
we sewed up?

I didn't ever think about it before, but I bet that's why he
built the hotel. He could go out there to Last Island and visit
with his fine friends, dance with their wives and drink a lot
of French wine. Except when he did all that at the hotel, his
friends were paying for their own keep. The master was rich
enough, but he still had to watch his pennies, at least until
he married the second missus and her money.

Before the hotel, every rich family south of Charleston
paraded through our doors. You saw the picture of this house,
the one that was painted before the paint peeled and the gardens grew over? (Faye desperately wished this painting had
survived.) This place was like a palace. Why do you think he
built a castle out here in the middle of the water? He never
had any children—at least not by either of his wives—so he
sure didn't need the rooms. He built himself a mansion so he
could impress the Yanceys and the Baileys and the Bachelders
and the Lamars and all the others.

There it was. Independent confirmation that Jedediah
Bachelder's family had visited Joyeuse during the years that Andrew
LaFourche was its master. What about later, when Courtney
Stanton had inherited all his stepfather's worldly goods? Had
Bachelder visited again, long enough to hide a fortune in emeralds
under Courtney Stanton's new summer house?

A quick scan of the rest of Cally's story gave her nothing concrete except for the occasional mention of a summer house—proof that it existed, though not proof that anything was buried under it besides sand. A careful reading for more subtle clues was in order, but later, when there was time to consider every word.

Because Cally was answering the interviewer's questions and just generally reminiscing, the narrative rambled to and fro through time, but Faye could find no entry that mentioned the summer house in such a way that showed it had existed before Bachelder's 1863 visit. So there was nothing to contradict his narrative.

She had looked for the summer house before, based on Cally's mentions of it, but she'd come to believe that it hadn't been intended as a permanent structure. She'd found no sign of any masonry foundations that couldn't be linked to known slave cabins and service buildings. That might mean that it had been built on an ephemeral foundation, perhaps wooden posts sunk into the ground. It might mean that the summer house was never there at all. Or it could just mean that she'd been looking in the wrong places. It was a big island, after all.

Still, logic had told her that there were only a few plausible locations for a summer house. It should have been close to the beach or the dock or the gardens or something else attractive. There seemed to be no reason to build a big gazebo-like structure for people to go outside and sit in, unless there was something to make it a better place to sit than the porches. Joyeuse was awash in porches. There was no shortage of places to lounge out-of-doors.

But perhaps her logic had been faulty, because she was missing a key piece of information. Maybe Courtney Stanton had built his summer house in a completely illogical spot, simply to obscure Bachelder's hiding place.

Her cell phone rang. Magda was on the other end, saying, "I found it. Oh, not everything you need. But some of it. Do you have copies of the notes handy?"

Faye absolutely did.

"Okay, look back to the September before the hurricane, when you were working by yourself. The label on the spine says, 'September 8-September 29.' You made a site sketch on the back page. See it?"

"Yep."

"See the point labeled '42?' Southwest of the house? That's where you excavated the gold finding."

"Hot dog! It's also near the spot where I found the hip flask."

"Faye. Did you just say 'hot dog!'"

"Yeah. What do you say when you're excited?"

"'Eureka!' worked quite well for Archimedes."

"Yeah? Well, he was Greek and 'Eureka' probably means 'hot dog' in Greek. He was also wet and naked. I'm not." Faye shuffled through the papers, looking for some more recent notes. "I think that's also pretty close to—"

"—to the spot where you found the emerald. See? On the site sketch you drew last month? The point labeled 24? It wasn't close enough to the finding to give us the whole story—if the necklace simply disintegrated during a few generations underground, the two pieces should have been inches apart, not yards—but the close proximity is suggestive."

"When you say 'close proximity is suggestive,' you sound exactly like a university professor. Would it kill you to do a little speculation, Magda? Like maybe the ground got disturbed when the summer house was demolished."

Magda's voice took on a raspier edge, making her sound less like a new mother and more like a contentious academic. "Okay, I'll play. Maybe Bachelder came back and dug up the necklace. Maybe it broke in the process and he lost a couple of pieces."

"Or maybe somebody else dug it up and became fabulously rich. Except it sure wasn't my family. Since the Civil War, we've never had two extra pennies to rub together."

"According to your site sketch, that copse of trees isn't there any more. Maybe the necklace got caught in the roots when one of your ancestors knocked down the trees. Or when a hurricane did it for them."

Faye had forgotten about the trees. She looked back at the notes describing the appearance of the soil at the time of excavation. The notes read, "Site stratigraphy is difficult to read, due to copious partially rotted roots."

Magda must have been reading her own copy of the notes, because she blurted out, "The roots! They were there!" at the same time Faye said much the same thing.

"This is the place," Faye said, stabbing at the site map with her finger, as if Magda could see. "You know this is the spot Bachelder buried that necklace. Don't get all skeptical and cautious on me."

"It looks good. But you need to get out there and look for the rest of those emeralds."

"I'll be looking all day tomorrow. If I find anything, I'll let you know."

# Chapter Fifteen

As soon as the next morning dawned, Faye wanted desperately to grab her trowel, walk out her front door, and run headlong to the southwest. She wanted to dig up some more emeralds.

She wanted it so badly that she conjured up a rainstorm. There could be no other explanation for the unseasonably dark cloud and torrential rains. If an equally miserable wind had been whipping off the water, she and Joe would have been stuck inside the house all day, but the seas were calm enough for safe boating. The two of them were simply getting wetter by the minute as they readied the *Gopher* for its first trip to shore in weeks.

Getting to shore on her skiff would have been no fun in the rain, and Joe's john boat would have been as bad, even if it hadn't been moored at Liz's. The *Gopher* was a different matter. She'd lived on the *Gopher* for years while she made Joyeuse livable. It would get her and Joe to the mainland, and it would keep them dry enough. Then, her car would get them to the library—but not the university library, with its forbidding librarian and jealously guarded manuscripts. Not at first, anyway.

First, she wanted to see someone who, unlike the rare books librarian Ms. Slater, was always thrilled to have his archives examined. Captain Eubank lived and died for Micco County history, and he couldn't quite understand anybody who didn't.

Faye didn't intend to waste today, not after the things she'd learned from Bachelder's letters and Cally's oral history. If she couldn't go digging for jewels, then she could certainly spend the morning sifting through Captain Eubank's informal library for more clues.

Too bad she stopped at Magda's house on the way there.

While Joe was stacking wooden blocks for Rachel to knock over, Magda delivered the bad news.

"Mike says you can't stay on the island any more. Not until we figure out this Bachelder mess."

Faye was speechless. Not go home? Now this thing was getting personal.

After a long breath, she found some words. "He wants to ban me from my *home*? Why? Nobody's died out there. Not lately, anyway. I think maybe we should all move out to Joyeuse where it's safe."

"Hear me out. There's a logical chain of events that suggest that Joyeuse Island is a dangerous place for you."

Faye half-expected Magda to whip out her laptop and display a slide show to accompany her scholarly explanation of this damnably logical chain of events.

Magda held up an index finger. At least she wasn't using a computer-based visual aid. "First, the data suggest that the criminals know about the necklace which, based on the single emerald we have, looks to be fabulously valuable. Or they *could* know about it. It's described in a book that's stored in a library that's accessible to a whole lot of people."

Magda had a point. This did not make Faye happy.

"Second, that self-same book describes the general location of this buried treasure. To be fair, it doesn't give the location of the island where it's hidden, but it does say that it's near Bachelder's childhood home. You found that home in a single day—a single *morning*—using easily accessible property records, maps, and photographs."

*Another good point,* Faye thought. *Crap.*

"Third, we know that the thieves have your notes describing the place where you uncovered the finding. The emerald's find spot isn't easily traced. You didn't know it was an emerald when you dug it up, and the thieves won't be able to do much with an entry labeled, "Unknown object, angular shape suggests it may be man-made, point 24." And they didn't get that notebook, anyway. But the gold finding's location is clearly labeled in the notes that they do have. So is the hip flask's find spot. That's why you have to leave the island. Those notes could bring the killers right to your doorstep. They may have already been there."

"Nita and Wayland." Faye didn't like her own voice. She sounded like a sullen child who wanted something she couldn't have. Not a woman to admit defeat easily, she tried to frame a winning rebuttal in her mind, but Magda's inexorable countdown continued.

"And last—the whole world could know where the finding was buried, not just the crooks who stole your notes. We published that data, Faye."

"We did what? I don't remember writing any such paper."

"I wrote the paper. You remember—there were two reasons we published your independent work. First, it was damn good work. And interesting, too. Second, you were on shaky ethical grounds, working half-trained and selling assorted baubles to collectors. Once I wrote the work up, slapped my Ph.D. on it, and got a respected journal to publish the paper, it was a lot harder for disapproving academics to slander you with names like 'pothunter.'"

Magda was right. It would be stupid to stay on Joyeuse Island, knowing what she knew. Stupid and careless. The thought of leaving her home, even for a little while, hurt like a hot rock in the pit of Faye's stomach. "So where will we go? I've still got my apartment in Tallahassee. Joe's been living there this semester. We could move up there—"

"There's no need to go that far. Emma says she's got more than enough room for you and Joe. She's also got a deep-freeze full of leftover funeral food, so you'll eat well."

"Good, because I'd never get my work done at the Turkey Foot Hotel if I had to commute from Tallahassee." An evil thought struck her. "You're not going to tell me I've got to stay completely out of the islands, are you? Because I have *got* to finish that project on time, or I'll never get funding again."

"Mike and I talked that over. It's not the safest place in the world. You know he had to turn those people who attacked you loose."

"Nita and Wayland? Sheriff Mike agrees with me that they were just pothunting, looking for a little something worth selling. They won't be back to Joyeuse Island, now that he's put the fear of God into them."

"Exactly," Magda said, in the tone of voice professors save for times when they're about to make an irrefutable point. "So maybe they'll try someplace else—like the ruins of the Turkey Foot Hotel."

"But how will I get my work done? I can't stay away from the hotel site…for a lot of reasons that I don't need to explain to you." Faye heard her voice modulate from "sullen child" to "whining child," but she couldn't help herself.

She hadn't considered until this minute that while she'd been distracted from her project by murders and emeralds, pothunters would have had days and days to destroy her work on the ruins of the Turkey Foot Hotel. And first among the pothunters likely to do that would be Nita and Wayland.

She needed to get out there and check on things. She needed to scope out Captain Eubank's library. There was no denying the fact that she still needed to get back to the rare book room in Tallahassee. And there might be a necklace-worth of emeralds lurking under the soil on her very own island. Faye was always a woman with a full plate of things to do, but this was ridiculous.

Magda stretched her bad shoulder, the one she'd wrecked by digging heavy dirt and hauling heavy artifacts. "My husband says those two scum have decent alibis for both murders. Granted, it's upstanding citizens like themselves offering the alibis, but there are a whole lot of people willing to say they were playing poker at some dive in Sopchoppy on the night Douglass died. And Liz says they were sitting at the bar, three feet away from her griddle, when Wally was killed. Mike's probably right. They're not our killers. They're not looking for you personally. You just happened to be there when they wanted to find something they could sell to offset their gambling losses."

"So—is it too dangerous for me to keep working out there?"

Magda pursed her lips and shook her head. "Hell if I know. Mike figures the really bad guys are most likely to show up at Joyeuse Island, looking for the necklace. If you're willing to work only in broad daylight and if you'll keep Joe by your side the whole time, then we'll say you're safe enough. Maybe I'll come out and help. Although Mike wouldn't like me taking Rachel someplace that requires bodyguards."

Joe turned an unsmiling face in Magda's direction. He didn't like the idea of his goddaughter being hauled to a dangerous island, either.

Magda paid him no attention. "I've got an even better idea. Take Ross out there to help Joe. He's big, and maybe he can shoot. I know for a certain fact that he could argue a criminal into submission. Damn lawyers."

◇◇◇

Faye loved the dusty smell of old books. Even the university library's up-to-date ventilation system couldn't rid the air of that scent, but modernity had robbed libraries of other strong, familiar smells of her youth. Here in Captain Eubank's home library, with its book-lined walls and its old-fashioned card catalog, she could smell age and ink.

She treasured childhood memories of visiting the bookmobile with her mother. Stepping out of the blazing Florida sun into dark, cool, air-conditioned space that was cushioned underfoot by industrial carpeting and lined with books from floor to ceiling, had always seemed like stepping through the gates of heaven to Faye. A tangy, chemical smell had been an unquestioned part of the bookmobile experience. She presumed it was the scent of the ink used to stamp due dates into borrowed books.

Computers and bar code readers had rendered that ink obsolete, but she still missed its odor. Captain Eubank had acquired the Micco County Public Library's obsolete equipment, thus updating his own library to 1970s standards, so Faye got her fill of library smell whenever she visited his collection.

Captain Eubank had been Micco County's unofficial historian for so long that the county manager had given him semi-official status—a certificate that read, *In Recognition of Long and Faithful Service to the Citizens of Micco County, Captain Edward Eubank Is Hereby Awarded the Title of Honorary Historian.* The position hadn't come with any money, but it meant that he got his hands on discarded library equipment and obscure books that would otherwise have been thrown out.

Faye had no idea which war Captain Eubank had served in, nor which branch of the service had made him a captain. For a while, she'd entertained the possibility that "Captain" was his actual first name. His meticulously kept library and soldier-like posture said otherwise.

Faye adored Captain Eubank. He was a man after her own heart.

She settled herself in the faded chintz armchair that faced the captain's desk. Joe sidled over to his favorite shelf, the one where the captain shelved documents related to Native American folklore.

"What can I do for you, Faye?" The voice was beginning to quaver, but the backbone refused to bend to age. "I haven't got anything new since you were last here. Well, yes, I have. But none of it could possibly pertain to your family."

"I'm not here to look for information on my own family. I'm looking for a family that lived in Wakulla County in the mid-nineteenth century. It's outside your area of interest—"

"Now, now. I'm not that provincial. My interests don't end at the county line. Besides, Micco County's boundaries changed three times in the nineteenth century. If I find a document that relates to the history of anyplace around here, I acquire it." He swept an arm through the air, to draw her attention to all the precious information he'd collected. As if she hadn't already noticed.

"Do you have anything on the Bachelder family, particularly a man named Jedediah who was probably born somewhere around the 1820s? The family property was on a river near the coastline, just across the Wakulla County border."

"The Bachelders? I don't have much on that family, but what I do have is probably still warm from the hands of all the folks who've been pawing through it. That's the most popular subject in the county this week."

Joe didn't turn around, but his finger stopped moving along the line of text he was reading. Faye knew he was listening.

"One of them was a Civil War re-enactor. Even had on half his uniform—the jacket was unbuttoned over his fat belly and grimy t-shirt and blue jeans. A real soldier would be sitting in the brig if he went around looking like that. I call folks like him 'fantasy soldiers.' I get those guys all the time. Some of them have as much stuff as I do. Although they tend to collect minie balls and cannonball fragments, 'stead of books."

"Do you remember his name?"

"No. I'd have it written here in my logbook if he'd checked out any materials, but I didn't have what he needed. I remember he was a big guy, though. Hefty."

"Was his name Herbie?"

The captain tugged on his neatly clipped moustache. "Yes. Maybe. Herbie sounds about right."

"Anybody else?" Faye realized she sounded like an officer barking an order. She softened her voice. "Who else, sir?"

"A young man. He didn't check anything out, either, so I don't have his name. He didn't stay long, didn't even sit down. So I'm not sure he ever gave me his name to begin with. But I'd know those tattoos if I saw them again. Lightning bolts all the way down one arm." He shook his head. "In Bachelder's day, it was a lot easier to shock people, so youngsters didn't have to go to such extremes. Maybe their system was better."

Wayland. The captain's visitor had to be Wayland. Faye wondered where Nita was while he was visiting the Captain.

"Did anybody else come in, asking about Bachelder?"

"Just you. And you're much better company than those men." He swiveled in his desk chair to peruse a shelf of bound documents to his right. "Let's see. I have copies of the property records from that period. Good thing the property wasn't in Micco County at that time, or we would've lost those records in the courthouse fire. I'm guessing you already looked at those down at the property assessor's office."

"Yep."

"Then you probably already visited the property. That's a good way to get the gist of who somebody was. Go the places they went."

Here was more evidence that Captain Eubank had been an actual captain. He had an instinctive grasp of human psychology. He certainly had her pegged.

"Joe and I uncovered the foundations of the Bachelder house and their cemetery."

Captain Eubank's eyes lit up at the prospect of reaping historical information from the dates on those tombstones. He leaned forward, elbows on the desk, and said, "When I was a boy, people used to talk about a Civil War battle near there, but I don't know if a professional archaeologist has ever been out there. You could—"

"Yes. There is—was—a battlefield out there, but treasure hunters have torn it up in a big way. I doubt there's much an archaeologist could tell you much beyond saying, 'Something military happened here.'"

"Well. That *is* confounding." The captain sat up straight again. "But you were asking about the Bachelders. There's a collection of Jedediah Bachelder's letters in the university library—"

"I know. We've been there. And we're going back as often as it takes to get transcriptions of them all."

"If you've already dug up all the information existing in the whole wide world, then why do you bother coming to my little collection?"

Joe didn't turn around, but his shoulders twitched like he was laughing.

"Because you have weird stuff that professional archivists might overlook."

Captain Eubank seemed to relish being called "weird."

"That I do, dearie. That I do. I even have a photo of Bachelder in his later years. He donated money to build a hospital for Civil War veterans near the medicinal springs in Panacea, naming it after his late wife in honor of her hospital work. It's gone now. The county let it rot down after the veterans died off. They've got better buildings now to put all their newfangled medical equipment in, but what call did they have to let that building go? One look at the place, and you learned more about a bygone time than a dozen textbooks could tell you."

Faye steered the conversation back to Jedediah Bachelder. "What does Bachelder's donation of money for a hospital have to do with the photo you've got?"

"The county government printed a handbill with a picture of the dedication ceremony. Posted it all over town, as a way to give Mr. Bachelder credit for his generosity. I've got one of 'em. Let me find it for you." The captain plucked a binder from the shelf and paged gently through documents stored in protective plastic covers—and all of that plastic was of archival quality, if she knew the captain.

The photo showed a crowd of people, all men in hats, clustered around an elderly gentleman whose face seemed to be all moustache and muttonchop sideburns. A pair of bright, dark eyes peeked out from under drooping brows and sagging lids.

This was Jedediah Bachelder.

The photo gave Faye no useable information, but it thrilled her to the core. "I'm so glad somebody saved that handbill."

"Big libraries can't keep everything. They say most of an archivist's job lies in knowing what to throw away. They have to do that. But real history is found in small things, too. A small-town paper, a routine letter to a faraway loved one, a photo hidden in a woman's locket—those are the pieces of history that I love."

:d by the thought that letters from Viola Bachelder waited
∎er deep in the bowels of the university library. She read on
∎e if the captain's fine mind had teased any more meaning
of the book.

*The Bachelders had no children to preserve the letters. It
was many years before Bachelder is known to have visited the
house where his wife died, and it had changed hands twice by
then. Who collected their correspondence and bound it into
this leather volume? We may never know.*

*However, upon study of the original letters, I have devel-
oped a theory. Mr. Bachelder's letters written before 1864 are
on expensive paper and were written with a finer pen than the
later letters. There are also discrepancies in the handwriting
that lead me to believe that the older letters are written in
his secretary's hand. Others may not have noticed these dif-
ferences, because both Bachelder and his secretary were highly
educated men, well-trained in the fastidious penmanship of
the day. The difference in paper and writing utensil may also
have obscured the change in handwriting.*

*Bachelder's secretary traveled with him in the early years
of the war, but Bachelder is known to have lost the man's
services by 1864. I believe that the book does not contain the
original letters sent to Viola Bachelder. Rather, the preserved
letters were copies made by Bachelder's secretary and, from
1864 onward, by Bachelder himself.*

*Photocopiers did not exist in those days, and carbon paper
was not widely used. It was not uncommon for gentlemen's
secretaries to maintain copies of all outgoing correspondence.
For these reasons, I propose that this book consists of original
letters from Viola and file copies maintained by Bachelder.
Perhaps Bachelder had them bound himself in his later years
as a form of protection for mementos of great sentimental
value.*

*Adding weight to this theory is the fact that Bachelder's
letters far outnumber his wife's. Due to his travel and to the*

stirr

for

to s

out

"Speaking of letters to faraway loved on[...]
to know where I could lay my hands on [...]
Bachelder's letters?"

"You know I don't. If I did, I'd have sen[...]
as soon as you asked me about him. Or I'd h[...]
a file drawer right here. I don't know of any [...]
I've seen the letters myself. I went to Tallahass[...]
of time with them, in fact. I wasn't allowed to [...]
but I do have my notes."

The man was amazing. Captain Eubank dipp[...]
of filing cabinets behind him without looking. [...]
a folder that held a few sheets of lined paper i[...]
soldier's regimented script.

> *The Bachelder letters bound into this volum[...]*
> *Civil War years. Jedediah Bachelder did not resi[...]*
> *County or the environs during those years, so these [...]*
> *are not strictly pertinent to my research, but his f[...]*
> *prominent in local history, so I have reviewed the le[...]*
> *an eye toward enhancing my understanding of the [...]*
> *regional affairs.*
>
> *Other than occasional mentions of his ancestral [...]*
> *Wakulla County, the most interesting topic to me doe[...]*
> *in the text of the letters, but in their very existence. H[...]*
> *were written to his wife, who died during a most tu[...]*
> *ous time of the war. Several of her letters are preser[...]*
> *this book, interspersed among his. He clearly receive[...]*
> *letters, because he answers questions asked in hers. She [...]*
> *ously received many of his letters, based on the same [...]*
> *How their letters were reunited, when his were maile[...]*
> *Alabama and hers were mailed to his last location know[...]*
> *her, is unknown.*

Faye could have kicked herself for failing to ask the ob[...]
question of who saved Bachelder's letters, when the man [...]
left behind no offspring to treasure them. And she was stran[...]

*disruptions of war, it is likely that she wrote many letters that did not reach him. If the collected letters are indeed Bachelder's file copies, then it may be assumed that we possess all of his letters to his wife during the war years, but only a partial record of her correspondence.*

Faye couldn't wait to get her hands on Bachelder's letters again. If she and Joe hustled, they could be in Tallahassee in time to get a reasonable amount of work done before the rare book room closed.

She waved the notes in the captain's general direction, saying "You're absolutely brilliant, sir. You should publish this work."

"I'm a learned man, but only in my trivial specialty. Nobody in the world cares what I think of the authorship of those letters."

"I care," Faye said, stacking the captain's notes neatly and replacing them in the file folder. "I care a lot."

# Chapter Sixteen

Ms. Slater cast a baleful eye on Faye and Joe as they signed in to the rare book collection. Her attitude stood in stark contrast to Captain Eubank's generous and helpful collegiality. Ms. Slater stared down at Faye's signature, giving no indication that she thought Faye deserved to get her grubby paws on any of the library's precious documents.

"Cotton gloves are provided over there," she said. "Touching materials with bare hands will result in revocation of your library privileges. All work done in this collection must be in pencil. Use of a pen will also result in revocation."

Faye found the nagging reminders irritating. She knew the librarian's canned spiel for what it was: a reminder that, at least in this little corner of the world, Ms. Elizabeth Slater possessed power.

The rare book room was never crowded. How long had it been since she and Joe were last there? During that last visit, they had listened politely to Ms. Slater recite rules they already knew. Had she already forgotten doing it?

Faye glanced over the sign-in sheet, looking for her last signature. Only half a page of names had been entered since then. Ms. Slater simply had to remember talking to her. Besides what woman, no matter how repressed, could forget Joe?

As she swept her eyes across the page, one of them leapt out at her. *Wayland Curry*. How many people named Wayland could there possibly be in this corner of the world?

Ms. Slater crisply removed the sign-in list from her hands and closed the binder holding it. Faye somehow doubted that she would hand it back over to a nosy snoop who wanted to pore over the names of the library's patrons. The sign-in sheet itself was a surprising breach of confidentiality, since it couldn't be used without the signer getting a good look at every recent patron's name and address, but Faye had found special collections librarians to be less ticky about privacy and more ticky about protecting the documents. If anybody absconded with a rarity, the names and addresses on that list would be a good starting place in finding the culprit and, more to the point, the goods.

Ms. Slater led them to her desk and handed over a stack of request forms. "These are required before any document other than reference works may be retrieved." Her insistence on repeating rules she knew full well that they already knew made Faye want to gnash her teeth.

She squinted up at the irritating woman. Ms. Slater's face had well-scrubbed, regular features that would have been attractive if she ever smiled. She had a slender body held upright by a completely straight back. Her starched shirt was as neat as the band that gathered her non-descript brown hair into a ponytail. Did she ever let that hair down?

Faye wished the woman would just relax. Or have a beer. Twelve ounces of hop juice might take some of the starch out of her. She understood the librarian's desire to protect the rarities entrusted to her, but really—if rare books couldn't be read, they might as well be rare bricks.

What good was an unopened book?

Faye filled out the request form for Bachelder's letters, but while she was waiting, Joe spotted it on the returns cart. His time in school had sharpened his library skills considerably. His powers of observation had never needed sharpening.

By the time Ms. Slater returned, shaking her head and saying, "The book is in use—" Faye was able to smile to smile sweetly and point to Joe who, gloves on, was already arranging his study aids the way he liked them. The Bachelder book had been placed carefully on the table in front of him like a trophy.

In the meantime, Faye had prowled through the reference materials that were stored in open shelving for easy access. A stack of books rested on the table in front of her—the volume of biographical sketches she'd seen before, a slim volume entitled *Confederates in the Reconstruction Years,* a history of the Confederate government, a lavishly illustrated edition of *Royal Jewels and the People Who Wore Them,* and *Civil War in the Sunshine State: The Confederacy's Florida Frontier.*

If fortune smiled, she'd find a photo of Bachelder with a string of emeralds in his hand that matched the emeralds hanging around Marie Antoinette's neck in an earlier portrait. In her dreams.

She spread the books across a table, while Joe started reading Bachelder's letters into his voice recorder. His voice was naturally quiet but clear, and there were no other patrons nearby who might be disturbed. Even Ms. Slater couldn't complain that he was disrupting her quiet haven.

Faye found no smoking guns in her reference books—smoking emeralds?—but she gleaned a few useful grains of information. From the book on royal jewels, she learned that the French Revolution, decades before the American Civil War, had scattered the gems of the King and his Queen, Marie Antoinette, and much of the French aristocracy all over Europe. Many of them were never seen again. So the unsubstantiated story told to Bachelder was at least potentially true.

The book gave no description of a necklace adorned with an emerald with the size and cut of the one she discovered, but she did learn that Marie Antoinette had owned and worn emeralds, which was something of a relief. She would have felt surpassingly foolish if she'd pursued the possibility that she'd found the French queen's jewels for months on end, only to find out that emeralds weren't available in Europe at that time or, even worse, that they were considered too common and vulgar for a queen. Or that Marie Antoinette just didn't like how she looked in green.

She learned that the Europeans' discovery of the New World had affected the emerald trade in the same way it had affected so many other things. When Spanish conquistadors had learned about the Colombian emerald mines, they'd promptly seized the mines, enslaved the indigenous people, and shipped home enough emeralds to make them wealthy beyond the dreams of avarice.

The Old World, accustomed to smaller, heavily flawed emeralds, couldn't get enough of the large Colombian gems—achingly green, clear as glass, and large enough to suit a sultan. The odds were excellent that the emerald Faye found on her island had begun its life in Colombia. Or under Colombia, to be painfully precise.

The book chronicling the history of the Confederacy yielded no direct mention of Bachelder, though there was a lengthy section on the beleaguered new country's request for assistance from England and France, just as he'd described. Bachelder had also mentioned a diplomatic mission headed by Duncan Kenner, an influential planter from Louisiana, and the history book confirmed that this mission had occurred. It also mentioned Kenner's failed attempts to convince President Davis to emancipate the Confederacy's slaves. Their shared interest in emancipation and European political ties explained the sole hit of Magda's Internet search of Bachelder's name: a biography of Kenner.

The pile of subtle confirmations of events described in the book of letters was growing taller. Jedediah Bachelder was shaping up as a reliable witness to the political upheaval around him.

The history of Confederates during the Reconstruction years mentioned something noteworthy about Jedediah Bachelder in his old age. He was a notable contributor to causes that benefited war victims still suffering long after the last shot was fired. No home for war widows and orphans, north or south, could approach the man without receiving a donation. He died without heir, and his will directed that his estate be liquidated, so that the cash could be given to the Confederate Soldier's Home at Jefferson Davis' final home, Beauvoir, in Mississippi.

Peering over Joe's shoulder as he worked, she got a quick overview of several Bachelder letters. She was disappointed to see that he didn't mention the necklace at all throughout 1864.

But why would he? Viola knew it existed. She knew where it was hidden. If her husband was concerned about his letters being intercepted, he certainly wouldn't advertise something so sensitive. He'd said as much.

The letters of this period were noteworthy primarily because of their depressing focus on the realities of life in a dying civilization. When boats are the only means of importing foreign goods, then a country with unusable ports will be slowly strangled. When most personal transportation is horse-powered, then a countryside littered with horse thieves and violent deserters is paralyzed. And when communication must travel by mail or telegraph, then impassable railroads and severed telegraph lines renders a country quadriplegic, unable to tell its hands and legs what they need to know to survive.

Faye had learned these things in history class, but Bachelder's first-person accounts made the suffering human and real. She craned her neck over Joe's shoulder so that she could follow along silently while he read the man's words aloud.

There were other, better things she could be doing with her time, but she couldn't help herself.

*April 18, 1864*

*My dearest love, Viola, my wife—*
*I should not burden you with my pain but I am heartsick. I see hunger around me everywhere. I would rather feel it myself than see it on a human face, so I share what I have. I no longer care how this war ends. I simply want it to be over. It is time to patch up our young men—those who survive—and find a way to feed our people. Everyone. If it were in my power, no human being would ever again go to bed with an empty stomach.*

*We have "Sherman's neckties" to thank for the recent exacerbation of our longstanding hunger. To render our* railroads useless, Sherman himself ordered that the ties be set afire and sections of rail be heated until they bend freely. The rails are then draped in trees and twisted into fanciful shapes. The "necktie" portion of their nickname is apt. I can say this because I have seen them with my own eyes.

I know that the soldiers who do such things are obeying orders. I know they are human beings with hearts focused on wives and children far away. They want to win the war, so they can go home. I cannot believe that they realize what the destruction of a rail that once carried food is. Every twist of the rail is a host of hungry children.

I know a lady, a war widow, who forages in the forest for roots and berries to feed her family. When I hear that you are running a hospital in our home, I am prouder than I can say, but I know you cannot possibly have proper medications. I pray that there are old women yet surviving who have knowledge of herbs.

My mother healed me of a grievously infected wound on my foot when I was just a boy. You have seen the scar. I wish I could tell you what went into the poultices that drew out the poison. Her blood-purifying tinctures would be of great use to you, too, I feel sure. Find yourself an old woman, Viola, and trust her knowledge.

Before I close, I must ask you something. I wrote you a letter that mentioned my recent visit to my father's plantation. If you received it, you will know the letter of which I speak. I have received no letter from you confirming its receipt. Please write me quickly as to whether you have the letter. It is best that I not take the risk of sending that particular information again but I will, if need be, because it is critical to our future. Or to yours, if I do not see home again.

I wait anxiously for your reply.

> Your devoted husband,
> Jedediah

Reading about Jedediah's "grievously infected" wound made Faye grateful for over-the-counter antibiotic ointment. She'd been cut with a dirty shovel only the day before, but a tetanus shot and a cheap tube of medicine had turned an injury that would have been life-threatening in 1864 into a minor, forgettable annoyance. Being reminded of her wound reminded her that it was sore. She shifted her weight onto the unaffected cheek.

The next letter was written on a tissue-thin stationery that looked gray, but it might once have been lavender. Faye reached around Joe to touch the delicate paper, then stopped herself, remembering that she'd taken off her gloves.

The writing was firm, legible, but gently rounded. It was a woman's handwriting. This must be one of the few surviving letters from Viola.

*June 30, 1864*

*My dear Jedediah,*
   *Even when your letters are filled with the sorrow that seems to pervade the very air in these grim times, I feel happier and stronger when I read them, and for days thereafter. One letter, in particular, has been entrusted to a faithful friend, as you requested. When peace comes, he and I will take the trip you suggested, then journey home to await your return. You needn't fear for our future.*
   *So you see how I treasure your words. Do continue to write them and send them to me, and know that I write as faithfully to you. If weeks pass between my letters, please know that many others have gone astray. I picture the countryside littered with envelopes addressed in my hand and yours. It is a distressing image, but so much more pleasant than looking clear-eyed at the countryside as it actually is—littered with the bodies of boys and horses and watered with their blood.*
   *I have had no word of my mother in Pennsylvania, nor of your aunt in Ohio. I will believe they are well, until I hear otherwise. The war hasn't come near their homes—at*

least, not to my knowledge— but they are both advanced in years. Either might fall ill and die, and we would not know nor be able to help. Well, we can help them through prayer. I sometimes forget to pray. I sometimes believe that I have forgotten how.

I see that the letter describing my little hospital reached you. I have found that even war does not satisfy the human need for argument. There is dissent around me, even in the matter of tending the sick and dying.

The mayor visited me last week. (Not Mayor Singleton, who has gone to the Army though he is nearly our age. His replacement is Simon Prine, who you recall was a doddering man with one foot in the grave when you left. He dodders still more now, though I wouldn't have thought such a thing possible.) It seems that he wanted to inquire delicately into my criteria for accepting patients.

I answered the door dressed all in black and the mayor's hand went to his heart. "Jedediah?" he asked.

I told him that you were hale and healthy, so far as I knew, but that I could bury no more young men without acknowledging their mothers' loss.

He asked whether it was true that I had accepted Yankee soldiers into my hospital, and whether Negroes were truly lying in cots in the same room as white soldiers.

I told him that I had but one room, so all the cots must perforce be in a single chamber. And I asked him how I was to tell an unconscious Confederate soldier from an unconscious Yankee soldier. Many of the men brought to my door are indeed in that dire condition.

He tried to say, "By their uniforms," but he had the good grace to stop there. Everyone knows that uniforms are, and have been, in short supply. Many soldiers would be half-naked, were it not for clothing taken from battlefield corpses. Freezing men cannot afford to discriminate against wearable clothing merely by its color.

*I waited silently, fingering the mourning locket my mother braided for me from my dead father's hair. The mayor seemed unable to further distress a woman wearing widow's weeds. There are so many of us these days.*

*He took my leave and went away.*

*Your recommendation that I find an old woman who is skilled with herbs and tinctures was well-considered. Mrs. Pylant has taught me that teas made from pleurisy root will ease breathing troubles, even sometimes the pneumonia that has carried off so many of my charges. Dandelion tea is a tonic for the digestion, a delicate way of saying that it can treat dysentery, which everybody seems to have, nowadays. A poultice of St. John's wort soothes muscles made angry by overwork or by bullets. Bathing the patient in willowroot water is far better for fever than a plain water bath. And wild lettuce will soothe an agitated patient, giving the best tonic of all—rest.*

*I could do far more with poultices made from onions or potatoes, but it would be the height of foolishness to waste food in such a way.*

*I tell you these cures in hopes that they will protect you, should some injury or disease threaten your health. Use these remedies liberally, as they are the only way I can care for you at this distance. I pray they will keep you whole until you are able to redeem your promise to come home to me.*

*You see—I have not forgotten how to pray, after all.*

*Your tender and affectionate wife,*
*Viola*

# Chapter Seventeen

Joe had just finished recording Viola's letter when a momentary dimming of the lights told them that the library was closing. Well, not precisely the library. The university library was open early and it closed late, as one would expect at a large institution. The rare book room, however, kept limited hours, opening at eight every morning and closing at four each afternoon.

Joe packed up his study aids silently, and Faye could tell he was upset. She wasn't sure how she could tell, since he was silent most all the time anyway, but she could.

"What's wrong?"

"There's just too many letters. The library keeps closing on me before I can get them all read. I wish I could read faster."

Faye wondered whether someone had told Joe about Ross' doubts about his intellect. If Ross himself had said anything like that to Joe, she would indeed kill him. Then she would tell him to take himself to Atlanta and to never come back.

"If you were to read the letters any faster, the computer and I wouldn't be able to understand you. You can only do so much in one sitting. Nobody could do it any faster. And it takes me a while to piece together the information hidden in Bachelder's letters. He wasn't writing for me, you know. He may have been telling Viola secrets in a way that only a married couple could. We'll come back to the library tomorrow—or soon, at least—and we'll get this thing wrapped up."

"I don't like wasting your time."

Maybe Ross hadn't needed to tell Joe what he thought of him. Joe's intuition had made him a fearsome hunter. Maybe he could read people as well as he read rabbits.

"Do I look like I'm sitting on my thumbs while you work? I'm getting lots of interesting stuff out of that stack of reference books. I'll tell you about it on the way home."

Faye and Joe took the elevator down to the basement, where a corridor took them to the parking garage, which was in an unusually convenient location. College campuses tend to spread like melting cheese—or like cancers, depending on your point of view. The longer a school has been in existence, the less one can hope for a reasonable quantity of parking at the campus center. And libraries are, as they should be, always near the campus center. Being able to walk to her car through a short underground tunnel, protected from the weather, was a welcome and unexpected convenience.

Sunlight leaked down from the upper levels of the garage as Faye and Joe made their way to her car. It lit a concrete cavern that would have been spooky if Faye hadn't been so very glad it was there. She was way too tired to hike across campus to the next nearest parking lot. When she cranked her car, the noise echoed through space that was empty of everything except endless rows of cars.

The garage's ramp ran in a very tight spiral. The need to maximize parking space had led its designers to skimp on the access drive. Faye was exhausted after spending the afternoon hunched motionless over a succession of books, so exhausted that she got sloppy with her driving and narrowly missed scraping her fender against the bumpers of several cars. She twisted the steering wheel back where it belonged, and past. The overcorrection nearly cost a few more cars their bumpers.

When she rolled five feet past the stop sign at the garage exit, she said, "I probably should have let you drive. I'm not doing too well here."

Joe made a move to open his door, but she waved him off, saying, "No, I'm fine. I just need to concentrate on my driving, instead of all those history books. I can see lines of type swimming in front of my eyes."

"I can see pages of handwriting—fancy writing with lots of curlicues. It's on light brown, blotchy paper. And it's written in kind of blurry ink."

"It's a wonder you can see at all. Those manuscripts are going to give you eyestrain. I'll take a turn reading them, next time."

"No. That's my job. It's something I can do. I couldn't scan over those other books like you do. I've watched how you do it. Interesting stuff seems to jump off the page at you, but I have to go word by word. I'll just keep poking along through Mr. Bachelder's letters."

Faye managed to merge onto the interstate to get across town, though she misjudged the gap between cars in the right lane and nearly plowed into the car in front of her.

Joe laid a gentle hand on her elbow. "Are you sure you're okay?"

This was insane. Even Faye wasn't hard-headed to a suicidal degree.

"You're right. I shouldn't be driving. Let me get off the highway at the next exit. I'll find a place to stop the car, and we can swap places."

Taking the exit at a higher speed than she'd ever been foolhardy enough to try before, she swerved onto the exit ramp. And kept swerving.

During the long sideways slide, Faye tried every strategy for regaining control that she could conjure up. She steered into the skid. She pumped on the brake, hoping it would miraculously grab hold. She flailed around with her other foot, fumbling for the old sedan's emergency brake. When she finally found it, she stomped hard, but it did no good.

When a car is moving sideways, at right angles to its proper direction, the action of the brakes and the steering wheel are more or less useless. Even the driver is superfluous. There is nothing to do but go along for the ride and brace for the inevitable impact.

Joe was falling toward her. But why? They hadn't crashed, not yet. He couldn't have been thrown from his seat already. Adrenaline had sharpened her perception and quickened her mind. As a result, her brain cataloged every detail of the world around her, as if it were taking a snapshot of her life as she entered the final few seconds of it. Joe was falling so very, very slowly. She could see his every motion as he spun in the air, flinging his arms wide open and turning his head in her direction.

As the car started its slow spin, she realized that he had worked his upper body out of the shoulder restraint and was wedging himself between her body and the steering wheel. He was trying to be a human airbag.

This realization reminded Faye that her car was too old to have airbags or anti-lock brakes or any of the other modern safety upgrades. This couldn't be a good thing.

The slide continued.

When the impact came, the clashing groan of metal grinding over metal filled the car. Faye could feel it in her teeth, her bones, her guts. She felt no sign that the car was rolling over, and she thanked God for small miracles, but it was still moving. The longer it moved, the more likely it was to hit something massive. Faye couldn't think of any way such an event could end well.

Then she noticed that the spin had stopped and that they were slowing down. She could see through the window that the metal screaming past her ears was a guardrail. It had guided them down the side of the ramp, keeping them from plunging over the steep drop-off just on its other side. The friction of its metal against the side of her car had been the decelerating force that stopped it from careening off the ramp and into multiple lanes of high-speed traffic.

Faye wanted to get out and kiss that guardrail, but Joe was lying in her lap.

"Joe! Are you okay?"

"Hit my head on the steering wheel, but I'm all right. How about you?

"I don't think anything's broken, but nothing seems to be working right. I can't think. I can't move. Well, I can," she stretched out an arm and jiggled a leg, "but I can't do anything useful with a body that's shaking like a leaf in a hurricane."

"You sound okay. You're probably just shook up. My arms and legs aren't paying my brain too much attention, either. How about we just stay like this for the time being? I'm guessing somebody's already used their cell phone to call for help. There'll be an ambulance here any minute."

◇◇◇

As Joe had predicted, the ambulance arrived quickly, but it had taken considerably longer for the emergency room personnel to pronounce them healthy enough to go home. Joe had a nasty bruise on his shoulder blade and a bump on his head, where he had made contact with the steering wheel. They had waited an interminable time for a CAT scan saying that Joe's brain was unaffected. Faye was powerfully relieved. Joe had been wrestling all his life with a brain that misfired on occasion. There seemed to be no need to compound his problems.

Faye's bruises traced an interesting pattern across her chest and lower abdomen, proof of the force that had been absorbed by her seat belt and shoulder harness...and Joe's body. Those bruises, in combination with the fresh cut on her rear end, gave her a body that only a ghoul could love. Other than that, she felt creaky, but otherwise okay.

The sheriff and Magda had bundled them into the back seat of their mini-van, behind Rachel, who was asleep in her car seat. Ross climbed into the far back seat.

The sheriff had taken Faye aside to say, "I guess you called Ross, because he showed up at my house and invited himself along on this rescue mission. I'm glad to have him. I like him a lot, considering that he's a lawyer and all. But you better sit back there and hold his hand, because he's about ready to explode.

You shoulda seen him pacing around and trying not to tell me that I need to give you a smarter bodyguard than Joe. Somebody smart like him."

Faye did as she was told. The sheriff might have been irritated by Ross' insistence on inserting himself into this situation but, in her current muddled state, Faye was rather charmed to have somebody who cared so much about her well-being.

After spending about a minute assuring Ross that none of her bones were broken and nothing essential to life had been damaged, she resumed blaming herself for the accident. "I should never have tried to drive in that condition," Faye said. "We could have been killed."

She expected Magda to jump in and help her rag on herself, but only silence came from the front passenger seat. The sheriff cleared his throat.

"What? What aren't you telling me?"

"Was it the brake lines? Or did somebody drug her?" Joe asked.

"Funny you should ask those exact questions," Sheriff Mike said. "Ross asked me the same things. And don't think I didn't ask myself the same questions before you two young pups got to me."

"What makes everybody think this was anything more than an accident? I was just too tired to be behind the wheel."

"You already said that," the sheriff said. "You said it to the emergency room people. You said it to the police. You said it to me."

Magda interrupted her husband. "Me, too."

Joe and Ross made it unanimous. "Me, too."

"You want to know why it never occurred to you that this accident wasn't your fault, sweetheart? Because if it wasn't your fault, then that might mean you don't have control over every little thing in your life, and admitting that might make you nuts."

Faye reflected on the fact that Sheriff Mike knew her thought processes so well, because they were virtually identical to his wife's.

"You want this accident to be your fault. You keep saying that it's your fault. But that doesn't make it so." The sheriff paused to shove a stick of gum in his mouth. "So I made sure your blood got checked for alcohol and drugs. Which they didn't find. Nobody expected them to, but it was worth looking into. They had a neurologist check your reflexes and response time and coordination and such—"

"You mean when they made me walk a straight line?"

"Yep. It was all routine, to make sure your brain didn't get too shook up by the accident, but it served my purposes, as well. There's no sign that you were impaired in any way, not even by a drug that we didn't think to test for. Certainly not because you were a little tired. Faye, you've been running on no sleep and hardly any food for years. It's a poor idea, but today wasn't any different from yesterday or the day before."

Faye's seat belt bruises ached. So did the shovel wound that she was sitting on. "So since I wasn't drugged, everybody's jumping straight to the conclusion that my car was sabotaged. I'm not actually a perfect driver, you know."

"When was your car built, sugar?" the sheriff asked, chomping on his gum. "Sometime during the Carter administration? Cars that belong to careless drivers don't live that long. You're as careful behind the wheel as you are with your money. That car sounded like it had emphysema, but I bet you would've gotten five more years out of it, if you hadn't totaled it yesterday."

Totaled. She was going to need a new car. Faye could feel her bank account shrivel.

"Don't declare it dead yet," Magda said. "I bet Faye gives it mouth-to-mouth. It'll be back for another few years."

"Where *is* my car?"

"See?" Magda's voice was smug. "Told you so. She'll bring in some paramedics and have it back on its feet—tires—before you know it."

"My car. I was asking where my car was."

"It's been towed and stored until your insurance company can take a look at it. And the Tallahassee police. I gave 'em a heads-up on all the people that had been dropping dead in your presence." The sheriff popped his gum. Even sitting in the back of the mini-van, Faye could see Magda cringe with every chew, but she said nothing to her gum-popping husband. The woman clearly loved that man. "They're gonna check the brake lines. Maybe they already did. I'll know soon enough."

"Who would've cut her brake lines?" Ross asked.

"Nita and Wayland?" Faye wanted to believe that the culprit was someone completely antisocial, someone that you could see coming, so that you could avoid them. Nita and Wayland fit that description.

"I wouldn't put it past them, but no. They've been in custody all day long."

"For what?" Faye asked. "You told me you had to let them go."

"They got caught digging in the National Wildlife Preserve this morning, and that's big trouble. As you well know. The Feds are talking to them now." His gum made some truly awesome noises, but Magda remained silent. Faye figured she knew that chewing helped Sheriff Mike think. "Nita and Wayland—those two are scared this time. If they know something, I think they'll spill it."

He gave the gum a rest and the minivan grew silent, except for an occasional sleepy sigh from Rachel. Faye couldn't get her brain around the notion that someone might have tampered with her car. Why? She didn't see Douglass' killer, nor Wally's. What was more, she was keeping her nose out of the investigation, letting law enforcement people do the criminal investigation, while she simply did a little archaeology. That was her job. How was she a threat to anyone?

Joe sat in front of her, as silent as she was. Again, she sensed that this was more than his usual quiet manner. "What's wrong? You mad at me for nearly killing us both?"

"Why would I be mad at you? You didn't do anything. I'm mad at me."

"Whatever for?"

"I should have thought of the car."

There was a long pause, and Faye thought he was going to drop back into his self-reproachful silence. Then he spoke again. "The sheriff told me to look after you, and I did, but I never thought that somebody might mess with the car. Maybe you need somebody smarter than me to keep you safe."

To Ross' credit, he didn't say a word.

# Chapter Eighteen

Magda and Sheriff Mike had urged Faye and Joe to sleep at their house, which only made sense, since it was the middle of the night before they arrived. They wouldn't be going home to Joyeuse for quite some time, since everybody in Micco County seemed to think her island was a more dangerous spot than…say…Iraq. Or the Sudan. And even though Emma was their official hostess, for the time being, there seemed to be no sense in waking her, just to find a place to lay their heads.

Faye had slept late and awoken to the smell of coffee left too long on a hot burner. The sheriff had left it in the coffee maker for her when he went to work, having no idea that it would be hours before she was awake to drink it. Joe, not being big on coffee, had gone for a walk for his morning pick-me-up. Faye was rather enjoying the overcooked brew's sooty, nutty, flat flavor, but she was enjoying Magda's misery more.

Magda had Rachel on her lap, trying to coax a burp out of her little mouth. She kept casting lovelorn glances at Faye's coffee cup. Faye didn't have the heart to tell her that most people would have said it tasted really, really bad. Instead, she dosed it heavily with cream and sugar and sucked it down, knowing that she was giving a caffeine-starved woman a little vicarious pleasure.

"So somebody really did sabotage my brakes?"

"That's what Mike says. Apparently, it's not all that hard to do, when you're talking about a car the age of yours. A crook who's a real artist can fix it so a little brake fluid leaks out every time you hit the brakes. You get a few miles down the road and—boom!—you're in real trouble."

"If they'd wanted to kill me, there are better ways."

"Mike thinks they were trying to scare you away…from something. We're not sure what. The important thing to remember is that they didn't care whether you were killed in the process. Or Joe. Or the people you could have hit. These are not nice folks."

"Maybe they don't like me going to the library—since that's what I was doing when they messed with my car."

"That would be an obvious answer. Or somebody could have followed you until that dark lonely parking garage gave them the perfect opportunity."

Remembering the way every sound had echoed through the empty garage, Faye realized that there were few better places to commit a crime that might be as simple as dropping to the cement and rolling under a car. It wouldn't be hard to do that, then to make sure all was quiet before rolling back out. Then the saboteur could simply walk away. It was an easy way to commit possible murder.

"Trouble is," Magda said, patting abstractedly on Rachel's back, "all our suspects are down here. Tallahassee is—what?—an hour or so away, but in some ways, it's the other side of the world. I mean, picture the nighttime crowd at Liz's. How many of them spend time on university campuses? If I saw any of them prowling the campus, I'd presume they were up to no good."

"Um…come to think of it…Liz's crowd seems to be flocking to Tallahassee."

Magda's eyebrows rose. "Who?"

"Liz tells me that Chip has been seen strolling around campus. She's all excited about it, since she figures it means he's going back to school. Also, he was in the company of a woman, so she's already buying yarn for the baby booties she's planning to knit."

"Liz? Knitting?"

"Okay. So the baby booties were metaphorical. But Chip has been seen at the university lately. And he knows his way around campus. He's the least of our worries, though. He actually has a decent reason to be there. Another of our suspects—one who doesn't seem the bookish type—has actually been to the library. He's been to the rare book room, in fact."

"Who? So help me, Faye, if you don't just spit it out instead of making me wait for you to spin a good story, I'm gonna scream."

"Settle down. You'll curdle your breast milk. I saw Wayland's name on the sign-in sheet at the rare book room. And the book of Bachelder's letters was on the returns cart so, unless Ms. Slater hadn't shelved returns since Friday—which I doubt, given her obsessive personality—somebody besides us looked at it in the past few days. Maybe it was Wayland."

"When was he there?"

"I didn't get a look at the date, but I was there the day after Wally died. No, wait. It was the day after that. Friday. Joe and I closed the place down. Wayland has been in the rare book room sometime since then." Another thought struck her. "We know where Wayland has been a lot of that time. Sheriff Mike said they were arrested sometime yesterday, down in the National Wildlife Refuge."

"It was pretty early," Magda said, eyeing Faye's nearly empty coffee cup. "Before lunch, for sure."

"There's not much chance that Wayland could have been at the library when it opened at eight, then finished whatever research he was doing so he could drive an hour south—"

"—and who knows how far out in the woods—"

Faye nodded. "Exactly. It would have taken an Olympic sprinter who owned a racecar to do all that in time to be arrested by noon."

"Mike had Wayland and Nita in custody practically all day Sunday, too."

"Saturday?" Magda had pulled a calendar out of her purse and started taking notes.

"We saw them at Herbie's pothunting party mid-morning on Saturday. You know—at Bachelder's homestead."

"And who knows how far out in the woods *that* place is. But I guess they could have driven to Tallahassee after you left. And they might have, if they thought you were getting too interested in Jedediah Bachelder. The rare book room's hours are short, but it seems like Saturday was Wayland's only chance to spend much time with Bachelder's letters." She circled Saturday afternoon on her calendar. "And for all we know, this wasn't his first trip to the rare book room."

"Saturday to Monday…" Faye tried to think how much traffic the rare book room could have seen in that amount of time. There wouldn't have been many people in and out, so Miss Slater—or whoever worked on weekends—should have had time to reshelf the book. Especially since it was so irreplaceable that she practically had kittens every time Faye wanted to see it. Faye imagined that the librarian had probably had some choice words for her employees if it had stayed out and unprotected for that long. "It's possible that someone else came in early on Monday to look at the book, but we can't know that for sure."

Faye wished for a little more certainty in their speculations. Maybe Wayland looked at the book when he visited the library. Maybe somebody else did. Maybe that someone had left when she and Joe arrived and headed downstairs to do a little brake-tampering. Maybe, maybe, maybe.

Her car, scraped and crushed into a lethal shape, rose in her mind's eye. She realized that she had been harboring a suspicion that Wayland was the saboteur who might have killed her. And Joe had thought so, too. Realizing that Wayland had been behind bars when it happened robbed her of a face to put on her enemy.

"The person who sabotaged your brakes must have known what you drive, or watched you drive into the parking garage."

"True. Neither of those are comforting thoughts." Faye thought of the Wayland's tanned, muscled arms, covered in tattoos from shoulder to wrist. His close-cropped hair and expressionless face made her think of a school shooter. His looks alone made him easy to suspect of attempted murder, but she'd have to let go of him as a suspect...which still didn't mean that he wasn't up to no good.

Faye brought her attention back to the subject at hand. "That's not all. Captain Eubank says Wayland came to his collection, too, looking for information on Bachelder. And there was something else...oh, yeah. When Joe and I saw Wayland and Nita at Bachelder's home site, Wayland said some things then that made me think he knew more than he was letting on."

"It all comes back to Bachelder. Which makes me think that it all comes back to Bachelder's emeralds, too." Magda settled Rachel in her automatic swing and pushed the on button. "She just loves to ride in this thing. That means I love it to pieces. Now, where were we?"

"I was telling you that Wayland had been to see Captain Eubank. What you don't know yet is that Herbie's been to see the captain, too."

"Well, as the owner of Bachelder's home site, Herbie's in a position to know a lot about him—including the existence of the emerald necklace. I think we're seeing a couple of people— Herbie and Wayland, maybe Nita, too—who are acting like they know about it, and it looks like they're darn close to figuring out where Bachelder hid it all those years ago. Which brings them perilously close to Joyeuse Island. And to you."

"Nita and Wayland weren't just close to Joyeuse Island. They were there. They were digging in the wrong place, but they had the right island." It was an island that was Faye's home, an island where she couldn't even live in peace, for fear that one of these bozos would kill her for the treasure buried there. The thought made her mad enough to spit.

"Anybody else got a link to the university? That's where your brakes got cut, you know."

"Believe me. I know."

As she thought of the university, an image popped into her mind...an image of the university seal on a torn and bloody scrap of paper. "Wally. I think Wally had been there shortly before he died. We know that he wrote me a note on university letterhead."

"Dang, that's a lot of potential criminals for one little campus." Magda reached for Faye's cup of bad coffee and drank the last swig. "It's enough to make a girl scared to go to work."

Faye's suitcase was bearing the brunt of her pent-up anger. She had wadded up several changes of clothes and thrown them at the defenseless piece of luggage, but they made no sound on impact, so there was no satisfaction to be had there. It had been slightly more rewarding to hurl face soap, shampoo, a toothbrush, and a tube of toothpaste, but they only made mild tapping noises when they hit the suitcase lid. More noise was necessary to express her frame of mind. Much more noise. Faye decided she needed something louder to throw. Maybe she should pack a big rock.

"That's not gonna help," Joe said, walking into the room as she missed the suitcase completely and a hardcover book thwacked on the floor.

"I don't want to leave my home. I don't want to live in a house with a bunch of people watching my every move, just in case somebody tries to kill me. Again." She threw her alarm clock in the general direction of the suitcase and missed again. "And I don't want Douglass to be dead."

She dropped to the bed, sitting on the side with her head in her hands. "Everything's wrong, Joe."

She felt in her bones that he was about to start spouting Native American philosophy about how everything was as it should be. The sun rose in the east and it set in the west. A billion stars wheeled endlessly in the firmament, but people weren't eternal. People were born to die.

She was not in the mood for philosophy.

But Joe didn't say anything. He just stooped down and took a seat on the floor, as if he planned to sit there and wait until she felt better. Faye found the silence oddly comforting. Sitting alone in a quiet room would have done nothing for her disposition, but sitting alone in a quiet room with her best friend was a healing thing. Soon enough, she was ready to start packing again.

She was zipping the suitcase when her cell phone rang. It was Sheriff Mike.

"The Feds let me take a look at the box of junk Nita and Wayland had in their car when they were picked up. I told them I had a consultant who knew all there was to know about archaeology in these parts, so they want you to go through it. They'll probably cut you a nice fat federal check, because I used the word 'consultant.' You can thank me later."

"What kind of junk are they consulting me about?"

"Old stuff. Old dirty stuff. The kind of stuff you live for. There's just one problem. I'll be hornswoggled if there's anything in that box worth selling. I've been hanging around you long enough to have some notion about that. That's for you to say, though. You come on over here and charge these Feds a nice fat fee to take a gander at something you'd have happily looked at for free. There's a broken plate I definitely think you should see, though."

"A broken plate? Sounds real exciting."

"It's stamped smack in the middle with a seal that says, 'Turkey Foot Hotel.'"

Faye felt the possessive part of her yell, *Hey! That's mine!*, but she tried to be reasonable. "I suppose it could have washed ashore long ago onto the land that's now the wildlife refuge, where they were digging. After all, the hotel was destroyed a hundred-and-fifty years ago by one hell of a hurricane. But I think Joe and I will take a little boat ride over to the Last Isles and check on the hotel site. Right now. I have a sick feeling that somebody's been mucking around on my property."

The hurricane that had howled through Faye's world nearly four years before had reconfigured the Last Isles. It wasn't the first time that a Category Five storm had redrawn the map of that part of the world. When Faye's house had been built around

1798, there had been just one Last Isle. That island had lived another half-century before being washed away in the 1857 hurricane that must have been as monstrous as the one that had nearly killed Faye and Joe. Last Island had been obliterated by the 1857 storm, broken into sandy pieces that were more sand bars than full-fledged islands.

Hundreds of lives had also been obliterated by that long-ago disaster. No one knew how many people died when the Turkey Foot Hotel was washed off Last Island, but Faye's great-great-great-grandfather, Andrew Whitehall, had been one of them. Her great-great-grandmother, a slave named Cally, had floated out of an upstairs window, clinging to a buoyant dresser drawer, adrift and alone in the angry Gulf of Mexico, but she had survived. The women in her family had always been survivors.

Giving further evidence of the family tenacity, Cally had achieved ownership of the Last Isles and Joyeuse—island and house, both—within ten years of the hurricane, and her daughter and granddaughter had spent their lives helping her hang onto that land. In the end, though, the destruction of Last Island had wrested a good deal of property out of the possession of those tenacious women, at least for a few decades. With no surviving landmarks to establish property boundaries, it had been easy for a corrupt judge to rule against the family's claim to the remaining islands, leaving them only their homestead on Joyeuse Island. Court decisions had frequently gone that way for people of color in the years after the Civil War.

Faye was intensely proud of reclaiming that land. When the most recent hurricane washed away the sand covering the ruined foundations of the Turkey Foot Hotel, she had been able to produce a document showing that her family had owned it. Those ruins had given her physical proof that she was the heir to what was left of the hotel…and thus the island—now islands—that it had stood on. Procuring funding for excavating those foundations was a particularly sweet victory, since she would have done the work, regardless.

There wasn't much left of the old hotel but, from a witness' description of its layout, she thought she'd located the kitchen. Thinking like a busy cook who needed to dump her trash quickly and get back to work, she'd used that information to intuit the location of a garbage pit.

A garbage pit. A hole full of hundred-and-fifty-year-old kitchen refuse…Faye might as well have been in heaven. The only thing better than a garbage pit would have been an outhouse. Overdressed Victorians had dropped the most interesting things into latrines back when getting dressed had meant fastening a plethora of buttons and pins. She hadn't had time to completely plumb the depths of the garbage pit, and the time she'd spent on Bachelder's history was time she could have spent shoveling old trash. The pit was calling her. She prayed Nita and Wayland hadn't ruined it.

Faye's skiff had eaten up the short distance between Joyeuse Island and the piece of Last Island where the hotel had stood. Joe was in his john boat, not because they had packed so heavily that it took two boats to carry their stuff, but because they might be ashore for quite a while, and they might both need water transportation while they were staying with Emma. Faye's skiff was fast, but Joe's john boat had kept pace with her. They'd no sooner dragged their boats up on the beach, than Faye felt a sick feeling wash over her. Drag marks on the sand told her that someone else had beached a boat lately, probably since the last high tide. Footprints pointing in the direction of her excavation told an even worse story.

Self-preservation reminded her that there could still be bad guys around. A bruised abdomen and a throbbing butt cheek reminded her of the damage those bad guys could do. A glance up and down the shoreline told her that no criminals were lurking on this side of the tiny fragment of an island. No one with a gram of sense would try to land a boat on the other side of this island, where mosquito-infested swamps predominated, so if anyone nasty was here, then they were very good swimmers. She judged that it was safe to proceed, and Joe must have agreed, because he didn't try to stop her.

Bad news greeted them at the hotel site. Randomly placed piles of earth and a few shattered sherds of white-glazed pottery gave evidence that somebody—probably Nita and Wayland—had been treasure-hunting smack in the middle of her neat and scientifically designed project.

Joe held out a hand, as if to quiet her inevitable outburst. "Don't fly off the handle. Let's just see what they did."

She found three or four pits randomly placed alongside the more well-preserved stretches of the hotel's foundations. Rectangular depressions in those areas showed that the pothunters had pried up some of the bricks and hauled them away. She didn't imagine they'd found much else besides bricks in that area. She didn't even want to think about the other parts of the site they could have messed up

Joe's voice, which said only, "Faye," came from the direction of the old garbage pit. She hurried over.

When she'd last been on this island, she had left a neat rectangular excavation with straight, sharp, vertical sides. There was nothing left now but a formless pit, surrounded by soil that looked like it had been plowed. Badly plowed. She'd had trouble with pothunters out here a time or two before, but it had never been anything like this.

The sheriff might have recovered the artifacts scavenged from this place. But how much information had been destroyed? Could she still sift through this churned-up soil and uncover the things she'd hoped to learn about the diet of the hotel's guests and employees? Or the kitchen help's cooking techniques? Maybe. Maybe not.

"Shit."

"I'll call the sheriff." Joe whipped out his cell phone and started punching buttons.

Faye couldn't think of any way to express her anger that wouldn't hurt more than it helped. She couldn't pick up a brick and hurl it at a tree. The handmade bricks, molded and burnt on-site, were artifacts in their own right. There wasn't a rock in sight, so she couldn't even chunk a rock at a tree. Besides, the trees never did anything to her, so there was no point in hurting them. She certainly couldn't yell at Joe, who never did anything to her, either, so she just stomped across the dunes and climbed in the skiff.

Soon enough, Joe appeared, folding his cell phone shut. They cranked their boats and pointed them toward shore, where the stuff Nita and Wayland had stolen from this site—from her, personally—was waiting for her to inspect it. She and Joe didn't talk, because there was nothing to say.

◇◇◇

"I don't get it," Faye said, sorting through the pile of dirty junk.

Besides the broken plate the sheriff had mentioned, there wasn't much to see. A piece of a bottle that had probably held vinegar. A plain metal button. The corroded blade of a butcher knife. The green neck of a wine bottle. She balanced the green chunk of glass on her palm, holding it up to the light. Nothing could have been less like the enigmatic emerald. The only things the two things had in common were that they were clear, smooth, cool to the touch, and green.

"Nobody's going to buy this stuff," she said to the sheriff and his friend, the man who was paying her a considerable consulting fee. The contract, hastily drawn up, rested comfortably in her purse. Given the chance, she could really get into this consultant gig.

She sighed. "I could've done something academic with all this trash. Maybe. I could've researched the wine to determine the country of origin and learn something about import patterns of the day. It makes sense that a large kitchen would have bought vinegar, even though housewives at that time generally made their own, so that broken bottle is mildly interesting. The button and the knife…I can't think of anything exciting to learn from them, but I might eventually come up with something. But collectors? They wouldn't give this junk a second look, much less pay good money for it."

"That begs the question of why Nita and Wayland are doing this." The sheriff held the knife blade, gently fingering its corroded cutting edge. "They could make more money per hour doing just about anything else."

Faye turned the broken plate over in her hands. The Turkey Foot Hotel's crest left no doubt that it had once graced a table at her ancestors' hotel, many years before. She studied the restrained but beautiful pattern of leaves that ran around its rim. "Maybe they've found better stuff in the past. Do you have a computer handy?"

She brought up the EBay home page. Just for laughs, she typed in "Turkey Foot Hotel" in the search box. She got no hits, but she hadn't expected to. Next, she pulled down the Categories menu and read over it for a while. After a thoughtful moment, she dropped down the "Antiques" menu and selected "Antiquities," then "The Americas."

An eyebrow-raising assortment of precolumbian artifacts filled the screen. Faye wondered how many of them were real, and whether any of those had been obtained legally or ethically. That question, however, was not pertinent to the problem at hand. She was looking for artifacts dating to the Civil War era and found in Florida.

She went back to the "Antiquities" menu and typed in "Civil War" and "Florida." No useful results appeared.

As a shot in the dark, she went all the way back to the home page and reset the search categories to search the whole site. She typed in the same search terms then hit "return"…and she also hit paydirt.

Buried within two pages offering fake Civil War uniforms and authentic Civil War musket balls and books on all kinds of Civil War artifacts, she saw a battered rifle being sold "as is." The description read:

GENUINE AUTHENTIC ANTIQUE RIFLE FROM THE CIVIL WAR ERA, DUG UP ON AN ACTUAL CIVIL WAR BATTLEFIELD. ALL ORIGINAL. NEVER RESTORED. STOCK LOOKS TO BE MAHOGANY OR RED MAPLE.

Faye wasted a moment pondering the notion of a "genuine authentic antique." Was it possible for an antique to be genuine but not authentic? Or vice versa?

Then she saw the name of the store offering this rifle, and she actually squealed. "Herb's Place! The outfit selling this rifle calls itself 'Herb's Place!' This just has to be the rifle we saw Chip dig up, and now Herbie's selling it online."

Joe leaned over her shoulder, so he could see the screen better. "Didn't he say he knew rich people and could be a broker for his customers?"

"Yeah. For a twenty-five percent cut."

"Is 'brokering a deal' the same thing as listing something on EBay?"

"Technically, I guess you could say that. But any of those people could sell their finds online without giving Herbie a quarter of the sale price."

She clicked on the "Meet the Seller" link, saying, "Let's see what else Herbie has in stock."

Herbie's virtual store listed belt buckles from the uniforms of both armies, as well as an assortment of buttons and military insignia. He had a couple of bayonets, in various states of preservation, and piles of rifle bullets. More interesting to Faye was a bullet mold that actually looked pretty good in the photo, despite long years in the ground and a hasty excavation by amateurs. She'd like to get a look at that.

She had sorted Herbie's store by price, from highest to lowest, so she'd scrolled through several pages before she saw the teacup. It was only slightly chipped, though its white glaze had been dulled by years buried in sand. There was no crest to label it conclusively, but the restrained and elegant garland of leaves around the rim was too familiar for coincidence.

Faye ran a finger along the leaves that rimmed the broken plate from the Turkey Foot Hotel. "Sheriff Mike?"

The sheriff closed the file drawer he was pawing through. "Found something?"

"I believe I have. Ask Nita and Wayland, one more time, who's buying their stuff. And get Herbie Canton in here. It's very possible that he's using his online store to sell things that belong to me."

# Chapter Nineteen

Being forced to live with Emma Everett wasn't all bad. Faye coveted the long, lightly populated beach that curved in both directions from Emma's dock. Her own beach was private and lovely, but very small. It wasn't made for leisurely sunset strolls. This one was.

Ross strolled beside her, looking significantly less like a city boy than he had when he arrived. He'd acquired some canvas shorts that were new but rumpled. His deck shoes no longer looked like he'd just pulled them from the shoebox. He looked so much more like an island man and so little like his usual persona that she half-expected him to start singing Jimmy Buffett tunes.

At first, she'd had no idea where he'd gotten the stained and goofy-looking hat shielding his face from the last of the sun's rays. When she realized that it had probably belonged to Douglass, her heart contracted with the pain of it. She took Ross by the hand, and the feel of his warm flesh helped some.

"We could come here on weekends," he said. "If you decided to move to Atlanta, I mean."

She didn't know what to say, so she just kept walking, looking at her feet and appreciating the way the sugar-white sand stuck to her dark feet.

Ross was a smart man. He shouldn't have pressed his luck. But love tends to make people behave as if they're brainless. He kept talking.

"I've looked into graduate programs for you in Atlanta. Emory has a top-notch anthropology department with an inter-disciplinary approach—"

"I'm pretty sure they don't do field archaeology, and I—"

"But it's interdisciplinary, Faye. You can draw from the field work you've already done, and branch out into some fascinating topics. They even have an emphasis in race and racism. Think what you could do with the work you've already done, excavating the slave cabins behind Joyeuse."

"My work is here." She let go of his hand. For some reason, she felt like she needed both her hands to think clearly. She didn't know why she felt that way, but she did. "My home is here."

"But it's too dangerous. Think, Faye. Douglass is dead. Wally is dead. You've been attacked with a shovel and rifle—"

"Joe took those bad guys out with some string and a few rocks. I'm safe enough."

"The next bad guy cut your brake lines, and Joe didn't even see him coming. You need to be with me, where you'll be safe. I love you, Faye."

She couldn't speak. She couldn't say she loved him. And she couldn't say she didn't.

"Joe's a nice guy, but you need somebody to remind you that you're not invincible. You're huge on the inside, Faye, but on the outside, you're a dainty thing. Fragile, even. Joe can't protect you here, and he can't take you any place safe. I can. We'd have a good life in Atlanta."

She knew he was right. Life with Ross would be good indeed. She would be comfortable every minute of the day. Emory was a fine school, and she could study everything that suited her fancy. She'd never have to stop learning, because Ross wouldn't care whether she ever graduated and did anything useful. He wasn't asking her to be useful. He just wanted her with him.

"You love me. I know you do. When you're with me, Faye, I feel...complete."

Again, she couldn't answer him, because she felt complete already. She'd never thought about it before, but now Faye realized that she'd never felt anything but complete—not even when her house was in ruins and she didn't have two pennies to rub together.

"What will Joe do if I go?"

It was the wrong thing to say. As soon as the words floated out of her mouth and into the air, it was clear to her that those were not the words she should have been using. She didn't know why she said such a thing, but Ross had the good grace not to be angry. He said, gently, "You'll need somebody to look after the place. And we'll see him when we come to stay at Joyeuse on weekends. I like Joe. He's growing on me."

She looked out across the water, but she couldn't see Joyeuse Island from where they were standing. Again, she couldn't speak.

"You know you have to do this. Joyeuse is beautiful. It's perfect. But you can't live out your life there. You need someone to love, someone like me. You need to live in the real world. You need people around you."

Why was he saying this? Was her home not real? Weren't Emma and Magda and the sheriff and Liz and Joe people? Did she really have to leave them?

"You've got to do this, Faye, for your own happiness."

But she was already happy. His words, *You've got to do this*, echoed in her head, and finally she knew what she needed to say.

"I'm sorry. I'm really sorry, but I can't let you tell me what to do."

When he was gone and her head cleared, she was able to finish her thought.

*I can't let you tell me what to do.*
*Joe would never tell me what to do.*

There would be no sleep tonight. She'd hurt Ross, and she'd hurt herself in the process. Why couldn't she just go to Atlanta and let herself be happy about it?

If she was going to lie awake in Emma's luxurious guest room, then she was going to need something to read. She'd chosen Cally's reminiscences to get her through this long night, because her guts told her that there was concrete information—information she could use—buried in the old woman's meandering stories. She knew Cally had met Jedediah Bachelder, probably more than once. Had she remembered him well enough to mention him when the government people came to record her oral history?

When she finally found that Cally *had* remembered Faye's new friend, Jedediah Bachelder, she learned that Cally had met him more than once, more than twice, in a day and age when visits spanned weeks, not hours. Cally appeared to have known Bachelder well, and she spoke of him with affection.

Faye was struck by the reason she'd overlooked Cally's reference to Bachelder during her first quick pass through the oral history. When he had visited Joyeuse Island the second time to ask permission to bury his treasure, Cally was no slave nor even a meek, submissive free person of color. She'd been in charge of the whole plantation ever since her common-law husband, Courtney Stanton, had died. Even before that, she'd been in charge of a large household.

It went without saying that a woman of Cally's dignity would never refer to the man she'd known for years as "Master Bachelder" or even "Mister Jedediah." As it turned out, she didn't even call him "Jedediah." Her references to Bachelder had been so familiar that they'd slipped right past Faye's sharp eyes.

*Excerpt from the oral history of former slave Cally Stanton, recorded 1935*

*The war years passed us by here at Joyeuse, mostly. Not that keeping everybody fed was easy when we couldn't count on buying much of nothing, but the fields made us enough food to get by, as long as I kept a sharp eye on how my money was being spent and kept a tight hand on my purse. So the war years went by quiet. We never had any armies trailing through the place, tearing things up and taking all our food, and we certainly never saw nor heard any shooting. Out here on the island, we didn't see much of anybody at all. Every time I thought I might be lonely, I recollected what things must be like on the mainland. That made quiet times on Joyeuse Island look pretty fine.*

*The Yankees did come, right before the war got over, but I talked them into leaving us be. I spoke good sense to them, and I did it politely, but the herd of strong, well-fed, well-armed field hands standing behind me didn't hurt our cause any, either. The Yankees paid their respects, we gave them a little food, then they went away.*

*The only visitor I recollect in all those years, other than the Yankee army, was my Courtney's dear friend Jed. I'd met him once before, when he brought his wife for a long visit, right before the war. By that time, I was a free woman, and I ate my meals a-sitting at the dinner table across from Courtney, like the lady of the house. I guess I was the lady of the house, considering that I ran everything but the farm, and I did my share of sticking my nose into Courtney's farm business, too.*

*He introduced me to Jed and Vee like he always did when we met people who might wonder why Courtney was living with a young lady who wasn't his wife. He told 'em I was "a cousin who came from Georgia to help me maintain my household." Him and his long blonde curls. We looked no more alike than a dog and an alligator, but I looked white—you can see I still do—so people swallowed whatever he told them. It didn't hurt any that my Courtney was known far and wide as an honest man. When you only tell one lie in your whole life, it's not terrible hard to make it stick.*

*Now, Vee was the kind of lady who saw things like they really were, and she usually said so. She was like me in that way. I always had a suspicion that Vee knew things weren't quite the way Courtney said, but she never opened her mouth. And she was my friend. I loved her for that.*

*As for Jed...I loved him, too, for being happy and jolly and kind and a loyal friend to Courtney, but he wasn't all that deep. He pretty much believed everything he was told. Courtney told him I was his spinster cousin, so he figured it must be true.*

*Jed came back one time during the war, without Vee. I was so glad to see him. I can't tell you how glad.*

*I had lost my Courtney by that time, and I was so lonely for someone who remembered him, someone who'd loved him, too. If I'd been a great lady, I would've sent a houseboy out to the dock to meet his boat while I waited inside for him, but I'm just me. I was there when the steamboat captain unloaded Jed and all his trunks, and I greeted him with more of what the great ladies of the day called "fervor" than I probably should've. It was sisterly fervor, but it was real, because I was feeling awful shut off from the world by that time.*

*I made sure his room was fitted out with comfortable, fresh linens, 'cause I could tell by the state of his shirt collar that he hadn't had anybody to wash his clothes for a good long time. And no other help, neither. His secretary, Daniel, had left him a while before that, and he just laughed when I asked him where his valet Philip was.*

*He said, "I can't let anybody know where I am these days, not even Daniel or Philip. But I warrant that there are people who are damn anxious to find me."*

*I remembered him saying that, after all these years, because Jed was not a man who cursed, at least not in front of ladies. And Jed always treated me like a lady. I told him to stay as long as he liked at Joyeuse. I said he could stay, if he wanted to, till the war got over and he could go home to Vee. I didn't like to think of people chasing him across the countryside, but I reckon that's what happens when you're in a war and your side's losing.*

*I'd brought some field hands to the dock to help him get his bags to the house and I had to send for more. I told Jed he traveled powerful heavy for a man who had people chas-*

*ing after him, but he just laughed. That was the only time I ever saw him laugh when Vee wasn't in the room. Lord, even now I remember how the field hands groused. They swore they never saw a woman travel with so many trunks, and all of them heavy.*

*I had a word with Jed after that. A man that's always had somebody to wait on him doesn't exactly live in the real, actual world, but I do. Always have. I told him that he'd do well to lighten his load, since it would probably be a good long time before he had enough cash laying around to pay a valet.*

*He said, "The war can't go on forever."*

*I said, "Just because the war gets over, it doesn't mean you'll live like you used to. Not at first. And maybe never."*

*Then, he said, "Cally, I plan to land on my feet. My wife deserves a life as gracious as she is."*

*I allowed as how that was true, then I said, "Still. Until that time, I'd lighten my load."*

*So he did. He left here with just one trunk that he could carry all by himself.*

*I only saw Jed one more time, after the war was over. After he lost Vee. He didn't smile much, and he didn't laugh at all. He talked about her pretty much the whole time he was here. But as the days passed, I saw him stand up straighter. He'd stand on the beach and look out over the water, like a man plotting a course to…somewhere.*

*I don't often go out to the beach without thinking of my friend Jed, and he's been dead these thirty years.*

Faye laid a writing pad in her lap and tried to summarize what she'd learned from Cally's story. The most important information was the record of Jedediah Bachelder's trips to Joyeuse Island.

First, he'd visited before the Civil War with his wife. One of his letters provided independent confirmation of that trip, which was a nice bonus.

Second, he'd visited during the war, alone. This must have been when he buried the necklace. If so, this visit, too, tracked with a story told in Bachelder's letters. As an added touch, Cally's narrative provided Faye with independent confirmation of Captain Eubank's assertion that Bachelder's secretary left him before the war ended. The captain would be tickled to hear that.

And third, Bachelder had visited one more time, after the war and after Viola's death. She knew he'd always planned to come back to retrieve the necklace, so this last visit added one more bit of evidence supporting her theory of the emerald's history.

Cally's retelling of her conversation with a man who was confident of "landing on his feet" in the wake of the total destruction of his civilization rang true. Jedediah Bachelder had left his future on Joyeuse Island. After the war, he came back to reclaim it, as he had always planned to do. Was he successful?

Faye knew that he'd spent the rest of his life building hospitals and giving money to widows and children. That sounded like a man who did indeed land on his feet. In the absence of more evidence, she'd have to say that Jedediah Bachelder had successfully retrieved the emerald necklace and used it as the basis for his post-war fortunes.

He would surely have buried the necklace in a sturdy box. It would have been made of wood or metal in those pre-plastic days, but perhaps it had rotted or corroded by the time he returned. Maybe a stray shovel blade had destroyed the box and broken the necklace, so that Bachelder lost track of one emerald and a stray gold finding.

This story fit the facts. If it turned out to be true, then Faye would probably be finding no more precious jewels in her back yard.

# Chapter Twenty

The sheriff had told Faye to be at his office bright and early, ready to help him and the federal officers draw up a list of questions to ask Herbie. And ready to be paid again at a generous hourly rate. She was beginning to wonder why she was wasting her time chasing a Ph.D., when law enforcement folks were so anxious to write big checks with her name on the line that said "Pay to the order of—"

Her clients knew that there might or might not be enough evidence to connect Herbie to the charges being pressed against Nita and Wayland, so Faye's expertise was essential. Where did Herbie's merchandise come from? Did he know that it had been illegally obtained? And what laws were being broken when it was sold?

When she arrived, she found the sheriff trying to calm a large, overwrought woman with bottle-red hair. Liz was a wreck.

"He's gone. Chip wouldn't go off without telling me. He's never done it before. Something's wrong."

The sheriff patted her hand and shot Faye a look that said, "Help me."

Faye perched on the desk next to the spot where Liz sat hunched and weeping. "Do you think it's the girlfriend?" she asked. "Most men Chip's age spend a night away from home now and then. They just tend to do a better job of hiding it from their mothers."

"Maybe. I'd like to think so. But he didn't show up for work last night, and I know he needs the money. I don't pay him all that much."

"Smart woman," the sheriff murmured.

"I still see him as my baby boy, but I know he's an adult. Is there anything you can do, Sheriff? Or is there a law that you have to wait for twenty-four hours or something before you look for him? Because twenty-four hours is an awful long time."

"Usually we wait forty-eight hours—"

Liz groaned and laid her head on his desk.

"—but that's not written in stone. We don't wait a second if the missing person's mental state could be impaired, or if we think he might be a danger to himself or to somebody else."

"Well, I don't think he's dangerous. And his mental state seemed fine to me, though a young man with a girlfriend can act real unbalanced. Does that count?"

"Testosterone is not a controlled substance." He shot a glance at Faye, as if he knew she was thinking, *Maybe it should be.* Rubbing a hand over his jaw, he said, "Do you have any reason to think he's in danger? Other than just the fact that he's missing?"

"No reason, other than the fact that somebody got stabbed to death in my parking lot lately."

"That's good enough for me. I'll have all my staff keep an eye out for him, and I'll assign somebody sharp to head things up. You have to understand something about missing persons cases, though, Liz."

She lifted her head from the desk and looked him in the face.

"There's more than one reason for those guidelines that say 'Wait twenty-four hours,' or 'Wait forty-eight hours.' First of all, an adult has a right to go where he pleases and do what he pleases."

"Chip's been telling me that for years."

"Second, most missing persons show up pretty soon, so looking for them right away can be a waste of time." He put his hand on the woman's wrist. "Are you listening to me, Liz? The odds are good that he's just fine."

Liz's nod was jerky. Faye took hold of her free hand.

"And third, most law enforcement people are way overworked. Those waiting periods keep us from wasting time looking for people who just took off in a huff, planning to come home in a day or two. That means we can't count on a whole lot of help from departments in other counties, at least not for a couple of days, but that's okay. We can do a whole lot from right here in Micco County." He reached in a drawer and pulled out a notepad. "So tell me about the condition of his room. Any sign of a struggle?"

"No. Nothing was out of place. His bed hadn't even been slept in."

"Were any of his possessions missing?"

"A duffel bag. And some clothes. All his underwear was gone, except for a couple of pairs in the hamper. His work clothes seemed to be all there, but that makes sense. I make him wear long pants and polo shirts to work, but he'd never wear that kind of gear anyplace else. It looked like he didn't take nothing but some t-shirts and shorts and socks and basketball shoes. And a pair of flip-flops."

"Toothbrush? Razor? Other toiletries?"

"His toothbrush and toothpaste were gone. His electric razor was still there. He doesn't use all that many toiletries, as you call 'em, but I didn't see any deodorant on his bathroom counter. Oh, and his New Orleans Saints cap was gone. He's loved the Saints since he was just a little boy." Her face sagged again.

"So he packed up and left peacefully."

"Or somebody made it look like he did," Faye added, trying to help. Immediately, she wished she could take it back. Or maybe she should just bite her tongue out. There was no point in speculating about foul play in front of a woman whose face was crumpled like a lost kindergartener looking for her parents.

The sheriff continued his list of questions, and Liz continued her truthful but unhelpful responses.

"No sign of a struggle? Any unsavory characters around last night…other than your usual wholesome crowd, I mean?"

"Nope and nope."

"You don't give a guy much to go on, Liz." The sheriff laid his pen on the pad and just looked at it for a second, as if he thought it should be able to write out the answer to this problem all by itself. Picking the pen back up, he said, "I'll need a description of the car. If you have the license plate number, that would save me from having to look it up."

"That stuff's not going to help you, Sheriff. Chip's car is right where he left it—in the parking lot next to the meat locker."

Faye couldn't say why this bit of information was more chilling than everything else that had been said. She couldn't shake the mental image of a young man carrying a duffel bag as he walked down a lonely road, then climbing into an ordinary-looking car or truck and riding away, never to be seen again.

After seeing a shaken Liz to her car, Faye couldn't recapture the total outrage she'd felt over the rape of her hotel site, not compared to the enormity of Liz's situation. She couldn't even completely recapture her repulsion at Herbie's completely mercenary approach to history, but she was trying. This odious man charged people for the privilege of destroying a battlefield. And battlefield was just another word for graveyard.

After that, he charged them to camp on that desecrated graveyard and he rented them equipment for camping and for digging. He profited still more by selling them food and drink. And he profited a fourth time by posing as an antiquities broker, then collecting a nice percentage for doing nothing more than setting up an EBay listing. Most of those things were not illegal, just unethical as hell. Faye wanted nothing more than to put a bunch of miles between her and Herbie.

Unfortunately, the sheriff had changed his tune about what he wanted from her. He didn't just want her to help him draw up a list of questions for the profiteering pig. He wanted her present during the questioning, because he thought her expertise would come in handy. He said it didn't make any sense for her to give him a list of questions, then study the answers, only to say,

"But you should have followed up that answer with a question about thus-and-so. Haul Herbie back in."

It would be a most unpleasant assignment, but Sheriff Mike still had access to the governmental dollars that were backing up her consultant's checks. Faye's money-grubbing little heart couldn't bear to pass this job up. Nor could she walk away from the tiny sliver of a chance that Herbie's pothunting business might somehow be related to Douglass' death, and Wally's.

She thought she knew why she couldn't work up any enthusiasm for grilling Herbie about his activities, no matter how much he disgusted her. So what if the sheriff or the federal agents or whoever had jurisdiction over this mess could prove he'd been doing all those things? What would it change? Herbie would still own the battlefield. He could still dig it up himself. He could probably still get away with charging other people to dig there. And she knew of no law against selling legally obtained goods online.

Faye didn't want to waste her time on the likes of Herbie, but the sheriff thought it was important. She'd figured she should rise above the queasy feeling he put in the pit of her stomach. So here she was, across a table from him.

Herbie was pale and he looked damp. Faye didn't know whether it was appropriate for her to shake hands with him, since she was just supposed to act like a fly on the wall. This was a relief, because those flabby hands probably had sweaty palms. His black hair stuck to his head like a wet swimcap.

The sheriff began talking with no more than the necessary greetings and introductions. They had been joined by the Wakulla County sheriff and a federal agent, but neither sheriff said much. Sheriff Mike ceded the conversation to the soft-voiced agent who began by saying, "We just want to ask you some questions about two people in custody who were caught digging artifacts on federal land. You haven't been charged with anything."

Faye thought she'd want a lawyer, all the same, if she were in Herbie's shoes, but he didn't ask for one. She kept her mouth shut, which is what she'd been asked to do.

"Nita and Wayland Curry tell me that they work for you," the agent added.

"I never asked 'em to do anything illegal. As far as I know, they never have. At least, not while they were working for me."

The agent rearranged the papers in front of him. "That may be so."

"It *is* so. And if those two tell you any different, just remember that it's my word against theirs. I know you checked my record, so you know I ain't never been arrested. And I have a regular job that pays my bills. Benefits and everything. You can't say any of those things about Wayland and Nita. My word is a helluva lot better than theirs."

Nobody said, "That's not saying much," but Faye was thinking it.

"They tell us that you pay them by the pound—that you don't even look at their goods before you pay them. Now why would you do that? I can't figure it out. Our archaeologist," he nodded at Faye, "tells us that there's nothing of value in the box of stuff we confiscated when they were picked up. Can you help me understand something? If it's not even worth selling on EBay, why would you buy it?"

Herbie's mouth gave a nervous twitch when the word "EBay" was mentioned, but he recovered well. "I'm a collector. If it's old, I want it."

Faye's temper crept up another notch. People like Herbie and his customers had cost the world a lot of history, just because they wanted stuff. They wanted to own stuff, possess stuff, keep it in a place where no one else could appreciate it or learn from it. Herbie's customers had no idea what they were doing when they tore up Herbie's property, and they would continue tearing it up until there was nothing left. What would Herbie do for extra cash then?

A thought struck her so hard that she had to suppress a nervous twitch just like Herbie's. Faye scrolled back through her last thoughts.

*Herbie's customers had no idea what they were doing.*

*They would continue tearing his property up until there was nothing left.*

*What would Herbie do for extra cash after that?*

She reached for Sheriff Mike's notepad, wrote down exactly what the interviewing officer needed to say, and passed it to him.

"We know what you do with the junk Nita and Wayland Curry bring you." Again, there was a not-quite-suppressed twitch. "What will your customers do when they find out you've been salting the battlefield with any old junk you can find?"

Faye mentally congratulated the interviewer on the phrase "any old junk." She hadn't phrased the question in quite that way, but it succinctly summarized precisely what Herbie was doing…buying old junk, burying it on his property, then selling people the experience of digging up "genuine" artifacts. And he could continue doing it forever because, so far as his customers knew, his property would never be stripped clean.

"It's not illegal." Herbie's voice had climbed a half-step. "I charge people to come dig up artifacts. They belong to me. I bought and paid for them. I didn't ever say how long they'd been in the ground. They just…assume…that the stuff's been there a long time."

"Nobody's said anything about it being illegal," the interviewer said in a soothing voice. "Is that the only reason you've been buying junk from the Currys?"

"Yes. Yes, it is. Only if they find something especially nice, I don't bury it. I keep it for myself and sell it online. And that's not illegal, either."

Faye could tell that he was trying hard not to look at her. No wonder he'd been in such a hurry to get her off his property. Customers like Herbie's insist that their antiquities be "genuine" and "authentic." With her archaeological training, Faye could have told them the truth about Herbie's battlefield in an instant, if she'd been allowed to look at it.

Though the sheriff had told her to keep quiet, she couldn't resist asking a single question. "I noticed quite a few holes next door to the battlefield, at the Bachelder house site. Are you digging there for artifacts, so you can salt the battlefield with them?" It would have been simpler just to open the house site to his customers and let them dig for junk themselves.

"Nobody digs there but me." Herbie had regained a bit of his composure. He answered her in a swaggering tone of voice. "And what makes you think that my property was in the Bachelder family?"

"The property records say so. So do the headstones in the family cemetery out back."

"You know all that, and yet you wonder why I keep people off that property?" Herbie was still a human puddle of perspiration, but this question seemed to stiffen his backbone a bit. He crossed his arms over his chest and leaned back in his chair. She could have sworn he was smirking. "Some archaeologist you are. You don't even know the history that's sitting right under your nose."

That's all Herbie would say.

# Chapter Twenty-one

Emma didn't even know Chip, and she was fretting about him. "How could he go off and leave his mother to worry? Look at her," she said, gesturing at Liz, who was slaving over a hot grill and tending bar. "And what if the boy didn't just go off? What if somebody took him? Or what if they tricked him into coming with them of his own free will?"

There wasn't anything to say to Emma. Faye could soothe her with reminders that young men wander all the time into places their mothers don't know about. Most of them come back home safe and grow up to be nice, respectable people. Chip was almost certain to come waltzing home that night, and he was almost certain to go back to college and do everything his mother dreamed for him. Get a degree. Teach high school history. Marry a nice girl and have strapping young man children who would come hang out at their grandmother's bar in the summertime.

Except he might not. Some nice young men didn't come home. Sometimes bad things happened to people who didn't deserve it. Nobody knew that better than Emma.

Emma stopped talking long enough to take a bite out of her hamburger. "It sure is good to get out of the house. And to eat something besides casseroles. Funeral food is delicious, but anything gets old after a week or so."

Faye bit into her own burger, enjoying the tangy mustard and the crunch of onions and dill pickles. The meat was juicy, with a perfectly browned crust. Liz had never, to Faye's knowledge, burned a burger, nor served one that was underdone.

How many patties of ground beef had Chip left behind, already patted up and ready for his mother to grill? He'd been gone all day. Had he made the hamburger she was eating, or had Liz already been forced to make them herself? She had a couple other part-time employees, but only because she had to sleep and eat now and then. Faye wasn't sure she would trust the burger-making to anybody who wasn't kin.

This evening, Liz wasn't even trusting an employee with the busboy chores. She had refused to bring anybody in to take Chip's shift, because she'd gotten through the day by hanging on to the hope that her son would show up for work. He was nowhere to be seen, so the dirty dishes were piling up.

Liz's well-brought-up customers had figured out what was going on. They were stacking their own plates on a cart parked at the end of the bar. Her more worthless customers just left their dishes where they lay.

Joe, displaying his keen powers of observation, had noticed the general filth of the dining room. Wearing Chip's apron and pushing another cart around, he was busing tables and whistling.

Emma, who was remarkably motherly for a woman who had borne no children, turned her penetrating brown eyes on Faye. "What did you do to Ross?"

Faye didn't know whether to cry or to bark, "None of your business." She opted for answering the question honestly. "I just can't see myself living in Atlanta. I told him so."

That wasn't strictly what she'd told Ross, but it was close enough.

Emma raised an eyebrow. "I figured as much when he suddenly had a work crisis and needed to go home. He said he thought Joe could take care of both you and me, now that we were staying in the same house. And he's right. I feel safe enough. How about you?"

Faye felt safe. Safe and alone. Was that why she'd pushed Ross away, so that she could be alone? Loners never had to compromise, and they always got their way. Was that her problem? Was she too strong-willed to share her life with anyone?

Rather than admit these doubts to Emma, she took the coward's way out. She made a joke of the question. "I don't see how we could be safer. You could drop Joe naked in the middle of the Sahara desert, and he'd find a way to make a deadly weapon."

Liz turned away from the grill long enough to say, "Joe? Naked?", but there wasn't enough heart left in her to craft an appropriately ribald comment. And there wouldn't be, not until Chip came home.

In the mirror above the bar, Faye had been watching Nita and Wayland eat. It seemed that the sheriff hadn't been able to come up with a good reason to hang onto them. Every now and then, one or the other cast an appraising glance at Faye's back. She'd seen them. Their interest in her wasn't just a paranoid fantasy on Faye's part. She knew it was real.

Nita said something to Wayland, and they both looked Faye's way, one last time. Then they pushed their chairs back from the table, stood up, and walked away, leaving their dirty plates behind.

There was no more infuriating way to cap off a miserable day than suffering petty theft. Joe had spent the evening doing good deeds like busing Liz's tables for free. He did not deserve to lose one of his few possessions.

"Somebody took your john boat?" Liz was too polite to add the next obvious word: *Why?*

Joe's john boat looked just like everybody else's. It was beat up, full of junk, and it smelled like fish. Joe used all the fish guts and scales that he cleaned off assorted fish carcasses as fertilizer, burying them in his garden plot on Joyeuse Island, which meant that his john boat didn't have a putrid smell. It smelled like fish in a good way. So if the thief wanted a john boat, Joe's might have smelled like the best option. But why would anybody steal something like that, when there were so many nicer boats moored at the marina?

"Kids," Liz had said to the sheriff, when he arrived to investigate. "I bet it was kids looking for a joyride. If Joe knew what was good for him, he'd use a padlock and chain to make sure that ugly boat never leaves the dock. I happen to know that Joe has never once done that."

"Neither does anyone else," Faye said. "Nobody ever took it before."

"What do you think, Sheriff? Kids?" Liz asked.

"Coulda been kids. Coulda been *your* kid."

Faye had watched Liz work like a slave all night, and she'd known that the woman was trying to block out her worry over Chip. The sheriff's comment crashed through Liz's protective armor, and she tottered for a second before flopping onto the bar stool beside her.

Faye, for once, remembered that she didn't have to say quite everything she thought. So she didn't point out to Liz, Joe, and the sheriff that the boat could also have been stolen by someone who had Chip, so that he could be taken...where? And what condition was he in? The Gulf was a very good place to hide a body, and a boat would be a necessary part of that plan. She kept this idea to herself, because everybody around her knew it as well as she did.

Faye's bed was comfortable. Really comfortable. Emma and Douglass had never spared a penny when it came to pleasant surroundings. The sheets were smooth, the comforter was light and soft, and the mattress cradled her body so well that she fully expected to see a Faye-shaped mold when she got out of bed the next morning. She was seriously considering parting with enough money to make her own bed just as plush as this one.

Too bad she was alone in this sumptuous bed. And she'd be alone in her own bed, if she ever got back to it. Maybe she always would be.

With these cheerful thoughts dancing in her head, Faye arranged three downy pillows as a backrest, so she could sit up in bed and read until she got sleepy. That way, she wouldn't have to think.

This was going to be hard, since thinking was what she did best.

She surrounded herself with paper—pages and pages of Cally's oral history, and pages and pages of the Bachelders' letters. She was having trouble making Cally's story dovetail with Jedediah Bachelder's, simply because of the difference in format.

The letters were chronological. Even better, they were dated.

Cally had just rested in a rocking chair and spun an old woman's tales. Her stories danced from her girlhood as a house slave to her old age in the Depression years and back to the waning days of the Civil War. Faye couldn't keep it all straight. It was time to construct a timeline.

She sharpened a pencil and laid a legal pad in her lap. On the first lines, she wrote,

> **Prior to the breakout of the Civil War in April, 1861:** According to Jedediah Bachelder's letters, he and his wife Viola visited Courtney and Cally Stanton on Joyeuse Island.

> **Corroborating note: Cally Stanton's reminiscences corroborate at least one visit by a family of Bachelders prior to the Civil War. There may have been more.**

On the next line, she added,

> **November 13, 1861:** Jedediah Bachelder writes a letter that begins proceedings to free his slaves.

The next few entries came in quick succession.

> **January 7, 1863:** Jedediah Bachelder writes his wife, telling her that he is being sent on a diplomatic mission to England. He believes he was selected to negotiate an alliance with the English solely because his lack of slaves gives him credibility in Europe.

> **Corroborating note: Such diplomatic missions are known to have taken place, including a well-known trip headed**

by a prominent planter named Duncan Kenner.

September 10, 1863: Bachelder writes his wife of the failure of his mission to England. He mentions an emerald necklace that was also mentioned in an earlier letter. The sale of his family's plantation has forced him to find a new hiding place for the necklace. He reminds her of their visit to Joyeuse and tells her of getting Courtney Stanton's help in finding a hiding place on the island. He tells her the necklace's hiding place, under a newly built summer house.

Corroborating notes: A contemporaneous account recorded by Cally Stanton mentions a summer house. An emerald and a gold finding found in the possible location of the summer house suggest that the necklace was indeed buried there.

Sometime in 1864: The pen and note paper used by Bachelder change, as well as the handwriting. This is believed to be the time when he lost the services of his secretary and valet and was forced to travel alone. There is little information on where he traveled during this time period, nor why "a minor public servant" has left Richmond for such a protracted period of time. A period of war and social turmoil seems like an odd time to embark on constant travel.

Corroborating note: Cally Stanton's oral history confirms that Bachelder had lost his secretary and valet prior to his single wartime visit to Joyeuse in 1863.

April 18, 1864—Bachelder writes a second letter to Viola about the necklace and its hiding place, because he fears that the first one did not reach her.

June 30, 1864—Viola writes her husband, confirming (though in veiled language) that she received the letter telling her where to find the necklace.

Cross-checking Bachelder's account with Cally's, Faye added an entry just below his letter of September 1863.

> **Corroborating note: Cally Stanton's oral history confirms Bachelder's wartime visit to Joyeuse, sometime after Courtney Stanton's death in**

Faye's pen stopped. She wracked her brain for the date of Courtney Stanton's death. It was fairly late in the war, but when?

Then she remembered. The Civil War began in April 1861 and it ended in April 1865. She remembered when Courtney Stanton had died, because it was just a year short of the end of the war, in April 1864. She penciled **April 1864** into the corroborating note, then she glanced back over the timeline to check for accuracy before she went ahead.

"Damn," she whispered.

Something didn't add up. That meant she had to follow the thread through time again, and again if necessary, until she could get it unsnarled.

Cally had mentioned that Courtney was dead when Bachelder visited, and Courtney died in 1864. But Bachelder's letter describing his trip to Joyeuse was dated 1863.

Even worse, there was a clear contradiction between Cally's account and Jedediah Bachelder's, one that was more fundamental than just a confusion over dates. Cally clearly said that Courtney was dead when Bachelder visited. And Bachelder clearly said that Courtney helped him hide the necklace, even going so far as to build a summer house over it.

Had Cally misremembered the visit? Her description of the loneliness that had made her so happy to see her friend Jedediah Bachelder—or Jed, as she had called him—rang so true. A widow would not forget when her husband died.

When Cally's reminiscences were taken into account, only one explanation fit the facts as presented in the Bachelder letters that she possessed: Cally's friend Jed visited Joyeuse Island twice during the war. The first time, he had worked with Courtney to hide the emerald necklace. It was possible that they worked in secret, without Cally ever even knowing he'd been there. Later, he returned, and this was the visit that Cally had described.

Now that the snarls in the timeline were untangled, Faye's mind should have rested easier, but this new information only stirred up more uncertainty. Cally's story mentioned Bachelder saying that people were after him. He'd said nobody could know where he was going, not even his trusted valet and secretary. Yet they'd presumably traveled with him when he purchased the necklace and during his previous trip to Joyeuse Island, when he and Courtney had buried the necklace. Why could they travel with him when he was carrying a fortune in emeralds, but not later? What information would have been more sensitive than that?

And why did people want to know where he was? Was it just because he was a Confederate official? Or was there something more?

She gathered her papers and put them in her briefcase. It was time to sleep. Well, it was time to *try* to sleep. She and Joe needed to go back to Tallahassee and get a look at the last few Bachelder letters. Maybe they would explain their author's peculiar behavior.

# Chapter Twenty-two

It took the hazy light of dawn, lit by the pink and gold glow of a sun still hiding below the Gulf of Mexico, for Faye to see her heart clearly.

*Why* had she sent Ross home alone? She didn't want to leave Joyeuse, it was true, but she'd always known that the day would come when she'd have to go back to the mainland. There was a reason that nobody besides Faye had lived full-time on Joyeuse Island since Cally died in the 1930s. Cally had lived so long that her daughter, named Courtney after her father, was old and infirm before her mother died. Courtney's daughter—Faye's grandmother—had moved to Tallahassee when she was widowed, so she could get secretarial work and, though her mother had been recalcitrant, she'd taken Courtney with her.

Faye's mother had been born in Tallahassee, and she'd grown up there. So had Faye. All the family's women had talked of moving back to the home place—for sixty years, they had talked about it—but only Faye had been bullheaded enough to do it. She'd managed to survive out there and be happy, it was true, but the cost had been high in terms of money and effort and heartache.

Paying work was on land, which meant she spent much of her time in boats and cars, trying to get to it. Pretty much everybody in the world, except Joe, was on land, too, and none of them wanted to live on a Godforsaken island. So she spent a lot more time in boats and cars, just trying to fulfill her human need for companionship.

Moving to Atlanta wouldn't mean selling Joyeuse. Ross had said they could go there on weekends, and Joe could look after the place. Only Joe wasn't going to stay there forever. When he'd come to Joyeuse, he'd needed a place to hide from a world where he didn't fit. Well, there *was* a place in the world for Joe now. He was driving, and in school, and making plans for...

What were Joe's plans? She'd never asked him, because she didn't like to think of him being gone.

Imagining her great white house, empty and alone, after she and Joe had left it behind felt like plunging a knife into a wound that had only begun to heal. No. She couldn't do it. Joe might have to leave, but she didn't ever have to go.

But the knife wouldn't leave her alone. Joyeuse without Joe was...unimaginable. She'd been terrified of Atlanta, afraid of being alone in a city of strangers, but this loneliness was worse. She couldn't bear it.

If Joe left, she couldn't bear it.

Before the sun cleared the horizon, Faye knew that she could move away from Joyeuse and be happy. But she would never be happy anywhere if Joe wasn't there.

What would she do if he decided to go anyway?

Breakfast was hard. Joe persisted in doing things that made Faye intensely uncomfortable...things like saying, "Good morning." When he asked if she'd slept well, she nearly jumped out of her chair.

He sat beside her, which was good, because she didn't have to look at him, and she wasn't in the direct line of fire of a sharp pair of green eyes that missed nothing. Trying to hide something from a hunter was a fool's game. Joe could surely read the tremble in her hand as easily as he knew which way a hunted rabbit would jump.

Faye soon found that the fact that Joe was outside her direct range of vision didn't help matters much. He'd neglected to tie back his hair, and she could hear the soft rustle as it moved over his shoulder every time he turned his head. She could see long bronze fingers lightly gripping a silver fork as it speared a bit of pancake. Forcing herself to focus on her own fork, she took a bite of her own pancake, but her mouth was dry. It would have been easier to chew dirt.

Emma slid into the seat across from Faye and smiled like a woman who knew a secret. Faye couldn't take it any more.

"I'm not real hungry. Just leave my plate here, and I'll eat something later." She needed to leave, and taking her plate to the kitchen would take too long. "I've just got to get some exercise, and if I don't take a walk now, it'll be too hot."

Joe put down his fork, and Faye's heart stopped. He was going to offer to go with her, and then she was going to have to make conversation. She couldn't talk to him yet, because she didn't know what she was going to say.

Emma, who continued to look like a woman who knew more than she should, forked another pancake onto Joe's plate. "Here. Eat this so it doesn't go to waste."

Faye had nearly gotten away, but Emma wasn't through with her. "Take your coffee," she said, holding the cup out to Faye. "It settles the stomach and clears the mind."

Faye needed both of those things pretty bad. She took the cup and made her escape.

Lapping water bathed Faye's feet. She was an islander, and water in any form usually soothed her soul. Not today.

Why did she even think that Joe might want her? She was thirty-eight—pushing forty, if she were to be brutally honest with herself. He wasn't even thirty yet. And he was so damn good-looking that his gravitational pull attracted women the way the sun drew comets.

When Joe walked into a public place, women drifted in his direction without even knowing they were doing it. Little girls smiled at him. Older women laughed at his jokes, even when he hadn't made any. Women his own age circled him like wandering planets, and he hardly even noticed. Every now and then, he took one out on a date, but it rarely went beyond that.

How did Faye look to Joe? Like one of those older women who lingered in his presence because they just liked to gaze at him? Telling Joe how she felt about him felt dangerous. It could be utterly humiliating.

She needed time to figure this out, which was unfortunate, because she needed to go to the rare book library and Joe would insist on going with her. He took this bodyguard thing very seriously.

While on the subject of serious issues, it occurred to Faye that she had no idea what to wear to the library. If she wore anything other than her everyday work garb—t-shirt, army surplus pants, and boots—Joe would notice. Of course, the point was that she *wanted* him to notice. But if he said anything as personal as, "You look nice," she was likely to scream.

That meant she'd have to wear the usual gear, but maybe she had something in her suitcase that would make her look a little less like Joe's dowager aunt. Maybe a red t-shirt, close-fitting, with a little scoop to the neckline. She felt sick to her stomach. Remembering Emma's advice, she took a sip of her cold coffee.

It would have been a lot easier just to run away to Atlanta with Ross.

Joe's car was about as old as Faye's had been before she totaled it, so the engine sounded like a steel barrel crammed full of aluminum cans, then flung into a rocky canyon. Faye found the noise distracting. This was good.

The car was small, forcing her to sit closer to Joe than her comfort zone—which was increasing by the minute—preferred. This was not so good. It was time to talk about something safe, like murders or emeralds.

"Did I tell you what we'll be looking for at the library today?"

Joe shook his head.

"Cally's tales and Bachelder's letters seem to contradict each other. The only way they could both be right is if he made two trips, and she didn't know about the first one."

"And that's important because...why?"

"Mostly because I don't like unanswered questions."

"I noticed."

"But also because Cally's words give me the feeling that there was something different about his second trip." Faye struggled to articulate exactly why she felt that way. "He said that people were after him, and he'd lost his traveling companions. Or maybe he got rid of them on purpose. I want to know why he came back. I really doubt he came to get the necklace while the war was still on. And he made another trip later that was a much more obvious time to fetch it."

"You think he talked about his reasons in his letters?"

"I sure hope so."

Joe turned his head her way and smiled. "Maybe he left some more emeralds laying around your island when he came back."

Faye didn't look him in the face, because that would be too dangerous. Keeping her eyes on the road, she just said, "Now, wouldn't that be nice?"

Joe shifted his weight in a driver's seat that was way too small for him. "Do you still think there's some connection between the emerald and the killings? 'Cause I just can't see it."

"I'm hanging onto that idea for no good reason. I mean, the logic is still there. We know somebody—Wally, at least—knew about Bachelder's letters, because he sent us straight to them. Presuming he wasn't the only one who knew, then there's somebody else out there who knew that Jedediah Bachelder buried a gold and emerald necklace somewhere around here. If that person reads the local paper, then they know that Douglass' very own archaeologist dug up Bachelder's flask. If they went to the museum, they know that Douglass' archaeologist dug up a gold finding. And if they're the ones who killed Douglass and stole my notes, then they know where I dug it up. Not the emerald...just the finding."

"I heard a lot of 'ifs' come out of your mouth."

"But suppose they were all true. It explains why Douglass is dead—because he got in the way of the people looking for my notes. And it explains why Wally is dead. He was going to tell me about Bachelder's letters. His killer knows that the knowledge in those letters will eventually take me straight to the necklace. I don't think Wally's murderer wanted that to happen. Not in the least."

Faye fell silent, and Joe just drove. She let her mind travel down the serpentine logic linking the killings to the emerald, because intense thought distracted her. And she needed distraction from the disconcertingly handsome man sitting beside her, oblivious to her discomfort.

◇◇◇

Faye reflected that parking on a crowded university campus is particularly nightmarish when you're trying to avoid a nice, quiet parking garage where somebody once tried to kill you. The good news was that they had carved a torturous path through campus, creeping up and down so many one-way streets and cul-de-sacs that a tail would have been obvious. There was no one following them. Faye knew, because she'd been watching.

Joe's car was a lot smaller than Faye's, so it was easier to park…if they could only have found an available parking place. The old joke about university parking permits—that they should be called "hunting licenses," rather than permits—was holding true.

When they finally found a place to put the car, it was in a commuter lot a mile-and-a-quarter from the library. Trams circled the campus at ten-minute intervals, but the first two were full, and there was no guarantee that there would be any seats in the next one, either. Faye and Joe opted to walk. It was pleasant outdoors, and they were both happier outside anyway.

The long walk had cut into their limited library time, so Faye bustled into the room when they arrived, determined to work efficiently. They signed in, and Faye noticed no familiar names on the sign-in sheet, though Ms. Slater snatched it out of her hands so quickly that Faye couldn't be sure she'd checked every single signature.

Again, she asked for the Bachelder book. Again, she was told that it wasn't available. And, once again, Joe found it on the returns cart. Faye wondered how many people were reading the thing and what they wanted with it.

Rather than gather a lot of other materials for her to plow through, she stood behind Joe, so she could look over his shoulder while he read. The shoulder was disconcertingly broad, but she made herself focus.

The book was open to a letter written in 1865.

*May 15, 1865*

*Dear Viola,*

 *I write in haste to tell you of an urgent matter.*

 *The green and gold has been secreted in the safest of places, on an island once owned by a dear friend, who has lately left this earth. Its metal is not the kind that will corrode, even if inundated in salt water, so it is safe, even against a mammoth storm. I'm told there have been mammoth storms there before. I daresay there will be again.*

 *There is a large structure sheltering its resting spot, built by a true friend. I was distraught to learn of his passing, but the young woman managing his interests until his heir comes of age is perhaps the most resourceful person I have met in my travels. No unfriendly boots will tread the island while she breathes. She will guard what I have hidden until I return to retrieve it, though she has no idea that it is there. The green and the gold are safe enough.*

 *You may have received this letter by the hand of my manservant, Isaiah, whom I trust implicitly. No one but he and I know the whereabouts of our treasure. I will go to retrieve what I left behind by the end of this year. If I do not bring it to you by that time, then you must find Isaiah. If you tell him that the name of my first pony was Whiskey, he will take you where you need to go.*

*I deeply regret the maelstrom that has consumed everything we have ever known, but we have done our part to earn this tragedy. The shooting is over. I look for the day when peace begins.*

*Yours loyally,*
*Jedediah Bachelder*

Joe's gentle voice was still reading the letter, because no one's lips could form the words as fast as Faye's quick eyes could read them. She flicked those eyes up to the top of the letter. Maybe if she read it again, it might make some sense. Everything on the page felt wrong.

Why was he telling Viola the necklace's hiding place again, when he'd already told her twice and received confirmation from her own hand that she'd received it? The phrase "the green and the gold" felt odd, though it was understandable that he might not want to mention the necklace in a letter that could be intercepted. But why did he call Courtney his "dear friend," without even referring to him by name, as if he were a stranger to Viola? And he wrote as if Cally were a stranger to her, too.

The language he used to describe Isaiah was even more off-pitch. Isaiah had presumably lived with and served the Bachelders for their entire married life. Why did he describe him as his manservant? No one knew better than Viola who Isaiah was. And why was this letter written in a crisp tone so different from any she'd read before? Where had the sense of romance gone?

There was no more "Dearest love, Viola, my wife." Just a bare "Dear Viola." Even his closing words were chilly. Rather than "Your devoted husband," or "Your loving husband," he'd simply signed himself "Loyally yours."

Surely their marriage wasn't yet another casualty of the war. Faye, set off-balance by her own emotional state, thought her heart would break at the very thought of it. She knew what Jedediah could not, that his wife would not survive the year. It was unthinkable that she should have died believing he didn't love her any more. Faye's own heart was nearly broken by the fear that the man she loved wouldn't love her back. If Jedediah and Viola Bachelder had lost each other, Faye didn't think she could bear it.

Joe reached out a gloved hand to turn the page, and Faye reached out her own gloved hand to stop him. The letter's date jangled like an out-of-tune guitar.

*May 15, 1865.*

Viola's biographical sketch said that she died before Appomattox, in the final days of the war. And the Civil War ended with the surrender at the Appomattox courthouse on April 9, 1865. Viola had been dead more than a month when this letter was written.

Had Jedediah known she was dead? How long would it take for word to get to him in the midst of the anarchy left behind by the fall of the Confederacy?

She reached for the book and Joe handed it to her. Flipping forward through the months, she saw that he continued to write Viola throughout the rest of 1865. The salutation of every letter was a cool "Dear Viola," and each closing was a crisp, "Loyally yours."

Scanning random letters, she saw nothing more personal than the general housekeeping issues common to a marriage, or even a longstanding business partnership. Jedediah told his wife how to dispose of certain assets and advised her on managing their much-altered post-war finances. And throughout all the letters ran a much-repeated theme. Viola must retrieve the green and the gold before anyone else did, and she must let him know as soon as the task was done.

Every letter depressed Faye more. How long did it take Jedediah Bachelder to learn that his wife had died? And if their relationship had been strained when he lost her, how it must have grieved him for the rest of his life.

# Chapter Twenty-three

Joe had finished reading Jedediah Bachelder's last letter, and Faye wanted to scream, but she couldn't because Ms. Slater's disapproving presence pervaded the room, even when she was out of sight.

The book of letters trailed off into an inconclusive list of financial irrelevancies. Faye wanted more. This man had met her great-great-grandparents, Cally and Courtney Stanton, though she felt sure he never knew that Cally had been his friend's wife. Common-law wife, actually, since a formal marriage between a white man and a freed slave would have been impossible due to the mores of the time. Illegal, too.

It was likely that he'd seen Cally's child, also named Courtney, who would have been hardly bigger than Rachel at that time. The fact that young Courtney was a girl had been almost as closely held a secret as the fact that she wasn't white, not by the standards of the day.

As a woman, young Courtney couldn't inherit her father's estate, so Cally had just kept her out on the island and remained vague about who the child's mother was and even what its gender was. Eventually, people were too caught up in the disastrous aftermath of war to care who inherited a bunch of worthless land.

Until that time, though, too much snooping into the facts of Courtney, Sr.'s "heir," would have brought Cally's world down around her ears. She had clearly pulled the wool over Bachelder's eyes, since no man of the Victorian era would have recognized a daughter's right to inherit her father's land and fortune. Viola might have, but not Jedediah. He was too much of his time to reflect on how well a woman like his wife could have managed several vast estates.

Faye smiled when she pictured her great-great-grandmother, barely out of her teens, dandling a baby on her knee and lying through her teeth to Jedediah Bachelder.

The man had called Cally "resourceful." He had no idea.

After Joe finished recording the text of the letters, Faye suggested that he go downstairs to the library's general collection and poke around in the section where Civil War history—particularly the history of the Confederate government—was stored. She needed time alone with Bachelder's letters, and she needed Joe to be far away during that time. The simple fact of his presence scrambled her brain waves.

"I'll meet you down there after the rare book room closes," she said, trying not to watch his manly back as he walked to the door.

After he left, Faye sat at the work table, unproductive and unable to shake the unbalanced feeling she got from Bachelder's later letters. And she still hadn't figured out why he made that second wartime trip to Joyeuse Island. The last year of a war that his side was losing didn't seem like a safe time to dig up the necklace. Besides, he spent the whole next year telling Viola to go to Joyeuse Island and dig it up. Why did he risk an overland journey, alone, through war-torn territory? And he'd done it while weighted down with enough travel trunks to make a team of strapping field hands grumble.

What drove him to make the trip?

No, that wasn't the question to ask. The right question was this: What was in those trunks? Because whatever it was had stayed on Joyeuse Island when Bachelder left.

On his first trip, Jedediah Bachelder's letters had said that he'd buried a fabulous emerald necklace. Cally had said that he left behind several heavy trunks on his second trip. After that, he wouldn't shut up about "the green and the gold."

What if he wasn't talking about the necklace any more? And what if he knew he was no longer talking to Viola?

All those odd letters written in 1865 had been signed, "Loyally yours." These were not the words of a husband. They were the words of a citizen.

Faye reached for Bachelder's letters again. Perhaps all that financial advice to his wife was a code for something else—the disposition of a dying country's financial resources. Disguising these governmental documents as letters to a wife who had received oh-so-many such letters would allow the instructions in those documents to easily slip past censors and spies who had seen Jedediah's besotted love notes before. The letters would have raised no suspicions before they reached the Bachelders' home, where someone would have been waiting to pass them on to the proper officials. If Faye had to say who that messenger was, she would have put her money on Isaiah.

Faye imagined that officials working for a government in its last days would be scrambling to hide things from an invading army—things like battle plans and the identities of their spies…and things like money.

There were a thousand stories about the final hiding place of the Confederacy's hard currency, but none had ever proven true. Maybe Jedediah Bachelder was the man entrusted with the Confederate treasury. Or the "Confederate Gold," as true believers referred to the legendary treasure. Looking back through Jedediah's later letters, the ones signed "Loyally yours," with that notion in mind, Faye thought she saw a clear pattern.

In these letters to a woman who he knew was dead, Jedediah Bachelder had directed the dismantling of a national government.

The letters instructing Viola how to dispose of their family assets in order to gain much-needed cash were veiled instructions to other Confederate officials, laying out in detail how to convert Confederate bills into assets less vulnerable to inflation.

The letters discussing their will and specifying the executor and the beneficiaries were coded messages telling those officials who was to be put in charge of the disbursement of the Treasury funds.

And the letters detailing the hiding place of the green-and-the-gold were describing the location of that Treasury—the fabled Confederate Gold itself.

Money is green and bullion is gold. And gold is very heavy…

Before long, a formidable pile of text was growing on the work table in front of Faye. She had searched the rare book library catalog for "Confederate treasury," "Confederate Gold," and any other variant she could imagine, gathering stacks of books from the reference shelves. Then she had signed out books shelved in the stacks controlled by the charming Ms. Slater.

Ms. Slater did not seem pleased by the number of volumes she would be reshelving at the end of the day, but she fetched book after book from the stacks, anyway. She had to, Faye reflected spitefully. It was her job.

Some of the books spread in front of Faye were written by reputable scholars with thoughtful opinions on the fate of the Confederate treasury. Some of them were written by conspiracy theorists and general nutcases, but Faye figured that, just because a person—or a whole group of people, for that matter—is crazy, that didn't necessarily mean any of them were wrong.

She'd also found a book of regional folk tales, hoping that old wives had passed Jedediah Bachelder's story down through the generations. The most important question plaguing her was this: Was there anybody out there looking for the Confederate Gold who knew that Jedediah Bachelder might have hidden it? Even worse, was it possible for anyone seeking the treasure to infer that the Confederate treasury had been buried on Joyeuse Island?

Because that person—or person—could be extremely dangerous.

The clock was ticking, but Faye was coming up dry. The people writing the books she was reading seemed to have never heard of Jedediah Bachelder. She wondered whether people who *didn't* write books might know more than these prolific scholars. When she and Joe had been exploring the ruins of Bachelder's home, they'd seen Nita glance around the property and say, "I heard tell…", but the young woman had been interrupted.

What had Nita heard about Bachelder's property, or about Bachelder himself? Wayland had made at least one trip to the rare book library. Had he and Nita been on the trail of a man rumored to have hidden a fortune somewhere in the backwoods South?

Herbie had said something that stuck in her mind, too. When she'd asked him why he didn't let anybody dig on his property, he'd sneered at her, saying she wasn't much of an archaeologist if she didn't know the history that was right under her nose.

Amateur history buffs like Civil War re-enactors tended to gather their knowledge indiscriminately. Serious history texts, far-out Internet ravings, oral history, rumors, legends…they knew it all. Herbie and Wayland had both asked Captain Eubank about Jedediah Bachelder. Were either of them close to solving the mystery of where he hid all that gold? And would either of them have killed for it?

The hands of the library clock were pointing at closing time, and Faye had found exactly nothing. No evidence that anybody had ever associated Bachelder with the Confederate Gold. No rumors that the Confederate Gold had ever been buried anywhere near her island. No nothing.

She reached for a reference book that didn't qualify as rare, and thus didn't absolutely require her to wear cotton gloves while reading it. Those gloves had wicked every last gram of moisture out of her hands, and they were making her nuts. She peeled them off as furtively as if she were removing her bra in public.

It was a wonder Ms. Slater let them get away with no other protection than cotton gloves. She pictured herself wearing white paper booties over her shoes and a hair net and some kind of an apron to cover her clothes, which were nasty with the dust of the outside world.

An apron…

Faye's ungloved hand fell on a rare text, leaving destructive skin oils behind, but her mind was too occupied to notice. She had remembered a disappearing apron.

Chip always wore an apron over his clothes while he was working, to protect them from people's uneaten food. He'd been wearing one the night Wally died. Faye could still see him hauling dirty dishes into the kitchen and returning with a platter of raw hamburger patties. He had fixed a misshapen burger and wiped his hand on that apron. Faye was sure of it.

Where had that apron been just a few minutes later, when he was comforting his mother on the dock beside the boat where Faye sat, covered in Wally's blood? She remembered Liz's face, pressed against Chip's polo shirt. The red cotton had been blotched with her tears, right where the bib of his apron should have been.

He could simply have taken it off because it needed washing. But what if he had taken it off because it needed to be washed clean of Wally's blood?

Chip worked in a kitchen full of knives, and his work took him outdoors to the storage shed several times over the course of an evening. Could he have seen Wally and known that he couldn't be allowed to talk to Faye? Could Chip have grabbed a knife and caught up with Wally in the parking lot, stabbing him twice? The sheriff had said there might not have been much blood, not at first. The little bit of blood Wally lost at the time of the stabbings could well have been intercepted by an apron.

It would have been so easy for Chip to take off that apron and throw it in the washer with all the dishcloths and towels that a busy restaurant generates every day. Even if someone saw him before he was able to hide the apron, they might not have noticed a red blotch…not when Chip was regularly stained with raw meat and ketchup and spaghetti sauce. And it would have been easy to put the knife in the commercial-powered dishwasher, along with dozens of others, and let the scalding water blast away Wally's blood and its incriminating DNA.

Her suspicions of Herbie, Wayland, and Nita, fueled by the fact that she just flat didn't like them, had blinded her to the fact that they weren't the only history buffs in her neck of the woods. Chip had been a history major, and he'd lived for years right here on the campus where Bachelder's letters had rested unnoticed on a library shelf. His name hadn't been on the sign-in sheet with Wayland's, but that didn't mean he hadn't already learned all Bachelder had to teach him.

Chip could have read the letters months ago. If he was as smart as his proud mother said, he might well have realized that the hiding place of the Confederate Gold was waiting for him, on an island somewhere within just a few miles of his mother's bar.

No wonder he'd dropped out of school and moved back home. Liz had worried over the obvious reasons he might have done that—drugs, alcohol, gambling, a woman—but the real reason hadn't been obvious at all. Chip was a drop-out busboy because he had his eye on a notorious treasure.

Why would Chip kill Wally? And had he killed Douglass, too?

Faye remembered Wally's last words, spoken through pale blue lips.

He'd said he needed to tell her he was sorry for everything. Then he'd said, "Tried to stop…never meant to…"

Had he tried to stop Chip from beating Douglass to death? . Chip and Wally were both big men, so they could have been the intruders Emma described. Maybe Wally was dead because Chip couldn't trust him not to tell anyone he'd committed murder.

This was all unprovable speculation, but the sheriff needed to know. There was no way Faye was going to lay out her case against Chip when there was any chance someone might over-hear. She didn't trust the privacy of the ladies' room or the stair-well, and certainly not the parking garage. She didn't feel safe out in the open, now that she had accepted the fact that someone had cut her brake lines and tried to kill her. She needed to get to the nearest utterly private place she knew—Joe's car.

She had just risen to go find Joe when he came into sight, asking, "What's taking you so long? This place is supposed to be closed by now."

"Joe," she whispered in a library-friendly voice. "We need to go."

He appeared at her elbow. "Like I said. It's about that time. Past it, actually."

She checked her watch. He was right. Ms. Slater was slipping. She had let Faye stay and work for fifteen extra minutes, and that quarter-hour had proven very enlightening indeed.

Ms. Slater was nowhere in sight when they left the rare book room, which was a relief. Faye had no patience for dealing with an unfriendly face, not when she was still chewing on the details of her theory.

The thought of Chip as a mastermind in the burglary of Douglass' home didn't mesh with her impression of him. The bur-glary had required significant planning and coordination. Somebody had to see the newspaper article, recognize Jedediah Bachelder's name on the silver flask, and concoct a plan to steal from Douglass any information he possessed about where it was found.

In Faye's mind, Chip was genial and pleasant, but not a take-charge kind of guy. Even his doting mother had said he tended to follow the crowd. So who else could be involved? Surely all the history buffs in Micco County couldn't be enmeshed in this web—Nita, Wayland, Herbie, and their treasure-hunting friends.

But Chip had another friend. Liz had told Faye all about her, even though she'd never actually seen her. Even better, he'd been seen with that friend on the campus of the university where Bachelder's letters were stored…and where someone had tried to scare Faye away. Or kill her.

*The woman was a little skinny and plain, compared to how good-looking Chip is. But she walked like somebody who knew where she was going.*

Who was that woman? Nita was skinny, for certain, but Faye wouldn't have called her plain. And her demeanor was languid but furtive. Nita didn't move like somebody who knew where she was going.

Faye pushed the elevator button and willed the car to rise faster, because she'd just figured out where Chip was. Could it be any coincidence that he and his shorts and underwear had disappeared just as soon as the sheriff talked her and Joe into leaving Joyeuse? The treasure was on Joyeuse Island, and she and Joe had abandoned it. Of course, Chip would take the opportunity to do some serious exploring…looking for gold that probably wasn't even there.

Nobody but Faye had read Cally's story of Bachelder's return to Joyeuse after the war. Faye would bet money that he'd taken the gold and paper money away with him then, not to mention a certain emerald necklace. The odds were excellent that her emerald was the only one left, lost when the necklace broke apart during its retrieval.

There was a posse of treasure hunters out there, some of whom might be killers, looking for a long-gone cache. If Faye was right about Chip's whereabouts, Douglass' murderer might be planning to sleep in her bed that very night. Faye slapped at the elevator button again.

Joe tapped on her elbow. She realized that this was at least the second time he'd done that, but her mind had been far away.

"I took the book for you."

"You did what? Which book? Not Bachelder's letters?"

Joe nodded proudly. "I watched the library lady put the book back on the shelf, then I swiped it when she wasn't looking. Stuck it under my shirt in the back. I figure it'll be a while before someone wants it. It's not like we're talking about George Washington's diary or anything. We take it home. You read it.

Take it to the copy shop, if you want to. Then I'll bring it back in a day or two. That librarian will never know."

Faye didn't know which was worse for an antique book—being exposed to the intense light of a photocopier or to the skin oils of Joe's intensely muscled back.

"Joe—what possessed you to do that? We've got to take it back before we're both expelled."

Trying not to think about things like signatures on sign-in sheets or security cameras, she grabbed Joe by the arm and hurried him—and the irreplaceable manuscript stuck into the waistband of his pants—down the corridor. When they reached the glass entry door, she tugged hard on the handle. Nothing. It must have locked automatically behind them, or Ms. Slater had been lurking close by so that she could lock it as soon as they left.

Now she was in possession of the book that had pointed Chip in the direction of treasure, then in the direction of murder. How many times had he visited this collection while he read and absorbed everything Jedediah Bachelder had to tell him? Ms. Slater must have gotten good and tired of pulling that book off the shelf for him, then worrying over whether he was handling it properly.

Faye turned away from the rare book room entrance and took an uncertain step toward the elevator bay, as the facts about the person controlling Chip fell into place. There was at least one other person who was as passionate about history as Herbie and Chip and all their friends. She had free access to Bachelder's letters and to shelves full of documentation on the Confederate treasury. She was thin and plain, and she always looked like someone who knew where she was going. She knew that Faye had spent the entire afternoon researching the Confederate Gold…and she had let her stay in the rare book room so far after closing time that there was no chance that any witnesses were still hanging around within earshot.

Faye let go of Joe's arm and slapped both hands flat on his back, pushing him toward the fire escape. "We've got to get out of here. We can't wait for the elevator. There's no time."

At that moment, the elevator doors opened to reveal an empty car, and the fire escape door opened, too.

A hand thrust a gun through the door, and Ms. Slater, looking cool and in charge, stepped through. "Ms. Longchamp. Would you like to take me on a little boat ride? I'm very anxious to see your island and all the lovely things that Jedediah Bachelder left behind."

# Chapter Twenty-four

Joe had driven the fifty miles from Tallahassee to this spot with great aplomb, considering that Ms. Slater had been holding a gun muzzle plastered to Faye's head. They stood on a secluded, muddy beach, watching Chip pilot a boat toward them, coming from the general direction of Joyeuse Island. As a final insult, he had brought Joe's own john boat to fetch them—the same boat he stole so that he'd have a way to get out to Joyeuse and dig for treasure. The flat bottom of the battered boat let him pull in so close that the shallow water hardly lapped against Faye's knees as she stepped over the gunwale.

She was momentarily seduced by the idea of using her weight to overturn the boat, gaining the upper hand against their captors. Johnboats were, on the whole, pretty stable, but Faye had been puttering around in boats all her life. She could probably have pulled it off, if Ms. Slater hadn't shifted the gun barrel to Joe's temple while Faye boarded the boat.

The poker-faced librarian had hardly spoken since she forced them into her car and handed Joe the keys. A boat ride over water as clear as diamonds did nothing to loosen her tongue, and the noise of the motor would have made conversation hard, anyway. Faye used the time to puzzle out what, precisely, Ms. Slater and Chip had done.

Even more importantly, she spent the time trying to figure out just what her captors did and didn't know. She had no doubt that the two of them were capable of teasing all of Bachelder's secrets out of the letters he left behind, but nobody had read Cally's reminiscences but Faye. There had to be some way of exploiting that one slight advantage.

Knowledge often translated into power. Not always—sometimes brute force translated into even more power—but knowledge and brains shifted life's balance often enough for a scholarly woman like Faye to put a lot of stock in the notion. Too bad her adversary was also a scholarly woman.

If that scholarly woman had only had access to Cally's oral history, she would have known that, though the Confederate Gold had indeed once been on Joyeuse Island, it was long-gone. If she'd known the truth, there would have been no reason to ask Chip to sabotage Faye's brakes when her research came too near the treasure's hiding place. There would have been no need for Wally and Douglass to die. And there would have been no sense in kidnapping Faye and Joe today, hoping to coerce them into showing her the place where X marked the spot.

There could be no reason to keep them alive now, treasure or no. Kidnapping charges would only be the beginning of Ms. Slater's woes, if Joe or Faye survived long enough to tell Sheriff Mike what they knew. There would be attempted murder charges for the sabotage of Faye's car. And all that paled beside the specter of murder charges for the deaths of Wally and Douglass.

There was no treasure, but that didn't mean Faye and Joe wouldn't die today. They were going to die for nothing, and she'd never even told Joe that she loved him.

Ms. Slater twitched the gun barrel in such a way that no one could mistake her intent. She wanted them out of the boat and onto the dock—Faye's very own dock on her very own island. If she survived this debacle, Faye planned to sanitize that dock. There had never been anything more noxious than fish entrails on it before. Chip was a murderer, so he was noxious for sure. Even if he'd killed on his own initiative, without prior instructions from Ms. Slater, the fact that the woman had continued to work with him afterward meant that she, too, was more disgusting than a harmless little pile of fish innards.

When Ms. Slater finally spoke, it was simply to nod in Joe's direction and say, "I'm glad you showed up. I was afraid Ms. Longchamp was just too puny to do the digging I need done."

"Until this afternoon, I wouldn't have had a clue what you're talking about," Faye said, wondering just how much she could get the woman to tell her. "I mean, even *you* could dig up a little tiny necklace."

Joe looked at her sideways, and she realized that she'd never had a chance to tell him that they were dealing with a treasure bigger than they'd ever dreamed. She also realized that he was, at that very moment, calculating how quickly he could get to Ms. Slater and snatch her gun, versus the amount of time it would take her to pull the trigger. Faye was not willing to risk Joe's life on those odds, but she wagered that he was. She caught his eye and gave a barely perceptible shake of her head.

*Don't do it, Joe.*

He looked away.

The best way she could help Joe, if he decided to take that suicidal chance, was to distract their captor. She fixed a confrontational gaze on Ms. Slater, in the hope that ancient instincts would cause the woman to focus on her threatening expression, instead of the powerful man preparing to launch himself in her direction. "You think Jedediah Bachelder hid the gold and cash from the Confederate treasury here on Joyeuse Island. You think it's still here. You're certain of it, certain enough to kill for all that money."

"I'm just glad you stopped digging before you got to it." Ms. Slater turned to Chip and said just one word. "Tape."

Chip pulled a roll of duct tape from the bottom of the boat and grabbed one of Joe's feet, knocking him onto his butt. Faye was reminded that Joe wasn't the only big man on this island.

As Chip bound Joe's ankles and wrists, Faye began to appreciate how coolly logical the librarian's mind truly was. While she'd waited for Faye and Joe to walk out of her library, she'd called Chip and told him to meet her. Faye imagined that Chip had been the one to suggest the pickup point, since he'd probably run around this part of the gulf in little boats most of his life, the way other boys lived their preteen years on bikes. He would have known plenty of good places to land a boat where they wouldn't be seen.

Ms. Slater's cold-blooded and logical mind had also foreseen the need to confine Joe, so she'd made sure Chip had duct tape. She'd also thought through the ramifications thoroughly enough to know that Joe would need his legs unrestrained when he got in and out of the boat. The first opportunity to bind him would have been when they reached dry land, which would be…right now. The woman took no chances, a trait which did not improve the odds that Faye and Joe would survive this encounter.

Ms. Slater put the gun against Joe's temple and supervised Chip's work. She had him use the tape to fashion makeshift shackles that allowed enough movement for walking but would hobble any attempt to run. Faye damned her attention to detail.

As soon as Chip was finished, Faye immediately saw the need to continue distracting their adversaries. She could see slight movement as Joe clenched and unclenched the muscles in his forearms, and she imagined that his mighty leg muscles were doing the same. He was trying to loosen the tape. It seemed to be a futile effort—Chip had pulled it brutally tight, except for the lengths of slack tape that allowed Joe to move his hands and legs—but Joe deserved a chance to try.

"Why do you need us, anyway? You're the librarian. You're the one with all the answers. You've had access to Bachelder's letters for a long time. You've had plenty of time to study my notes. You probably have a better idea of where the necklace is buried than I do."

Ms. Slater didn't speak—which wasn't necessary, since the gun was speaking for her—but she also didn't move. Was she reveling in the sheer power of her life-and-death hold over two human beings? Faye would have suspected as much from most people, but Elizabeth Slater wasn't into power. If she had been, she'd have chosen some career other than library science.

Well, that wasn't quite accurate. Like Faye, she knew that knowledge was a powerful thing, but it wasn't the kind of power that required the use of deadly force.

What motivated a woman like Elizabeth Slater? What desires had driven her to this point?

Faye would wager that the woman's first motive had been curiosity. Reference librarians did what they did because they *just had to know*. She had no doubt that the first step in Ms. Slater's slide toward murder had been an insatiable curiosity about how people lived in the past. Bachelder's letters would have sung a siren song to the librarian, just as they had sung to Faye. The two women weren't so different. Faye was simply not willing to do the things that Ms. Slater had done to ferret out the past's secrets.

The librarian's second motive was simple and obvious—greed. Gold, cash, and emeralds had all triggered many murders in the past, and they might spur two more today.

Subtle body language told Faye that love might have played its own part in this drama. A softness in the woman's eyes, a slight inclination of her head in Chip's direction, a change in her tone when she spoke to him...all these things suggested that she might have been drawn into this treasure hunt by a simple desire to be near the handsome young man who'd called her attention to the book of romantic letters.

These thoughts flashed through Faye's mind in seconds, causing her to pause only a few heartbeats to look inward. Still, those heartbeats had been too long. Ms. Slater had stood there, gun aimed, and waited for Faye to think. Why hadn't she forced Faye to move toward the goal? A woman with an obsession for treasure did not wait patiently for people to think. Why was Ms. Slater hesitating?

It was because she didn't have a clue where Bachelder had buried the Confederate Gold.

Elizabeth Slater was waiting for Faye to lead the way. But she should have known the exact spot. What information was the woman missing?

"You don't know where it is." Faye almost laughed when she said it. "Why don't you know? You've had the field notebooks for more than a week, and they document the exact spot where I dug up the hip flask. That's what led you to me...and to Douglass. Right? When you read in the newspaper about an artifact linked to Bachelder that was dug up on an island near here, you knew he probably buried it with the necklace and for the same reason. It was made of a precious metal that would be worth something when the Confederacy's economy collapsed, even if his paper money wasn't. Any reference librarian worth her salt would have known that. And she would surely have figured out where he buried it by now."

Ms. Slater was still silent.

"You had Chip cut my brake lines. Why would you try to kill me if I'm the only one who can find the treasure for you? That doesn't make a bit of sense."

"I thought you were expendable. I was wrong."

Reality dawned. Faye would have laughed if the situation hadn't been so dire. "You don't have all the notebooks. I pulled one notebook out of the box and took it with me when I left Douglass that night. I took the one I was using when I found..."

She stopped. Ms. Slater had no way to know that she'd found the emerald. She was simply hoping Faye would lead her to the necklace and the Confederate Gold, based on the discovery of Bachelder's hip flask.

"I thought it didn't matter. I thought you could find the gold, even without that notebook, but you're missing the critical information. Yes, you have the notebook where I documented the hip flask, and it should have taken you to the treasure. But I found it before the hurricane took out the tree I used as a reference point and changed the shape of the whole island. You sent Nita and Wayland here to do your digging, but they couldn't find the spot because the landmarks were gone."

Ms. Slater twitched the gun toward the shovel in the bottom of her boat. Faye picked it up and kept talking, "You were going to kill me, so that you and your flunky would be the only people who knew the treasure was here. Aren't you glad you didn't manage it? Loser."

Ms. Slater foot lashed out and kicked Faye in the butt, forcing her to take a step forward. "Walk, or I shoot your handsome friend."

Faye stole a glance at Joe, who was still unobtrusively stretching his bonds. She took a single step, then started talking again. "Wally. Why is Wally dead?"

"It's Wally's fault you're here right now. He was supposed to help Chip get all the information he could about where you found that hip flask. Then Mr. Everett surprised them by being home that night and Wally got all prissy about getting rid of him. Fortunately, Chip understood the importance of keeping the old man quiet."

"It seems that even Wally had more morals than you. That puts you pretty low on the ethical totem pole."

Ms. Slater didn't bat an eye at Faye's comment. She just went on defaming the dead. "Wally was gung-ho about this project when it was all about money. He'd been laying low since the hurricane, but Chip's mother has a soft spot for Wally. She and Chip have always known where he was. And Chip knew that Wally had been pothunting these islands for years. If there's a place to bury something around here, Wally knew about it. Chip asked Wally to help us find the necklace, and he was happy to do it, until you and Douglass got in the way."

Faye's eyes watered. So Wally had learned something since she saw him last. He'd been perfectly willing to double-cross her back then, maybe even send her to jail, for a chance at big bucks. If he'd clashed with Chip over Douglass' killing, then he'd clearly grown a conscience in his old age. And it had cost him his life.

"Wally was going to tell you everything," Ms. Slater continued. She was clearly angry with Wally, even now, and it was making her chatty. This was good. While she was chatting, she wasn't shooting. "He was afraid you'd get hurt like Douglass did. He should have known that Chip would never let him warn you, but he tried anyway. Look where it got him."

Faye's tears burned. Wally had known he was risking his life by trying to warn her, but he did it anyway. He'd died before he could tell her anything, but he'd managed to pass enough information to lead her to Bachelder's letters...and to his own killer. His sacrifice more than made up for his earlier betrayal. There weren't many people in the world to weep for Wally, but he had earned Faye's grief.

Ms. Slater didn't share her sorrow. "Without that scum Wally, you'd be nothing to me but some initials on a field notebook. Without him, you wouldn't have come snooping in my library."

"You'd have gone looking for the archaeologist who wrote those field notes sooner or later. Because you don't know where the treasure is. And I'm going to die today. Why should I tell you?"

"Because you're hoping I won't kill you. Maybe I'll try to buy you off with part of the treasure. And maybe you'll let me do that, if I promise not to kill him." She reached out a hand and shoved Joe, hard. With his feet hobbled, he couldn't stop himself from toppling. It broke Faye's heart to watch him fall, but then she noticed something. Sprawled as he was, with his hands and feet under him, he was freer to struggle with his bonds. And his position put Ms. Slater a slight disadvantage.

With Joe on the ground and Faye standing up, the librarian couldn't keep them both in a single field of vision. To look from one prisoner to another, she had to shift her eyes slightly. It wasn't much, but it was something. Faye stuck out a foot to the right and shifted her weight in that direction, widening the gap between her and Joe. Making it harder for Ms. Slater to look at Joe made it slightly easier for him to work at freeing himself.

"No, I don't have the magic field notebook that tells me the key to your sampling plan. So I don't know the exact spot you found Bachelder's flask. But I've finally got something better than a bunch of field notes that maybe, just maybe, will point me to the spot where you dug up that flask. I've got you. Start digging."

Faye reflected that Ms. Slater must think she was a supernaturally good archaeologist, if she expected her to walk straight to an excavation she'd dug and backfilled years ago. She had only a general idea of where it was, but it was certainly near the spot where she'd found the emerald a few days before. No way was she going to dig there and risk giving Ms. Slater what she wanted. Not while Joe continued to unobtrusively stretch his bonds.

An inspired idea struck her. She would lead Chip and Ms. Slater to the messy pit that Nita and Wayland had left behind. It was near enough to the true location to be realistic, and someone had obviously been excavating there. Her captor was surely smart enough to know the general vicinity of Bachelder's treasure, so it was important that the decoy spot be plausible. Otherwise, Faye would have taken this expedition to a spot right on the waterfront and hoped that a passing fisherman would notice her distress.

Joe followed along, but his hobbles caused him to lag behind. Faye could see him taking slow strides, but long ones. He was stretching that tape with every step. If she could just give him a chance to break free, they could...what? She knew she didn't want Joe to rush a murderous woman with a gun. Still, if he could break those bonds, the two of them would be that much freer to exploit an opportunity for escape. She quickened her pace, trying to force Ms. Slater to divide her attention between two captives who stood slightly farther apart with every step.

Chip was another factor to consider. He was no idiot—Liz had been right when she bragged on her boy's smarts. He was steering a path slightly further away from Faye and Joe than necessary, and to their right. Faye could tell he was trying to position himself to keep them both within eyeshot at the same time. At least his hands were empty of weapons. Still, he was nearly a match for Joe in size, and he'd been proven capable of murderous violence. Chip bore watching.

Standing on the lip of the muddy hole Nita and Wayland had left behind, Faye took the shovel Ms. Slater had forced her to carry and carved a bite of dirt from the bottom of the hole. The rhythmic digging tranquilized her, as it always did, and it focused her thoughts. If she could just get her enemy to stand beside her and look down, the woman's balance would be thrown ever so slightly forward, and her focus would shift away from her gun. Faye's notion of what she would do at that point was fuzzy, but it might be her only chance to do anything at all.

It was clear that she'd have to find a way to neutralize the gun. Joe would be stretched to his limit by taking on Chip, one-on-one, especially if his hands and feet were still severely constrained. Joe was big, strong and fit, so he might be able to pull it off. Unfortunately, Chip was also big, strong, and fit, and he was several years younger than Joe. Was there a significant difference in physical prowess between a man who was twenty-two and another who was twenty-nine? She didn't know. Probably not, but this situation was critical enough that having even a small edge might give their captors the ability to take their lives.

She sneaked a look over her shoulder at Joe, without having any hope that he'd already worked himself free. He opened his hand a millimeter to give her a look at the piece of flint that it held, and she let a little hope take hold. Ms. Slater might have been trying to humiliate Joe when she shoved him to the ground, but she had accomplished something else. When his hands were trapped under him, his body had shielded them from view. He'd used that chance to work open the leather pouch that always hung at his waist…and that pouch was always brim-full of deadly weapons.

She was dead-certain that Joe had already used the blade in his hand to slice through the tape binding his hands. Nothing could be done about his feet without alerting Chip and Ms. Slater, but a fair fight between Joe and Chip might now be possible. Chip would have the use of his feet, but Joe had a weapon that could slice Chip right open, and he knew precisely how to use it. Faye just needed to give him the opportunity.

She raised the shovel higher than strictly necessary and paused, taking aim at a target that just might save them.

"Would you get on with it?" Ms. Slater barked. "I know you dig faster than this when you're on the clock."

Faye thrust the shovel down hard into a tree root, and she got what she wanted--the clacking sound of metal on wood. Peering down, she asked, "Is that a wooden box?"

Ms. Slater, hearing what she had expected to hear, stooped forward slightly for a look at her hoped-for treasure chest. There was no doubt that Joe would see this opportunity and realize that Faye was about to take it.

Afterward, Faye was amazed how clearly she could recall the next seconds. She could visualize the sudden and unexpected reactions of three other people with so much detail that her memories felt like movies, shot from above. It was as if she could look down and see how all four of them were reacting to unforeseen events—Ms. Slater, Joe, Chip, and even herself.

Their actions intertwined like a demented minuet. Faye and Ms. Slater, facing each other, bowed to peer into the pit. Joe leapt in Chip's direction. The younger man's arm rose gracefully in front of him to shoulder height.

And then all hell erupted.

That brief glance between Faye and Joe had communicated everything they needed to coordinate their assault. Faye would distract Ms. Slater, then attack, hoping to get control of the gun. In the hubbub, Joe would take on Chip.

The flaw in this plan was to presume that when Joe charged Chip, the younger man would defend himself.

# Chapter Twenty-five

When Faye remembered those moments…when she could no longer avoid remembering those moments…she saw Ms. Slater lean forward slightly over the hole to see what Faye had found, and she saw herself yank the shovel out handle-first, aiming for the librarian's throat. Perhaps things would have gone differently if she'd only connected with that throat. Instead, the handle poked hard in Ms. Slater's upper chest—hard enough to knock her on the ground, but not nearly hard enough to eliminate the woman as a danger.

Joe, in a single motion, had lifted himself from the ground and charged Chip. He needed to cover a fair distance to reach Chip, which cost him the element of surprise, but he still might have been able to pull it off through sheer athletic prowess. The odds should have been at least even—one well-muscled man beating the hell out of another well-muscled man—but neither Faye nor Joe had even considered that Chip might be armed. He just didn't seem subtle enough to have let the tiny little handgun in his pocket remain a secret until needed.

He'd always given the impression of being a gregarious and affable young man—intelligent, maybe, but not terribly shrewd. Today, Faye had learned that he had a serious violent streak. And, at this terrible moment, she'd been reminded of what Liz had been telling her for years. The boy was smart.

Joe should have been dead in an instant, launching himself at nearly point-blank range toward a man with a gun, but that instant passed, because Chip had another target in mind. His arm swung to the left, so that he could take aim on Faye, and Joe saw it happen.

Why had Chip done that? Why would he have wanted to shoot her, rather than taking out the more immediate threat?

Faye now saw the answer as clearly as she saw the intricate moves of their desperate dance. Chip hadn't committed all his grievous sins out of a lust for treasure, though the promise of treasure was what had brought him to the rare book room in the first place. Chip had done burglary and kidnapping, and he'd done murder twice, because he loved the woman that Faye was trying to beat into unconsciousness.

Chip had seen that he only had time for a single shot before Joe was on him, and he had chosen to use it on Faye, because she was trying to hurt the woman he loved.

How could Chip have possibly known that Joe would make the same choice?

Joe had passed up the opportunity to rush Chip while the gun was pointed elsewhere, because he couldn't take the chance that he'd be too late to stop a bullet from hitting Faye. Instead, he had called Faye's name in an effort to warn her, prompting her to take the dangerous risk of turning away from a woman with a gun. This meant that she saw it happen. She would never forget that she saw it happen.

Joe had twisted around to call out to her and, at the same time, he had launched himself sideways, putting himself between Faye and a loaded gun. He was quick—Joe had always been quick—so he was in the air, acting as a human shield, when Chip pulled the trigger. The bullet hit him dead-center in the middle of his back.

At this point, it no longer mattered to Faye that there were two loaded firearms pointed in her direction. Her shovel had hit the ground as she fled to Joe's side.

She'd screamed, "There's no treasure! It's not here. It hasn't been here in a long, long time!" then she'd leaned down and put a trembling hand on the side of Joe's throat, looking for a pulse.

Dropping to the dirt beside him, she'd dropped her wet face into her hands and shrieked, "You've killed him. You killed him for nothing, because Bachelder took everything away, the first chance he got. Why would you think he didn't? Greed, that's why. You wanted that gold and those emeralds so bad, it never occurred to you that it made no sense for them to be here."

Her sobbing had echoed across Joyeuse Island as she sat, rocking back and forth, waiting for a bullet or two to come and take her out of her misery.

The bullet came. She couldn't tell where it struck her. She just sensed the physical shock of a tremendous collision, followed by pain radiating through the entire upper left quadrant of her torso. She couldn't keep her body upright any more, so she let herself drop down beside Joe.

She had a clear sense that consciousness was ebbing, and an equally clear sense that she had control over that. She could succumb to shock, and let the fear and rage and anger go. She could die in peace. Or she could try to live.

She decided in favor of living, because Joe needed her. He needed her bad.

She had lied about the weak, thready pulse she'd felt in the hollow beneath his jaw. If fortune smiled, then Chip would believe her, and he would fail to walk over and put a bullet through Joe's head.

It was possible. He had failed to make sure Douglass was dead after he'd beaten the life out of him—after he'd beaten almost all the life out of him. And he'd walked away from Wally without taking the time to be certain he was dead. In both cases, he'd been right in the end. He had indeed inflicted injuries that were fatal. But for whatever reason—squeamishness, denial, or the simple need to get away before he was caught—Chip had walked away without making sure his victims were really gone.

It was possible that her lie had convinced him that he had no need to finish Joe off. Now she needed to convince him that one bullet had been enough to kill Faye, too.

Maybe it had. A bullet in the upper left part of her body might have passed through her heart or her lungs or any one of the huge vessels transporting blood to and from those organs. She didn't know how badly she was hurt, but she had fallen with her chin tucked down toward her chest, and she didn't see blood spurting with every heartbeat. That was the most hopeful thing she could think of at the moment. If she lay still and tried to look like someone who'd been shot through the heart, maybe Chip would go away so she could save Joe—though how she might manage that was anybody's guess.

"You're insane!" Faye heard Ms. Slater scramble to her feet. "Why do you keep killing people? I never said to kill anybody. Now…God. I don't know whether it's safe to go home. I don't know whether there are witnesses out there who saw us with these people. I can't…"

"But we were going to go away together. It doesn't matter whether anybody thinks we killed them."

"Idiot. We were going to go away with the treasure. With Bachelder's necklace and the Confederate gold, we could have gone anywhere. Now…I don't have enough money to get us out of the country. Do you?" She continued to back away from him.

"None of that matters. Not if we're together. Elizabeth…"

Faye had tried to keep both eyes half-open. She imagined that a hooded, blank gaze would make her look good and dead. Also, it gave her just a tiny sliver of vision. She couldn't see much, but she sensed that her adversaries were distracted. She needed to find a way to exploit that.

Chip took a step, as if to follow Ms. Slater. Then Faye saw her do what Chip had done…and what Faye had done, and what Joe had done. She acted instinctively to save the person closest to her heart.

Herself.

The gun rose from her side. She aimed it squarely at her young lover's heart. "Don't take another step. I'm getting out of here, and you're not. I can make the police believe that you kidnapped me from the library when you snatched these two. I can make them believe you killed the other two men, because you did. I am not going to lose everything because of you."

She scuttled backward and disappeared down the path that led to the dock…and to Joe's john boat, the vessel that held Joe's only hope for life. Faye had been doing a mental inventory of her fleet of watercraft, and it told her that the *Gopher* was at Liz's marina and her skiff was at Emma's house. If she was going to get Joe to shore, she needed that john boat. Even worse, Chip had taken both their cell phones, and they were on that boat. If it sped toward shore without her, she'd have no way to call for help.

Faye watched Ms. Slater retreat until she was out of sight then waited until Chip disappeared, too, in hot pursuit. Then Faye tottered to her feet, pausing just long enough to say, "I'm coming back to you, Joe. And I'll bring help."

Chip and his faithless lover had a head start on her, and they weren't losing blood with every step, but Faye had a single advantage. She was on her home turf.

The path back to the dock wasn't hard to follow. Ms. Slater and Chip would have no trouble getting back to the boat, so Faye couldn't hope to gain any time because they'd gotten lost. There was an even more serious obstacle to Faye's hopes of stopping them. She needed to get to the house before she went to the dock, if she had any hope of keeping that lifesaving john boat from leaving the island.

There was another path that led to the house, and it was an easy walk from there to the dock—fewer roots to trip over than Chip and Elizabeth Slater would encounter, and fewer holes to break an ankle in, too. Faye was grateful for that advantage, but it hardly outweighed her severe disadvantages. She was badly wounded, and she needed to spend a few critical seconds in the house. She forced herself to move, and she found that she could still run.

It was an odd sensation, moving so quickly, when she sensed that each step might sap the last ergs of energy from her battered body. These next few minutes would be all-or-nothing. She would move at top speed, or she would fall down and never get back up. She plunged down the narrow path, wondering what she would do if she arrived too late.

When she burst from the wooded path into the peaceful clearing that surrounded her home, Faye searched for the welcome feeling of homecoming that this place always brought her, but it was gone. And it would always be gone if she lost Joe.

She stumbled into the house, energy ebbing, and bypassed her own room. The thing she needed—the thing she had to have—was hiding in Joe's room. She prayed that it would be easy to find.

◇◇◇

It wasn't in the drawer in Joe's bedside table. It wasn't in the cedar chest at the foot of his bed where he stored his clothes and his moccasins and the leather he used to make them. It wasn't behind the perforated tin door that kept the dried berries and meat stored in his pie safe well-ventilated. Where would Joe have hidden the handgun that Liz gave him?

*Please tell me that you didn't trash it.* Faye had never realized that she talked constantly to Joe, even when he wasn't there. *I know you don't trust guns and you think they smell funny, but you wouldn't have dumped something that cost Liz a lot of money. Where did you put it?*

If she were Joe, she could have smelled it. She could have sensed its presence disturbing the peace of the room. But she wasn't Joe.

Where would he put something with an odor that disturbed him?

A breeze wafted into the room and brought an idea to Faye. Joe's window was fitted with a double set of shutters. Outside, the shutters were crafted of solid wood to shield the window from the onslaught of hurricanes. These shutters were folded back to expose almost all of the window opening. Inside the room, the window was fitted with louvered shutters that let in air, but kept the room cool by filtering the sunlight. These shutters were closed.

Faye rushed to the window and folded back the louvered shutters. There, on a windowsill made broad by the house's thick masonry walls, rested Liz's weapon, tucked out of sight behind the folded-back outer shutters. Faye prayed that she wouldn't be required to use it on Liz's son.

Faye was too late. And Chip was too late, too.

As she stumbled from the house to the dock, trusting her body to find reserves of strength that probably didn't exist, she heard the john boat's motor start. At that moment, Chip burst out of the woods. When he saw Ms. Slater backing the boat away from the dock, he kept sprinting straight into the water, his gun still in his hand. It was as if he thought he could run right across the Gulf of Mexico, if that's what he had to do to reach the woman he loved.

He could have reached her, and they could have escaped together. The boat had hardly traveled ten feet from the dock. He could have plunged through the water and lifted himself over the gunwale before the boat picked up enough speed to leave him in its wake. Unfortunately for Chip, Elizabeth Slater had already decided that her chances of escape were better without him. And she had already shown that her own safety far outweighed any concern for Chip's wellbeing, and probably anyone else's.

The handgun was off her lap in an instant. Her hand was steady as she raised it and aimed. Despite everything he had done, Faye felt a sharp stab of pity for the man as he watched the woman he loved fire a bullet into his forehead.

Chip disappeared beneath the water and Ms. Slater laid the gun back in her lap so that she could maneuver the boat away from the dock, away from Joyeuse Island, and away from the victims of her venality. At that moment, Faye knew that Joe couldn't be saved, not even if she ran clear across the Gulf of Mexico. Without that boat, and without the cell phones it carried, there was no way to get help to him in time.

She stood there with a gun in her hand and wished Elizabeth Slater dead. Of its own volition, her hand rose in front of her, taking aim with Liz's handgun. She found herself quite willing to shoot another human being because, second by second, that human being was killing the love of her life. If she squeezed the trigger right now, before the john boat was throttled up to full speed and pointed at the mainland, there was a glimmer of a chance that she could swim out to it and go fetch Joe a doctor.

Elizabeth Slater saw her take aim and raised her own handgun, taking aim. Faye was glad. If she succeeded in killing Ms. Slater before the woman got her weapon steadied enough to fire it, fine. If she didn't then maybe the woman would kill Faye, and this nightmare would be over.

Faye pulled the trigger.

The bullet didn't tear into Ms. Slater's head or her chest or her belly. It did something worse than that. It hit the john boat's gas tank.

The explosion was deafening.

The water rippled with the concussion, then its surface was dimpled by bits of boat and motor, as they dropped out of the air. If any large chunks of boat still existed, Faye presumed they had gone to the bottom of the channel. She presumed that Ms. Slater had gone there, too.

Decency demanded that she try to retrieve a woman who was drowning, if she wasn't already dead, but Faye was still leaving a trail of her own blood everywhere she went. The shock of seeing the boat explode had dropped her sprawling into the sand, and she wasn't sure she would ever stand again. The boat that had been Joe's only lifeline was gone, and she needed a doctor pretty bad herself. Faye decided to let Elizabeth Slater stay where she was.

If she only had a radio…but that would have meant having one of the boats, in which case she would have a cell phone, obviating the need for a radio, so her futile wishes were circular. If she had one floating boat or one working cell phone or one functional radio, then she and Joe might live. Since her boats and radios were together—and since they weren't here—her only other chance was a cell phone, and they were all at the bottom of the channel with Ms. Slater and Chip.

Joe's survival, Faye's survival—everything depended on getting help fast, but there was no way to do it. Faye would have traded anything on earth for a cell phone. Even Joyeuse.

There had been a time when she couldn't afford a cell phone. Before that, there had been a time when cell phones didn't even exist. Cally had made do with an occasional mail boat, but she had lived in a time when a wound like Joe's would have been mortal, unquestionably. Faye's grandmother had used a radio to talk to shore when she visited the island, and so had Faye, back when she couldn't afford to keep a phone in her pocket.

She'd been so poor that she'd cleaned layers of grime off the connections on her grandmother's old radio and kept it functional through sheer willpower and a soldering iron. Did she still have it?

Of course, she still had it. Faye was not one to get rid of something that still worked. But did it work? She remembered disassembling it, hoping to cannibalize some parts so that she could avoid spending money to fix one of her boat radios...but that salvage effort had failed. Her grandmother's radio was just too old to have any parts that were useable in a modern set. Sort of modern. Faye didn't buy many things new.

But could she get it functional? Oh, yes, indeed, she could. If she had access to a screwdriver and a soldering iron—and she did—Faye knew she could fix damn near anything.

# Chapter Twenty-six

A cracked collarbone and extensive soft tissue injuries can hurt like hell, but they don't do much to keep a patient in the hospital. Faye received nothing more than a battery of x-rays and CAT scans and MRIs that proved she wasn't at death's door. Then she was handed some tape to stabilize the shoulder, a sling, and some woefully inadequate painkillers, and she was told to go home. This was the only time in her life that she ever expected to *want* to stay in the hospital, but nobody asked her opinion.

Ms. Slater and Chip had been fished off the bottom of the Gulf of Mexico, and Faye reckoned they'd both been buried by now. She hadn't asked. She didn't have a clue what she would say when she next laid eyes on Liz.

Under questioning, Herbie had told the sheriff that, months before, his re-enactor friends had told him of old rumors that the Confederate treasury had been hidden somewhere nearby, and that a man named Jedediah Bachelder was said to have known what happened to it. When pressed, Herbie said that he was certain that Chip had been part of those conversations. Shortly after that, Chip had quit school and moved in with his mother, probably so he could be closer to the loot's reputed hiding place. And busboys have a lot more free time to go treasure-hunting than serious students do.

Having spent his childhood listening to his mother tell people how smart he was, Chip would have been certain that he was plenty smart enough to find a treasure that had eluded the world for nearly 150 years. More scholarly than the jocular but aimless re-enactors, he wouldn't have been willing to rely on rumors. It only made sense that he would have gone to a reference librarian known to specialize in local Civil War history—someone like Elizabeth Slater. In the rare book room, he'd found the trail of the Confederate Gold, and he'd found love. As it turned out, he'd also found death.

Either he or Ms. Slater would have seen the newspaper article describing Jedediah Bachelder's hip flask, and either would have known that it might be a critical piece of the puzzle. Ms. Slater would, by nature, have been the one who did the planning, carefully keeping her hands clean. Gullible Chip would have done the out-of-the-library legwork, which ultimately included two murders.

Faye wished she were Christian enough to forgive those two and to let the past go. It was what her grandmother would have told her to do. And it was what her mother would have told her to do. Cally, on the other hand…Faye had a feeling that Cally would have known that some grudges have to be nursed a little while before they're set free, and she had a feeling that Cally would have known exactly how to nurse one.

Joe deserved for Faye to hate those people. He didn't deserve what they did to him. Neither did Douglass. And neither did Wally.

Today, she was carrying a plastic bag as she walked down the familiar hall to Joe's hospital room. She'd carried it every day that week, and she was going to keep on carrying it until his extensive medical staff gave her a few minutes alone with him.

She found him alone, praise God, but his eyes were closed, so she just laid her gift on his bedside table. It was the book of Jedediah Bachelder's letters, and there was a round hole squarely through its middle, surrounded by copious amounts of dried blood. She saw no need to return it to the rare book room, not in its current condition. Libraries lose materials all the time, even rare books like this one. Besides, she figured Joe had earned it.

His eyes flickered, so she took the opportunity to say, "I brought you a present." She waved the book at him.

"I'm real sorry. I meant to take care of it, Faye," Joe murmured. His eyes opened a little more. They were so green. "I stuck it in my waistband before we left the library, so Ms. Slater wouldn't see that I had it. I thought you might need it."

"Oh, I did need it. Very much."

Joe closed his eyes again and drifted off to sleep.

The hardbound volume had taken the first impact of Chip's shot, and it was just possible that it had diverted the bullet's path a very providential millimeter or two. It had burrowed through the ropy muscles of Joe's lower back and exited from his side, nicking his colon and narrowly missing his spine. There had been an operation to repair the damage to his internal organs, and he had received massive amounts of antibiotics and other miracle drugs to deal with the infection that sprang up in the surgery's aftermath, but the doctors were finally talking about sending him home.

She picked up the old book and paged through it, as she'd been doing for weeks now. Time and again, she returned to two letters written in early 1865. The first was written by Jedediah Bachelder, and the second was written by his wife Viola. Faye felt Jedediah's presence every time that she saw that Viola's letter had been bound out of sequence. A whole month had passed before he received her response to his letter, a whole month in which he'd continued to write her almost daily.

There were no more letters from Viola after this one. Faye felt like she knew Jedediah Bachelder after reading so much of his most personal correspondence, and she believed she knew why this last letter was misplaced in time. It was because he'd asked his true love a question, and she'd given him her answer.

*February 21, 1865*

*Dearest Viola, my only love,*
*I must ask you what you were doing last night. I know that the evening of February 20 will have receded well into*

the past before this letter reaches you—if this letter reaches you—but please try to remember.

You will be wondering by now why I obsess over one particular night, when we have been apart for so many nights. Here is why. Last night, I dreamt a dream.

I was walking in a night that was cool but not cold. The sky was pricked with more stars than I could ever count and I knew, deep in my soul, that all was well. There was no war, yes, but even the absence of war could not explain my utter peace. I have never before had the certainty in my religious faith that you wear so beautifully, but today I do. I had the unshakeable sense that the world around me was not real, merely crafted by a loving Creator to suit my understanding. Because I am not capable of understanding the world as it truly is.

I stepped through a copse of trees that had served as a veil for what lay behind it—our home. I had come upon the place of my dreams from an unexpected direction and was treated to an instant of pure joy. I knew that there could never be room for any more joy in my soul than I felt at that moment, or so I thought until you walked out the door and flung yourself into my arms. I no longer fear death, because I believe that I have been blessed with a rare gift. I know what heaven is like, and I know you will be there.

So, tell me, Viola—what did you see in your dreams last night?

> Eternally yours,
> Jedediah

March 18, 1865

My cherished Jedediah,

Nearly a month has passed since you wrote me of your dream of heaven. With my whole soul, I hope and pray that you still carry that peace within you.

*You have asked me what I saw in my sleep on the night
you had your beautiful dream, believing all the while that
I could not possibly remember an evening that has receded
further into the past with every step taken by the horse that
has carried your letter to me. How wrong you are!*

*I know the precise content of my dreams on February 20
of this year, because I know what I have dreamt every evening
for time out of mind. On that night, you were in my dreams.
You always are.*

*Your eternally devoted wife,
Viola*

◇◇◇

Faye closed the book and settled back into the chair that sat
beside Joe's bed. She tried not to dwell on how pale he was, and
she failed. To distract them both, she began spinning fanciful
stories, the way a loving parent dreams up tales to soothe a child
who isn't ready for bed. Her tales always involved animals and
magic and spirits who lived in trees. Sometimes the thunder
rumbled through her stories. Once, a hurricane even blasted its
way into her imagination. But all the stories began in the same
way, just as a parent's stories always begin with "Once upon a
time…"

Faye leaned back in the uncomfortable visitor's chair and let
the story roll out of her. It began, as all of her stories did, with
the words, "When I get you back home to Joyeuse…"

# Chapter Twenty-seven

When the hospital finally decided to let Joe go home, they didn't give Faye much warning. One of his battery of doctors simply announced one morning, "He's ready to go home. I'll sign the paperwork, and we can have him out of there before noon." A cynical part of her presumed that his student insurance, which was adequate but not generous, had reached the limit of what it would pay, so the doctors had hurriedly pronounced him ready to go home and be cared for by somebody cheap like Faye.

Except Faye hadn't had time to go home and get the place ready for a convalescent who would need a lot of care. She hadn't gone home at all, not in weeks. She'd just camped in Mike and Magda's guest room whenever the hospital staff announced that she was abusing the concept of "visiting hours."

She needed to put fresh, clean linens on Joe's bed. For all she knew, Chip had slept there. Germs, evil karma, bad smells... Faye planned to scrub all invisible threats to Joe's health right out of the house. If the timing worked out right, then she would dry the sheets on the clothesline and his bed could smell like all outdoors.

There was so much she needed to do, but she had friends to help her, and they knew that there was no chance that Faye could be convinced to let Joe go anywhere but to Joyeuse when he was finally sprung from the hospital. Sheriff Mike volunteered to wait with Joe until he was discharged, then trundle him onto the

*Gopher* and give him a slow smooth boat ride out to the island. Magda volunteered to raid her own pantry for the groceries Faye needed and meet her on the dock at Liz's with the goods.

Faye was afraid to ask Magda how Liz was dealing with Chip's death, and Magda didn't offer her any information. The answer to that question was so obvious: Liz was assuredly not taking it well.

When Faye arrived at the marina, she found not one but two of her dearest women friends waiting for her. Three sacks of food sat on the dock at Magda's feet. Standing beside her were Emma and one of the sleek and luxurious lounge chairs that adorned her patio.

"Joe's not going to be happy lolling around indoors all day. You'll need to get the man outside. Put this thing on the porch where he can feel the sun and listen to the birds. He'll get well right quick."

◇◇◇

The boat ride out to Joyeuse Island had been…interesting…with Emma's lounge chair aboard. Even folded, it crowded Faye's skiff significantly. Now it sat on the back porch of the big house, overlooking the deep green woods. A tray table and a coaster sat beside it, because Joe's doctors wanted him hydrated. Faye figured she could pour water down his throat, if he refused to drink.

The soup was simmering. The laundry was done and the sheets were drying. Magda had tucked a stack of the sheriff's hunting and fishing magazines among the groceries, so Joe had easy access to his preferred reading material. And a pile of rocks had been moved from the corner of his room to the floor of the porch, so Joe could chip stone any time he felt like it. Faye was way past ready for her patient to arrive. But she was being thwarted by hospital bureaucracy.

The doctor who had said Joe would be home by lunch had neglected to sign a piece of paper that must have been very important, because the staff was trying to track him down for that signature. Sheriff Mike had been calling Faye with regularity, keeping her posted on their status, but even if Joe were released right now, by the time he was taken to the car, driven to the dock, helped onto the *Gopher*, and hauled out to the island, hours would have passed. Faye was not prepared to spend all that time staring at the walls.

There was still a question to be answered, and Faye was not the type to tolerate that. Jedediah Bachelder had hidden a fabulous necklace on her island. She knew this to be true, because he'd left behind an emerald and a tiny bit of gold, and she'd found it. She didn't get that same sense of resolution when she thought of the legendary Confederate Gold.

Her gut told her that a ghost of a chance remained that the Confederate Gold had left a shred of physical evidence behind. Faye would not be Faye if she didn't look for it.

The sun was shining, Faye had no more housework to do, and she was a worthless ball of nervous energy. Maybe a little exploratory digging was in order.

Faye had dug in this spot once, and she'd found an emerald. She'd dug here again, and she'd found nothing but dirt. Now she was back a third time. Why was she wasting energy on this thing?

Because she'd thought of one more place to look. Not left. Not right. Not east, nor west. She had realized that she needed to look down. She needed to go deeper.

On her previous visit to this spot, she'd located the coordinates where the emerald had been found, then she'd looked laterally, excavating a pit that was wide but shallow. It hadn't seemed logical for Bachelder to have buried something small like a necklace very far beneath the surface, so Faye had never looked there.

But several trunks full of gold? He would have had to go deep to bury that much treasure. Faye intended to start where she'd found the emerald and dig until she couldn't dig any more. She'd dig until she hit water, and further, if that was what it took to be sure that no trace of the Confederate Gold had been left for her to find.

The irony of the situation was that, though the treasure was long-gone, it was still wreaking havoc. Gold-lust had driven Elizabeth Slater and Chip to murder, and it would likely make Faye's own home life miserable for quite some time to come.

They were gone now, so they wouldn't be skulking around her island looking for gold, but every history buff within three counties had heard rumors that the hiding place of the Confederate Gold had been found on Joyeuse Island...but the gold had not. Yet. Faye was bracing for a blitzkrieg of trespassers.

She peeled back the soil, layer by layer, looking for a treasure that she knew wasn't there. It was clear that Jedediah Bachelder had returned and retrieved his necklace, leaving behind a single stray jewel and a broken finding. And she believed he'd retrieved the Confederate Gold, too.

Or maybe she was wrong about everything. Maybe his necklace had never been here at all, and she had found only the remnants of one of her ancestors' jewels. French historians were even now scouring records of the royal family's possessions for her, hoping to find something that matched the paltry evidence she'd uncovered so far. The sentimental part of her would rather have found Mariah's necklace than Marie Antoinette's, but a newsmagazine article detailing the connection between her island and the executed queen had assured that popular culture would always recognize the green-and-gold fragments in Douglass' museum as belonging to Marie Antoinette.

She hopped down into the pit to clear a layer of loose soil off its bottom. Even though she was half-expecting it, she was startled to hear her trowel strike metal. Carefully peeling back the earth, she found a single rusted hinge and a layer of discolored soil left behind by rotting wood. Try though she might to find it, there was nothing else.

There were many ways to interpret this find, but there was one interpretation that she particularly liked: Jedediah Bachelder came here on two separate occasions, first burying the necklace and then the Confederate Gold. He retrieved them later, on a third visit, leaving behind only an emerald, a gold finding, and a hinged wooden box that had once enclosed the fabulous lost treasure of the Confederacy.

When the Confederate government finally collapsed, Jedediah Bachelder had been left holding a treasure that he was too ethical to spend on himself. He would no doubt have sold the necklace and used the proceeds to make himself comfortably rich. But the Confederate Gold...that was a different matter. It would have made him ridiculously rich. What better use for that money than to relieve the suffering left behind by a ruinous war?

No one would ever convince Faye that the man who wrote those tender letters to Viola could have done anything else. It could be no coincidence that Jedediah's final bequest had given everything he owned to a home for penniless Confederate veterans.

It was time to call that reporter to come back for a follow-up story. If word got out that she'd found the treasure chest, and that its gold was long-gone, maybe she could keep some of her cherished privacy. Particularly if she could get the paper to print of a picture of Joe, taken before a bullet laid him low. Her extremely intimidating security guard should keep the riff-raff away. Most people would think twice about stealing from her if they knew they'd be tangling with Joe.

# Chapter Twenty-eight

Joe must have felt really terrible, since he hadn't fussed when Faye spread a blanket over his legs. He'd just sat propped up in Emma's chaise lounge and stared at the sunlit trees. Faye had been steeling her nerves all day to talk to him, to pour out her heart, to ask him never to go away. Even if he couldn't love her, she'd be okay if he never went away.

"I'm glad you're home, Joe," she began, but Joe interrupted her, possibly for the first time in his soft-spoken life.

"I never ever had so much time to think as I did when I was lying in that hospital bed. I figured out that there are a few things I want to do in this world before I leave it."

Faye held her tongue, possibly for the first time in her outspoken life, but she was thinking, *I want you to do those things as much as you do. But please do them with me.*

"I want to finish school. It'll be hard. I believe I'd rather take on a panther, bare-handed. But you showed me I could do it, and I thank you for that."

Faye's mouth tasted bitter. He was telling her good-bye.

"I don't rightly know what I'll do when I get out of school. Heck. It may take me till I'm forty to get that degree."

Faye couldn't imagine Joe at forty. He already had the centered, settled, solid air of someone who'd grown into himself. Middle age might not change him at all, but she would have liked to have had the chance to find out firsthand.

"I want to do something that's useful to people, but I don't want to sit at a desk. I looked out that hospital window so long that I know I never want a pane of glass between me and the world, not ever again."

Faye could no more imagine Joe working at a desk than she could fly.

"And I want children. I can talk to children. Sometimes better than I can talk to adults."

Something inside Faye broke. "I want you to go where your dreams take you, Joe, but I'd dearly love to see your children."

He turned his eyes her way. They had always been green, like the leaves of the live oak trees that sheltered Joyeuse, and they always would be, even if he traveled farther than Faye wanted him to go. "Why wouldn't you see them, Faye? Won't you be there?"

Would she? Would she want to watch Joe make a life with somebody who wasn't her? She didn't know. Finally, the tears came.

"Faye. I'm telling you all this so you'll know who I want to be. I want to be the right man for you. All this time, I've been telling myself that you're too smart for me and too pretty and too…well, I've been telling myself that I wasn't good enough. I laid flat on my back for a long time while I was getting well, and I didn't do anything but think. Do you want to hear what I think? I mean, do you want to hear what I know?"

Faye nodded, wiping her eyes on the back of her hand.

"I know that I love you. I've loved you ever since you caught me camping on your island, but you were too tender-hearted to make me go away. And I know that I would be good to you. I think maybe that's enough. If I can give you those two things, then maybe I'm good enough for you, after all. I want to be."

She threw both arms around him, but she did it carefully. He'd been through hell and back, and he'd gone there because he put his own body between her and death. "I love you, Joe. I always have. If I'm so smart, why didn't I know it?"

Joe rested his chin on her head and smoothed her hair with his big, calloused hand.

"Marry me, Faye."

# Guide for the Incurably Curious: Teachers, Students and People Who Just Plain Like to Read

1. **For those who have read *Artifacts*, what did you think of Faye's return to her home on Joyeuse Island in *Findings*?**

When I took Faye to Alabama in my second book, *Relics*, some of my readers were concerned. They had enjoyed the island setting of *Artifacts* so well that they thought it would be risky to move the action. I think they thought that Faye wouldn't be Faye if I plucked her off Joyeuse.

I was convinced that I needed to take Faye on the road for a couple of reasons. First, how many mysteries could she possibly solve from the vantage point of a single island? And second, how could I explore her character if I never took her out of her comfort zone?

In *Artifacts*, I put Faye through hell, but I left her on her home turf. In *Relics* and *Effigies*, I tested her in unfamiliar territory. When I began plotting *Findings*, I felt sure that it was time to take her back home.

It was fun for me to revisit the setting of my very first published novel, and it was a bit relaxing. I didn't have to spend effort on designing Faye's world, because I'd already done that. I'd already read about the way barrier islands are built, and I knew an awful lot—both from reading and from personal experience—about the ways the environment recovers from such a hurricane's brutal assault by wind and water. And I knew almost all the characters intimately. With *Findings*, I was able to concentrate on crafting a story that functions as a pivot point in the lives of each of those characters.

2. **As I finished writing *Findings*, I realized that it was different from my other books in some important ways. I consider mystery fiction to be the "literature of justice," in the way that science fiction has long been called the "literature of ideas." So it is no surprise that I considered my first three books to be explorations of the notion of justice. The real surprise for me was realizing that *Findings* was about something altogether different. What would you say was the central theme for this book?**

Reading my own book after it was already written, from the point-of-view of a reader, gave me an interesting perspective on *Findings*. Suddenly, it became apparent to me that I had written a book about love. This story is permeated with romantic love— Faye and Joe, Faye and Ross, Douglass and Emma, Jedediah and Viola, Magda and Mike, Curry and Sharon—there is hardly a character in this book who is not affected, for good or ill, by romantic love. Romance has never been a major theme in my previous books. How did these love stories work for you?

3. **I originally created Jedediah and Viola Bachelder and their Civil-War-era world strictly for plot purposes. As I wrote, they all came alive to me. Jedediah and Viola developed a habit of saying and doing things that I never planned or expected. Joe's character developed in that same way while I was writing *Artifacts*, and he continues to "tell" me what I should do with him. Do these characters feel real to you? And are there any other characters you particularly enjoyed?**

I always choose an unusual corner of history to explore in each book. I want to take readers to a place or time that they know little about. For this book, I wanted to take a peek at the short-lived government of the Confederate States of America. Many books, notably *Gone with the Wind*, have given us an image, factual or not, of everyday life in the American South before and during the Civil War. Battlefield scenes have been described in both fiction and nonfiction works. However, I don't think the Confederate government is given much thought when most Americans think about the Civil War. Yet I wondered how one would go about setting up a government for a brand-new nation that was born at war.

Jedediah's description of the CSA's constitutional convention was based on descriptions of discussions said to have been held during the writing of the Confederacy's constitution. His diplomatic trip to Europe was based on the real Duncan Kenner's actual diplomatic efforts. Kenner is said to have recommended freeing the slaves as a way to solidify diplomatic ties with Europe to CSA President Jefferson Davis, but this plan never came to pass. It makes sense that a man like Jedediah would be chosen for just this sort of diplomatic mission.

Jedediah and Viola, when I first created them, existed only to provide an illustration of real situations that are often forgotten when we view the people affected by the American Civil War from this distance. Many citizens of the Confederacy owned no slaves simply because they could not afford them. A few, like Jedediah and Viola, owned no slaves because their conscience forbade it.

Though we often hear the cliché that our Civil War pitted brother against brother, we forget that this conflict extended to the non-military citizenry. Though I don't say so, Viola was likely born in the North, since she mentions her mother in Pennsylvania. The story establishes that Jedediah spent his childhood on a Florida plantation, yet Viola mentions his aunt in Ohio. When war closed the channels of communication between family members, people were harmed in a way that's not apparent by reading history books. To read Viola's concern about their northern relatives puts the modern reader directly into this terrible enforced separation.

Viola Bachelder was simply created as a foil to receive the letters Jedediah sent. I never intended to include any of her letters in the book, but she wouldn't agree to stay quiet. In the end, I realized that any woman who would so captivate a man like Jedediah after years of marriage would have to be loving, yes, but also strong and independent. I had already "killed" her during the plot development phase of the book, and it grieved me that I could think of no way to "save" her without weakening the story. The final two letters that passed between Viola and Jedediah were among the last passages of this book that I wrote, and it pleased me to give them a happy ending, even if it couldn't come in this world.

4. **How did you feel about the fact that Faye was looking for gold and emeralds in this book, rather than the arcane archaeological finds she's usually hunting?**

I've always felt that archaeology made such a good setting for mystery novels because, though it is a science, there is also the air of a "treasure hunt" about an archaeological dig. No, modern archaeologists are not looking for King Tut's gold. They're looking for rotted kitchen scraps in order to reconstruct a civilization's diet. Yet the fact remains that they could, at any time, unearth a bag of gold or even a huge emerald that was buried for safekeeping years ago. You can never know where you might find hidden treasure. If you knew where it was and where it wasn't, then you couldn't call it "hidden."

I was already toying with a story about Jedediah Bachelder and the Confederate government, when I realized that this story could send Faye on a real treasure hunt. The fate of the Confederate treasury still generates books and magazine articles and web pages galore. Some stories say the Confederate Gold passed through Florida. Other stories put it in just about any other place you could imagine…which made it easy for me to put it exactly where I wanted it to be. How did you feel about the fictional Faye discovering the fate of a real treasure? Does that blur fact and fiction too much? Or does it just make the fiction feel more real?

5. **Now we know how Faye and Joe feel about each other. Is this the end of the series?**

Of course not. When a romance resolves itself in real life, do the lovers' lives come to an abrupt halt? Faye and Joe need to finish school, find jobs, enjoy the company of their friends and each other...and we know they both want children. Life goes on, but if all goes well, they'll be living that life with each other. I will continue throwing life-and-death ordeals at them but, in the end, I want them to be happy.

To receive a free catalog of Poisoned Pen Press titles, please contact us in one of the following ways:

Phone: 1-800-421-3976
Facsimile: 1-480-949-1707
Email: info@poisonedpenpress.com
Website: www.poisonedpenpress.com

Poisoned Pen Press
6962 E. First Ave. Ste. 103
Scottsdale, AZ 85251